BLACK MAGIC MURDER

A MELTING POT CAFÉ PARANORMAL COZY MYSTERY #6

POLLY HOLMES

Gumnut Press

Western Australia

DEDICATION

To the one and only Angela Lansbury,

For so many years I watched you play the iconic character, Jessica Fletcher, in the award-winning series Murder, She Wrote.

Little did I know that you would be my writing inspiration to create two of my every own cozy mystery series.

Thank you for the many hours of fun and entertainment you provided. You are a legend and will always have a special place in my heart.

Also from Polly Holmes

Melting Pot Café Series

Pumpkin Pies & Potions #1

Happy Deadly New Year #2

Muffins & Magic #3

Mistletoe, Murder & Mayhem #4

A Deadly Disappearance Down Under # 5

Black Magic Murder #6

Cupcakes & Cauldrons #7

One Hex Too Many #8

Cupcake Capers Series

Cupcakes and Conspiracy - Prequel

Cupcakes and Cyanide #1

Cupcakes and Curses #2

Cupcakes and Corpses #3

Murder and Mistletoe #4

Dead Velvet Cupcakes #5

CHAPTER ONE

"I cannot believe you're not going to have a birthday party!" Harriet said, dropping on the edge of my bed, disgruntled. "It's not every day you turn twenty-five and become a full-fledged witch. Why would you not want to have a party? It's a milestone to celebrate."

"Parties are over-rated," I blurted, holding a pink and black blouse against my chest and checking out the vintage look in the full-length mirror in the corner.

Not bad, if I say so myself. Lookout, Tyler, here I come.

"Harriet's right." Jordi joined her on the bed. Both my best friends stared blankly at me. These two women meant the world to me, and that was precisely why I was *not* having a party.

"I'm sure lover boy has a great night planned this evening, but what about the rest of us?" Harriet giggled. "How are we going to celebrate your birthday?"

I bit the inside of my cheek, choosing my words carefully. "Do you remember what happened when we hosted our last party at The Melting Pot?"

They glanced sideways at each other, and then Harriet piped up, "Please don't tell me it was New Year's Eve?"

My forehead tightened. "It certainly was."

A grimace turned Jordi's expression upside down. "I remember. Prudence McAvoy turned up dead in your pond. But when you think about it, that's no great loss."

"Jordi!" I said, three octaves higher. "That is a terrible thing to say."

She shrugged. "Sorry, but we all know she was not at the top of my Christmas Card list. She made my life hell at school and after. She made my life hell…period."

I pursed my lips and stared straight at her. "I know, but we're not at school anymore."

"Come on, Evelyn." Harriet's grin spanned from ear to ear. "Forget that party; it was one occasion? It's time we had a party to rock the pants off Saltwater Cove."

Rolling my eyes, I searched the base of my wardrobe for my brown boots, tossing aside several pairs of heels that rarely graced my feet.

"What about Florence Chesterfield?" I straightened, pausing, eyeing both ladies. "I don't think I'll forget her birthday party in a hurry."

My stomach tensed at the memory of Tyler lying in a pool of his own blood on the cellar floor of The Four Brothers. The crazy woman was determined to claim him for herself by forbidding anyone to stand in her path. Even me.

Like I'll ever let that happen.

"Look," I said, jumping on the bed and squishing my derriere between the two of them, "we will celebrate my birthday together. I promise. I just don't want a big party, that's all. Just the people I would give my life for."

Harriet's eyebrows shot up. "Like me?"

"And me?" Jordi added, leaning forward, waiting for a response.

I poked each of them in the ribs and nodded. "Yes, both of you."

"Ouch." Harriet swatted my finger away. Her gaze narrowed, and she tilted her head. "I suppose we can live with that. You gotta admit being a full-fledged witch is going to be a-ma-zing. I wish I was at that stage with my witch skills."

"You'll get there," Jordi said, checking out the nail wicks on her left hand.

A full-fledged witch. Am I ready for this?

Butterflies pummelled back and forth in my stomach, sending a wash of nausea floating up to the back of my throat. It's not the first time they've made

7

an appearance and I'm sure it won't be the last. Aunt Edie and Miss Saffron were always saying my true powers have yet to be seen. They've helped me solve a murder or two. What could go wrong, right?

"Where's Tyler taking you this evening?" Jordi asked.

Scooting off the bed, I took another look through the tops in my wardrobe, searching for just the right one to go with my freshly blue-streaked chestnut hair. "I'm not sure. I expect we'll just eat at some place in town. Anywhere is fine with me."

"I'm sure it'll be great." Harriet grabbed my make-up mirror off the bedside table. Holding it inches from her face, she puckered her lips and blew her reflection a kiss before dropping it in her lap. "He's been asking all these questions about you lately. It's been driving me absolutely batty."

My throat tightened, and I spun on my heel and glared at her. "What do you mean? What could he ask about me he doesn't already know?"

"You know, things like what's your favourite flower and which sort of jewellery do you favour, silver or gold."

Jordi gasped and flew off the bed. "OMG...OMG, I bet tonight's the night."

"For what?' I asked.

Jordi's hands started flapping around like she was drying her nail polish. "I bet he's going to ask you to marry him."

"What?" I yelled. My jaw dropped, and ice shot through my veins. "Marry him?"

I'm too young to get married.

I flicked my hand, brushing her comment away. "No, he's not. Don't be silly. You're jumping to conclusions. Whatever gave you that idea?"

Harriet squealed at the top of her voice. She clasped her hands together at her sternum. "That makes perfect sense. You guys have been dating for a while now, so it's only natural he wants to spend the rest of his life with you. He loves you."

The rest of his life?

"And," Jordi added, "it's not like he wasn't doting over you throughout our senior year. You were oblivious, of course. He rocked the nerdy, shy persona back then. But I caught him checking you out when he thought no one was looking. That was before his life-changing trip to Nepal."

My breath hitched just thinking about Tyler walking off the plane minus the dreadlocks looking all hot and sexy, like Zac Efron—not the teenybopper Zac Efron from *High School Musical*, but the tantalising seductive chiselled Zac Efron from *Baywatch*. A flush of heat worked its way up my neck, and I bit my bottom lip, working hard to keep my body's reaction hidden from sight.

I cleared my throat. "Yep, that trip to Nepal was something. I'll give you that."

"What are you going to do if he proposes?" Harriet asked, her voice all serious. "What will you say?"

"I'm not sure." I paused and flopped on the bed. My heart beat heavily in my chest while my pulse thumped against my temple. "I love Tyler with all my heart. I think I always have, but marriage? That's a big step, and I'm only twenty-four."

Harriet held up her hand. "Twenty-five in three days."

"I mean, I'm still learning how to use my powers, which, according to Miss Saffron and Aunt Edie, are still to develop fully. Is he going to want to live with a witch for the rest of his life?"

A frown marred Jordi's expression. "So, you're not going to marry him if he asks?"

My chest ached, and my mind struggled to process the conversation. I threw my arms in the air and bolted to the other side of the room to fiddle with my jewellery box on the dresser. "Can we just drop all the marriage talk, please?"

A moment of tense silence met my request, and I spun to see both of them still standing where I left them, wearing puzzled expressions. "I guess I'll know what to say if and when Tyler proposes." Warmth filled my chest, and I relaxed knowing these two women would have my back no matter what. "I can promise you one thing...when it happens, you ladies will be the first to know."

"I'll take that," Jordi said, giggling and laying back on my bed.

Harriet harrumphed and folded her arms across her chest, a frown slowly creeping into her expression. "You'd better. I'll keep you to that."

"Keep you to what?" Aunt Edie asked as she entered the room.

My chest seized, and I flinched back. "Ah, keep me to the promise of agreeing to teach her how to make my famous chocolate eclair cake." I tilted my head and glared at Harriet. "Isn't that right?"

Harriet first stared at me and then at Aunt Edie. A smile broke out across her face as the penny dropped. "That's right. I've been wanting to learn how to bake it for a while now, but every time I ask Evelyn, she always has an excuse. Well, not this time, young lady."

"Okay," Aunt Edie said, looking a little unsure.

Help. Change of subject needed.

"What brings you up here?" I asked. "Please don't tell me my trusty furry familiar has gotten into your spice pantry again."

Aunt Edie huffed. "Hardly, not after the last time. She knows better than that now." She slid her arms into her red coat and buttoned it up. "I just wanted to wish you a lovely evening tonight with Tyler."

"Thanks."

"And to tell you Micah and I are popping over to Dawnbury Heights to look at engagement rings."

"Oh, how perfect." Harriet smiled, her cheeks turning a rosy pink. "Have you set a date for the wedding yet?"

Aunt Edie shook her head. "No, we are going to wait until after Evelyn's birthday and graduation. No use trying to do it all at once. A ring shall suffice for now."

"How romantic," Harriet said, looking off into the distance, all dreamlike.

Aunt Edie pursed her lips together. "I don't know if I'd call it romantic. I'm not one to make a fuss over these things. If truth be told, I've kept him waiting so long I thought he would have run for the hills by now."

"Never. He loves you way too much," Jordi said. "I mean, first he takes a bullet for you when that crazed witch tried to shoot you last year at the town show. Then the man insisted on accompanying you to Australia to help find my missing parents—"

Harriet's hand shot up and interrupted Jordi mid-sentence. "In a luxury plane, mind you."

"That's right," Jordi continued, now with Aunt Edie's full attention. "In a luxury plane he pulled in all his favours to get, so you'd travel in style. I'd say he's a keeper, and you're stuck with him."

I watched Aunt Edie's face as Jordi's words sunk in and a crimson blush flushed her cheeks. "I suppose you do make a few good points."

A few? Stop playing hard to get and marry the man.

I made sure she heard me this time. There was no escaping me when I used my telepathic voice on her. She looked straight at me and gave a nod.

I know you're right. She pulled at the edge of her jacket sleeve.

What is it, Aunt Edie? What has you so nervous about a future with Detective Huxton?

Oh, love, how you know me so well. I'm afraid.

Of what?

Of him leaving again. I gave my heart to him once before, and he broke it. I don't think I'd survive if that happened again.

Aunt Edie, you're being silly. He explained that, remember? His brother was murdered, and he had to find out who did it, for his family's sake.

I know you're right, but what if he is killed in the line of duty?

Been there, done that—except I healed him, remember? You can't stop yourself from being happy because of what might happen.

"Okay, you two, enough of the telepathic chitchat." Harriet snapped her fingers. "You forget, you're not the only two in the room."

"Yes, you're right, sorry ladies," Aunt Edie said, brushing down her winter coat. "I will try to remember it, now if…" She paused and looked down at the furry familiar rubbing up against her legs carrying a letter in her mouth.

"Seriously, Miss Saffron. Sucking up will get you nowhere," I said, shoving my foot into my black boot.

"What's this?" Aunt Edie bent down and pulled the letter from Miss Saffron's teeth.

"It's for Evelyn," Miss Saffron said, purring as she sprang up onto my bed and planted herself on Harriet's lap.

Harriet giggled and ticked her under her chin. "Aw, if that isn't the cutest. I always knew she liked me best."

I huffed and glared at my furball.

Traitor. That will get you nowhere, either.

Harriet's brow creased, and she looked from Aunt Edie to me and sighed. "You know, this telepathic thing the three of you have is growing old. Sometimes, I feel like the fourth wheel in the conversation the way you, Aunt Edie and Miss Saffron all talk to each other in your heads and none of us can hear it."

My chest tightened, and I wanted to scold myself for not thinking about how our internal conversation would affect others.

"I think it's cute," Jordi said, shuffling down on the bed to give Miss Saffron a tickle on her belly. "I wouldn't worry about it. If it's something we need to know, they'll tell us. Think of the positives."

Harriet tilted her head and glared at Jordi. "And what are they?"

14

Jordi smiled and tickled harder. "We don't have to listen to this familiar's whiny voice all day long."

Miss Saffron's ears and tail shot up, and she glared at Jordi, hissing. "How dare she? I do not have a whiny voice."

"No, of course, you don't." I struggled to hold my laughter at bay, but it tumbled out and before I knew it, everyone was laughing and smiling with their attention focused on the feline. Just the way Miss Saffron liked it.

Harriet's sweet voice broke through the joyous moment. "Aunt Edie, I was wondering if you could solve a problem for me?"

"I'll do my best." She smiled and brushed cat hair from the hem of her jacket.

Harriet's brows pulled together, and she put on her best puppy dog pleading expression. "Evelyn refuses to have a birthday party. You're the closest she has to a mother. Can't you insist she has one? It's not every day you turn twenty-five and become a full-fledged witch."

An eerie shiver went through my body at Harriet's mention of my mother. Both my parents were killed in a car accident when I was eleven which was how I came to live with Aunt Edie, and that was also when I found out I was a witch. Except the wreck was no accident—it was murder. Just hearing the word in my head made me nauseous.

I will find out who killed you, Mom and Dad. You can count on it.

"Oh, love, I can't make Evelyn have a party. That's her decision and hers alone." Aunt Edie handed me the envelope and turned to leave, pausing by the door. "Although I am not getting any younger. It would fill my heart with such love and joy if she did have one so we could celebrate this milestone. Bye now." She was gone.

My jaw dropped. *That's not fair.* How could she use the guilt treatment on me and then just leave like that?

"She has a point," Jordi said, nodding.

I squeezed my hands into fists, dropped the letter on the dresser, and applied the finishing touches to my hair and make-up. "This is my birthday, and I'll do what I want." Even as the words left my lips, I knew in my heart if I didn't have some sort of family celebration, it would destroy Aunt Edie. I spun on my heel, folded my arms across my chest and glared at my besties. "I'll think about it. That's all I'm going to promise at this stage."

Harriet's high-pitched squeal blasted my eardrums, and out of the corner of my eye, I saw a lump of cat fur catapult through the air as Harriet sprang off the bed, launching herself and throwing her arms around my neck. "Yay. You're not going to regret this."

"I haven't said yes. I said I'd think about it, nothing more." Harriet squeezed harder, and I sucked in a breath. She pulled back and sent me one of her best evil glares. I'd have been scared if I didn't know her better.

"Think fast; your birthday is three days away," she snapped.

"All right, I will." I rolled my eyes. My head hurt. It was like keeping up with the Energizer Bunny.

I grabbed the letter off the dresser and ripped it open. My heart sank, and a cold shiver inched across the base of my neck. I bit my lip to stop blurting my annoyance.

"Who's the letter from?" Jordi asked, Miss Saffron now snuggled down in her lap. I looked up into the two sets of eyes gluing me to the spot. I swallowed the lump caught in the back of my throat.

"Well," Harriet said, "don't keep us hanging."

CHAPTER TWO

It irritated me to say his name, but I forced it out. "Eli. It's from Eli"

"Oh my gosh…no way…"

"Are you serious?

"Yep." Heat warmed my neck, and I pulled at my collar.

"What does the dirty scoundrel have to say for himself?" Jordi asked her voice monotone with a touch of sarcasm.

"I don't know that I'd call him a dirty scoundrel," I said.

"Really?" Jordi dumped Miss Saffron on the bed and joined us at the dresser. She stood with her arms folded, glaring at me. "Let's see, shall we? Number one, he's supposed to be your protector, here to guard and protect your life from black magic that has arrived in Saltwater Cove. Two, he bailed on you when you needed him to come to Australia to help find my parents. Where was he then, hey, when you needed him on the other side of the world?"

Jordi's words rang true in my head, but I couldn't help feeling there was more to it. My gaze read each word, and the niggle in my neck said, *Hold out until you can find out the truth.* "He says he'll be back for my birthday, and then we can find out once and for all what was so life and death he had to stay away this long."

"Ha, the nerve of the man," Harriet said, snatching the letter from my fingers, her eyes gazing over the words. "He does say he's sorry and that he'll explain it all when he gets back."

I chewed the inside of my cheek and paced over to where Miss Saffron had burrowed herself under my pillow. "I get that something came up, and he said a replacement protector would be here as soon as one was available. That never happened. What annoyed me the most was that he just up and left. No explanation or anything. He left Aunt Edie in the lurch. She had to hire someone to cover his shifts at The Melting Pot Café. Don't get me wrong. Kellin Olson is a great fit. She even opened up this morning, but what is Aunt Edie supposed to do when Eli gets back? Fire her?"

"Kellin is my favourite," Miss Saffron said, purring in my direction.

I gave her a tickle under the chin. "That's because she spoils you with chocolate cake. I'm just looking out for your health. You're a bit on the cuddly side as it is."

Miss Saffron's ears stuck up, and I could have sworn her lips curled into a snarl as she jumped off the bed and elegantly strutted toward the door, her tail swishing in a continuous line of figure eights as she went. She paused and looked over at me, her long neck stretched. She pointed her nose in the air and walked out. I smiled at her cheekiness, but I wouldn't trade her for another familiar, even if my life depended on it.

Harriet picked up my hairbrush and twiddled with the end. "I'm sure Aunt Edie will keep her promise to Kellin and sort something out with Eli." She paused and looked me up and down. A cold shiver danced up my spine, lodging in the base of my skull. "What?" I asked.

Her eyes grew brighter and the mischievous twinkle Harriet was renowned for made an appearance.

Oh no, what is she up to now?

She clasped her hands together in front of her heart. "I have *the* best idea ever. Wait for it…why not have a double wedding?"

"A double wedding!" I felt the blood drain from my face as the room started spinning. "Are you out of your mind?"

"Harriet, you really have outdone yourself today," Jordi said, placing her hands on her hips. "A double wedding? What gave you that idea?"

My chest ached under the heavy weight bearing down on it. The thought of marriage was confronting enough, but a double wedding with my aunt…that had disaster written all over it. An eruption of heat burned through my chest, and I pinched the bridge of my nose. The verbal banter between Jordi and Harriet continued, slowly turning into white noise in the background.

"Okay, enough," I said, a tad grumpier than I anticipated. But it worked. Their lips promptly snapped shut, and they both stopped dead in their tracks. "There will be no more talk of marriage or a double wedding. Aunt Edie's wedding is going to be amazing and exactly what *she* wants. Let's focus on that for now. If and when there is any progress with Tyler and me, you ladies will be the first to know, apart from Aunt Edie. Then the wedding plans can commence. Agreed?"

I held my breath and waited for the usual rebuttal. To my surprise, they both nodded and smiled, and the tension in my shoulders eased. "Glad that's all sorted. Now, if you wouldn't mind voting for which top goes best with my dress jeans and black boots," I said as I held the two tops up.

"My vote is the pink," Harriet said, picking up her bag and slinging it over her shoulder.

"I agree," Jordi said, retaking her spot on my bed.

"Pink it is, then. What would I do without you two?" The thought of losing my two best friends sent a shudder down my spine.

Harriet stared at me like I'd been speaking gibberish, one eyebrow raised, and her top lip curled up. "Like that is ever going to happen? You're stuck with us, and I personally wouldn't have it any other way. That's my cue to leave."

"What? Where are you going?" Jordi asked.

"I've an appointment to get my hair done at Salty Snips before my shift at The Melting Pot this afternoon. Misty squeezed me in." Harriet checked her hair in the mirror and ruffled it between her hands. "Look at it. It's way past my shoulders, and you know how I hate it when it does that."

"Okay, catch you later," I said, giving her one last hug before she turned and left. I'd only made it a few steps toward Jordi who was sitting on my bed when a sharp slap on the wooden door frame had my head spinning so fast, my neck cracked.

Harriet stood with her head bowed, one hand flat against the door and the other on the door frame. They pressed so hard the tendons were bulging against her skin.

Oh no, a vision.

I raced to her side and whispered, "It's all right, Harriet. You're just having a vision. Work through it."

Jordi stood on Harriet's other side, biting her fingernails, and staring at me for answers. "You're safe in Evelyn's room." She leaned away from Harriet and cupped her hand, hiding her mouth as she whispered, "What do we do now?"

I shrugged, and my stomach tensed. "Let it play out but give her space." I turned back to Harriet, and to my surprise, she looked in total control. I said in my best soothing tone, "I'm here for you, Harriet. Nothing is going to hurt you."

Harriet's arms wrapped around her waist, and her whole body shivered. Her teeth were even chattering as though she'd walked through a rainstorm in the dead of winter. And then it stopped. Her body folded forward, her hands found her knees for support, and her breathing came in short gasps.

I rubbed her back lightly. "It's okay. You're okay, Harriet. Deep breaths."

Please don't be a disastrous vision of my birthday.

Harriet stood and sucked in a deep breath, placing her hands on her hips, her eyes still closed. Letting it out slowly, she looked at me, and her face paled.

"What?"

"That was the weirdest feeling I've ever felt."

Jordi's brow creased as she guided Harriet back to the bed, and they both sat on the edge. "How do you mean?"

She looked at me, then Jordi, and back at me again. "I'm not sure how to explain it. I couldn't see anything. I was all by myself, with darkness surrounding me. My body was weightless as though I were submerged in water, but I wasn't drowning or anything. I was floating, but I had no idea where I was."

"That's just creepy," Jordi said, pulling back.

Harriet pressed her lips together and then continued. "That's the weird thing. I didn't feel lost or scared. I was exactly where I was meant to be, and then I was cold, so cold...and then it was gone."

"That is strange. Was it a vision of the future?" I asked.

She shrugged. "I couldn't tell, and I have no idea if it was from the past. I guess I'll just have to wait and see." Harriet shot up from the bed and shook off the vision. "I'm getting much better at controlling the aftermath of my visions now thanks to Hannah."

"Hannah?" Jordi and I said in unison.

Jordi sent me a blank expression, but her eyes screamed anything but blank. "As in, *the* Hannah Graverson that works nights at The Four Brothers?"

"Ah huh." Harriet nodded. "Did you know she's into meditation in a big way? I mean, she's been guiding me on how to regain my focus after a vision and helping me open my chakras. I had no idea mine were so blocked. How can anyone feel completely at peace when your chakras are so unbalanced?"

What the...your chakras?

Jordi's eyebrows shot up. "Okay, who are you, and what have you done with our best friend?"

Harriet giggled and play-punched Jordi's shoulder. "Oh, stop it, you. Hannah is pretty cool once you get to know her."

"Excuse me," Jordi said, holding her hands up in a defensive position. "I'm sure she is, but I would rather spend my spare time with a werewolf than a gorgeous ginger-haired vampire. Thank you very much."

"Don't be ridiculous." Harriet huffed and rolled her eyes. "It's not like she's going to bite me. You know her mother is human, and she detests the taste and smell of human or witch blood."

Jordi folded her arms. "Still...that doesn't mean she won't have vampire friends."

A restlessness hung in the base of my gut, and if I were honest, I didn't much like my best friend hanging out with a vampire either. "Jordi's right. There's nothing wrong with Hannah, but you don't know the company she keeps. I'd hate you to become the main meal in a situation where you might not have any idea what you're walking into."

"I won't, I promise." Harriet threw her arms around my neck and squeezed. "Thank you." She did the same to Jordi and then bounced toward the door. "I'm so lucky to have two best friends who care so much about me. Okay, bye, I don't want to be late for my hair appointment, and I still want to pop home first and change."

"Stay safe," I called as she disappeared down the staircase.

"I will." Echoed up from the ground floor.

That's Harriet for you. But I still love her to bits.

"It never ceases to amaze me how much energy that woman has," I said, my gaze still focused on the empty doorway. Silence hung heavy in the room, and

I spun to see Jordi staring out the window. Her gloomy expression put a sudden downer on the moment. She thought I never noticed, but I saw how she drifted off into her own world when she thought no one was watching. There was only one person of late who could turn Jordi's smile upside down—the enigmatic Constable Wade Antonio.

I tip-toed over and leaned against the other side of the window frame. "I suppose I don't have to guess who you're thinking about." A few seconds passed, and she finally registered I was standing opposite her.

Oh man, she's got it bad for Wade.

She straightened her back and wiped stray strands of black hair from her face. She blinked a few times, but it was as though her mind were still elsewhere. "I'm sorry?"

I grabbed Jordi's hand and guided her toward my bed. Sitting on the edge, I pulled her down, so she was sitting next to me. Watching her subtle downcast movements, my heart ached for her. "Talk to me, Jordi. I know you still like Wade."

Jordi's posture slackened, and she let out a sigh. "Is it that obvious? I thought I was hiding it well."

"You are, but it's obvious to me." I smiled and placed my hand over hers. "I know it when I see it, and, girl, you are still head over heels for the guy. What is going on?"

She shrugged. "I don't know what to tell you. After I got back from Australia, I knew my feelings for Wade were real, and I was sure he felt the same way. After almost losing Mom and Dad in that terrible bushfire in Australia, I realised time is too precious to waste."

I closed my eyes and took a deep breath washing away the tightness in my chest. Jordi's mention of the fire conjured up images I thought I'd buried deep down. Of all the ways to die, I could only imagine the horror one would endure being burned alive in a bush fire. I didn't even want to think what burned flesh would smell like.

"I'm just glad it all turned out okay in the end."

She continued. "I was adamant that if he wasn't going to make the first move, I was. I wanted to, and I thought he was open to it. When I approached him, he basically brushed me off, and then he was gone on some work assignment that had him leaving Saltwater Cove."

"Why didn't you tell me any of this?" I asked, my throat tightening.

Jordi's cheeks reddened. "Because you had enough to worry about. Eli was still missing. Your shifts at The Melting Pot had doubled, not to mention Aunt Edie was adamant she was going to redecorate the café, and she wanted all hands on deck for that."

"You still could have told me," I said, a slight growl in my voice.

Jordi lowered her gaze. "I know, but in all honesty, I thought I'd be over him in a few weeks.

27

But it turned into a few months, and I'm still not over him. I just wish I knew what he was working on and if he's coming back."

"Maybe Detective Huxton knows something."

She shook her head. "Nope, I asked. If he does, he's keeping silent about it." She paused and looked at me, then sprang off the bed as though she'd remembered something. "Evelyn, why did you let me wallow on so long? You have a date tonight, and the last thing you need is me confessing my dreary love-life woes. Come here," she said, holding her arms open and waving her beckoning hands at me.

My heart overflowed with love, and I engulfed her in the tightest hug I could muster without breaking her. "I am always here for you, no matter what else is going on in my life. You're my best friend, Jordi, and you're stuck with me for life."

"Thank you." She pulled away and wiped the moisture from her eyes. "Okay, enough soppiness for one day. I am out of here so you can finish getting ready for your date with lover boy."

Gosh, I hate it when she calls Tyler lover boy.

Jordi paused by the door and sent one of her cheeky grins my way. "I want a full report tomorrow. Scratch that, maybe not a full report, just the juicy parts." She blew me a kiss and vanished out the door.

The seconds flew by, and by the time I put my hair up in a messy bun and applied the finishing touches on my make-up, my stomach was jumping and twitching like a swarm of butterflies was throwing their own birthday party.

I shook out my trembling hands and paced the room. "What the hell is going on? It's just dinner with Tyler, for goodness' sake. Just like a gazillion other dinners we've had together."

Heat rose from my neck to my cheeks as the speed of my pulse doubled. I was hyper-aware that every inch of my body was on high alert. "I love Jordi and Harriet, but I am going to wring their necks. With all the talk of marriage and proposals, I'm a walking jitterbug now." I stopped in the middle of the room, closed my eyes, and took a few deep breaths.

In two...three...four and out...two...three...four. In two...three...four and out...two...three...four.

"There, much better. I can breathe again." I grabbed my black coat and my brown coat and tried on both to see which one went better with my outfit.

Would it be so wrong if Tyler proposed? My heart started hammering in my chest, and it radiated warmth as I checked out my reflection in the mirror. It was suddenly as if the stars aligned, and I knew exactly what I'd say if he popped the question.

I gave myself a satisfactory spin and nodded. "Why wouldn't he want to me marry me? I happened to think I'm a catch. At least life would never be boring married to a witch." I winked at my reflection in the mirror and burst out laughing.

A vibration jumped my phone across the dresser, followed by a chorus of *Dance Monkey*. I picked it up to see Jordi's smile plastered on the screen.

Now what?

"Hello, Jordi. Did you forget something?" I asked, prepared for a quick talking answer.

"Um, no not really."

The awkward tone in her voice put me on edge. My free hand gripped the edge of the dresser. "Jordi, what's wrong?"

"I think we have a problem," she said, an urgency in her tone that sent my blood cold.

"What are you talking about?"

"I was on my way home and drove past Salty Snips. There were police cars with sirens and flashing lights, and they'd cordoned off the entrance with tape."

Please don't say it. Please don't say it.

"Being the sticky beak that I am, I pulled over to check it out. Although they won't confirm it, I think you better get over here and fast. I believe we have a murderer loose in Saltwater Cove."

She said it.

CHAPTER THREE

Jordi wasn't wrong. As I turned down the road toward Salty Snips, blue and red police lights flashed while sirens pierced the air. A pile of cars had blocked off different parts of the street and the entrance to the hairdresser. That didn't stop the nosy onlookers from planting themselves at any available advantage point, mobile phones ready to take a photo or recording of what or who was the main attraction.

I pulled to the curb in the first available parking spot and grabbed my phone to call Jordi. I needn't have bothered; she was on a beeline for my car. My stomach tensed as I got out to greet her.

Three days out from my birthday and we have a new dead body in town. And I didn't even need a party!

"Boy, am I glad you're here. Can you believe this?" Jordi asked, her eyes wide and full of eagerness. "I haven't been able to find anyone who will tell me what's going on, and now the crowd has thickened, I doubt they are going to tell us anything."

Jordi linked arms with me, and we headed back toward the action. My chest tightened as I caught sight of Detective Huxton who was busy giving instructions. He looked the part in his long brown Sherlock Holmes-style coat, collared shirt, and brown dress pants. My mind wandered back to the conversation in my bedroom, and my throat clogged as though I'd eaten a full teaspoon of peanut butter.

When he and Aunt Edie get married, does that mean I have to call him Uncle Micah? Surely not.

He turned and gave a half smile, then waved us over. Officer Cameron Martins was behind him, snapping photos of the surrounding area before stepping inside.

Jordi squeezed my arm. "See, I knew it would be easier getting answers if I was with someone in the know."

"I wouldn't exactly say that." I pulled my arm from Jordi's, rubbing the sudden ache in my stomach.

"Evelyn…Jordi, what are you two doing here, or do I even need to ask?" Detective Huxton said, shoving his hands in his pockets.

"I think the more appropriate question is, what are you doing here?" I stood strong and folded my arms, tapping my fingers against my elbow. "Aren't you and Aunt Edie supposed to be engagement ring shopping over at Dawnbury Heights?"

His eyes widened, and a flush crept across his cheeks. "We were. We hadn't gone too far before the call came in about the homicide and we had to turn back. I feel terrible about it. I finally get Edith to agree to it and then this happens."

"Where is Aunt Edie now?" I asked, a tad bolder than I expected.

"I dropped her over to Sweets'n'Treats, the new confectionary slash cake shop. She has been wanting to go there for some time to check it out, so she swapped ring shopping for cake and dessert shopping, and I'm stuck here. We are aiming to reconvene after I'm done."

"That sounds fair," Jordi said with a shrug. "If you can't have diamonds, cake has to be the next best thing, right?"

I swatted her arm and shook my head. "Trust you to think of food at a time like this."

"You never answered my question; What are you two doing here?"

"If you must know," Jordi said, folding her arms across her chest, "I was the one who called Evelyn. Harriet had an appointment with Misty to get her hair done before her shift at The Melting Pot this afternoon. I was driving past and saw the commotion and all the police and thought it best I let Evelyn know."

He cocked his head to the side, and his eyes narrowed. "I see."

I cleared my throat. "Now that we're both here, you may as well tell us what is going on."

He glanced back toward the front door. "You said Harriet was getting her hair done by Misty?"

I nodded. "This afternoon."

He pressed his lips together and shook his head. "Not anymore, at least not with Misty. This is a crime scene."

My jaw dropped open, and a slight gasp left my lips. My hand covered my mouth, and I fought the tears forming behind my eyelids. "That's awful."

Copious mutters and murmurings echoed from all directions, but it was the female crying and hiccupping gasps drifting over from the other side of the taped area that caught my attention. "Is that Ashlyn?"

Detective Huxton followed my gaze. "Yes, she was the one who found the body."

"Oh, how terrible," Jordi said, shaking her head.

"Apparently, she and Blair had been out on their lunch break, and when they returned, she went in first and found the place empty…except for the body."

My heart went out to the woman. I can't imagine finding your boss's dead body. I was surprised she could keep her lunch down, unless it had already made an unscheduled appearance. Nausea swished around inside like a washing machine in my stomach.

My mind was awash with confusion. "Do you think it has anything to do with magic?" I asked.

Huxton pursed his lips. "Why would you ask that?"

Jordi butted in. "We do live in Saltwater Cove, and most dead bodies we've dealt with in the past had an aspect of magic hooked up with them. I think it's a fair question. I'm sure you'd like to know what or who you're up against."

A smile curled his lip. "While I can't be one hundred per cent certain as I've not long arrived on the scene, I'm pretty sure there is no magic involved, at least as far as I can tell. This one is pretty much straightforward—a simple case of blunt force trauma to the back of her head."

Heat filled my cheeks, and I let out a sigh. "Blunt force trauma, you say?"

Detective Huxton's head tilted to the side as though he were mentally weighing my comment. "Why do you say it like that?"

"Like what?" I shrugged. "I was just thinking aloud. From the track record of dead bodies, it always works better when we work as a team. You know, two-way street and all."

He stood and rubbed his chin, his gaze shooting between Jordi and me. "You do have a point. I have been impressed on more than one occasion with how you have put the clues together and pointed the finger at the correct culprits."

Jordi piped up. "So does that mean you'll let us see the body?"

He paused only a fraction before nodding. "Follow me."

Oh great, seeing a dead body was totally on my agenda today. Not!

The bounce in her step puzzled me. "Okay, what gives?"

"I don't know what you mean," Jordi said, her eyebrows raised as though she had no idea what I was talking about.

"You've never been this eager to see a dead body before. What is going on?" I asked once more, using my tell-me-or-else tone. "I'll give you one more chance to fess up."

She huffed and rolled her eyes as we approached the rear of the salon.

An outline of tape surrounded the body.

Jordi leaned in and whispered, "I'm not keen on seeing a dead body. I just thought if I had something to occupy myself, I wouldn't have to think about Wade and where he was or what he was doing and with whom."

I stopped and stared at my best friend. "I cannot believe you just said that. Are you seriously happy someone is dead just so you don't have to think about Wade?"

Jordi paled as my words sunk in. "Oh, my goodness, I must have sounded like a monster. I didn't mean for it to come across that way. I swear. I just thought if I had something else to occupy my thoughts, I wouldn't be thinking of Wade that's all. I'm sorry."

"I guess I can understand, but maybe next time you want to take your mind off a man try finding a new hobby instead."

Jordi nodded, her gaze regretful. "Agreed. Point taken. Thank you."

"Okay, guys, can I have a bit of space here for a few minutes?" Detective Huxton called out to the men gathering evidence around him. They downed their tools and cleared the space.

Pays to have that kind of power.

The detective turned and beckoned us closer to the body. My stomach dropped as I looked into Misty's cold dead eyes. I sucked in a quiet breath, and the taste of bile rose in the back of my throat. Pulling my gaze away, I searched the surrounding area, mentally forcing the queasiness rolling around in my gut to disappear. *I'm sure the last thing Detective Huxton needs is me contaminating his crime scene.*

"You can see the bloodied trophy is sitting by the body. It's clear that's the weapon used in the attack. I'm hoping we can get fingerprints from it," Detective Huxton said.

It was already in an evidence bag. "That's if they didn't use gloves," I said softly. His Mediterranean green eyes drilled into me. I swallowed, a shiver racing up my spine. "I was just saying."

I moved around the body and took in the scene. There didn't appear to have been a struggle, but they could have cleaned up before they left. I moved farther back into the salon, and I stopped. Something wasn't right. My gaze scanned every possible location in the salon, but I couldn't see anything that had pricked my senses. Taking a few more steps towards the wash basins and the door leading outside the back of the salon.

I froze. A familiar scent accosted my nostrils. My eyes tingled, and I balked at the smell. I gasped and shook my head in small movements, flinching back. Rubbing my forehead, I muttered, "This is not good, not good at all."

Both Jordi and Detective Huxton stopped and looked at each other with raised eyebrows and then at me.

Jordi was the first to break the icy chill that had seized the room. "What is not good?"

"If you know something, Evelyn, now is the time to tell me," Detective Huxton instructed.

I nodded and licked my dry lips slowly backing away from the rear of the salon. "If I'm right—and I sincerely hope I'm not—but if I am, then we have a far more serious situation on our hands."

He shoved his hands on his hips. "Okay, now you're just talking in riddles."

I spun on my heel and glared at both of them. "You said you didn't think this murder had anything to do with magic."

He nodded. "That's right."

"Well, I can say with full confidence that you are completely and utterly wrong."

"What?" he said, his pitch raised. "How can you be so sure?"

"Because of what I can smell down there," I said, pointing to the wash basins and the back area of the salon. "The last time I smelled it was last year at the annual Saltwater Cove Show, and it wasn't something to be sneezed at."

Jordi huffed and folded her arms across her chest. "Just say it, Evelyn."

"Licarbre fern," I blurted. "It's faint, but it's there."

Jordi's sharp intake of breath was audible as she flew at me and practically lifted me off the ground carrying me to the front door.

"What are you doing?"

"Um, I would think it's obvious. Licarbre fern is deadly to witches—or have you forgotten?" She stood glaring at me blocking the entrance to the shop.

I loved the woman dearly, but sometimes she could be infuriating. "I am very aware of that. But you don't have to worry. It was nowhere near strong enough to affect me."

"Still," she said, maintaining her protective stance and blocking the entrance.

Detective Huxton moved up beside Jordi and patted her on the shoulder. "Well done, Jordi, it's nice to know who your true friends are, isn't it, Evelyn?"

"Guys, I'm okay," I said, pursing my lips and pushing some stray hair behind my ears.

Detective Huxton continued. "And because of this Licarbre fern, you believe Misty's murder is connected to magic?"

Jordi turned to face him, and her eyebrows shot up. "Well, duh. Why would the smell of an illegal magical substance be in your shop if you weren't using it or dealing it? It's not like it's used to make pumpkin soup."

Oh, Misty, what did you get yourself caught up in?

"Let's not jump to conclusions, Jordi," Detective Huxton said, moving back to the body. "We don't have all the facts yet, and until we do, I am calling this a suspicious death that may have a possible link to magic."

I edged my way around Jordi, which was pointless as nothing got by her when she was in protective best-friend mode.

"Where do you think you're going?"

"I'm just going to take one more look at the body, and then we can go. Okay? I just think it's strange that Misty rang me and specifically booked a time to catch up for coffee after my birthday. She's never done that before."

Detective Huxton's head shot up, and his gaze caught mine. "What did you say?"

"Misty rang me two days ago and wanted to catch up. She said she wanted to run something by me. I said I was happy to catch up, but she said it could wait until after my birthday." I paused, and my gaze dropped to where her body lay, a cold tense shiver skirting across my shoulder blades.

"Do you have any idea what she wanted to talk to you about?" Detective Huxton asked.

I shook my head. "No, sorry. We normally just wave and say hello. The last time I stopped and actually spoke to Misty was when she walked straight out on the road in front of Tyler's car, and he almost ran her over."

Jordi clicked her finger and pointed at me. "That's right, I remember you telling me. Didn't you say she was in a trance or something like that?"

"Kind of, it was really strange," I said, looking at Jordi.

Detective Huxton flipped over a page in his notebook and held his pen at the ready. "How so?"

"She wasn't so much in a trance as just oblivious to her surroundings like she was caught in a world of her own and her mind was solely focused on her thoughts. Misty was always one to dress impeccably, rarely seen not wearing one of her gorgeous 1950s-style outfits." I pointed over my shoulder at her lifeless body. "Even in death she's still dressed in style, but the day she walked out in front of Tyler's car, she had a drawn, fatigued appearance about her. She wore track pants, sneakers, a long gray woollen coat tightly wrapped around her waist and no make-up."

Jordi piped up. "That is unusual. Whenever she did my hair, she always wore a classic Misty outfit, and I've never seen her without make-up."

Officer Martins headed our way, and Detective Huxton held his hand up. "Hold that thought." They chatted and hands pointed in different directions until Detective Huxton seemed to give his approval.

"Apologies," he said, rejoining us. "Now where were we?" He glanced down at his notepad. "You were saying Misty looked different the day she walked in front of Tyler's car."

"Yes. She put it down to the stress of running the business, but I had a feeling there was more to it."

Jordi stepped in closer, her eyebrows squishing together. "Hold up. I may be spitballing here, but didn't that happen around the time of the annual show as well?"

I nodded.

She continued. "The same time Licarbre fern was first sighted in Saltwater Cove?"

I nodded, and my chest cramped.

"I may only be a shapeshifter." Jordi twisted a clump of her long raven-black hair around her finger. "But in my book, that is way too coincidental."

It sure was. Who would deal in illegal substances, especially ones forbidden under magic law? Just getting caught with Licarbe fern in your possession could get you disbarred or banished; imagine what dealing it on the black market would get you. I shook my head not even wanting to imagine the punishment.

Was Jordi right? If Misty's murder was linked to the appearance of Licarbre fern that surfaced during the annual show, then we had our work cut out for us.

The air hung with a thickness that weighed down my heart. I bit my bottom lip. The mutterings of police flitting around doing their assigned jobs interrupted the moment.

"Oh, no," Jordi said, slapping her forehead.

"What's wrong?" I asked, my heart jumping into the back of my throat.

"What's the matter?" Detective Huxton followed in a gruff tone.

"Harriet, that's what's wrong," she said, looking from me to Detective Huxton and back again.

"I don't get it."

"She's supposed to be getting her hair done this afternoon." I cringed at the thought of telling her about Misty. Turning to Jordi, I said, "Have you got your phone handy?" She took it out of her back pocket and waved it at me. "Great, can you ring Harriet and tell her about Misty before she hears it on the local gossip vine?"

Jordi's jaw fell open, and she dropped her arm as though it were dead weight. A smile crossed her face. "No problem. It will be fine. Harriet isn't the same woman she was when she found Camille Stenson's dead body at the bank."

"Really?" I folded my arms across my chest and tilted my head waiting for Jordi's response.

"Pfft," she said, waving her phone around. "For starters, she's a witch and has seen much more than she ever thought she would since that day in the bank. I'm sure she'll handle the news better this time."

"So that would mean you forgot her reaction to finding the body in the ladies' toilet at the show last year?"

Jordi paled then snapped her fingers at me. "Yes, but remember her reaction to the mysterious dead elf that turned up on the night of the annual Christmas concert. You said she didn't scream and handled it all right."

"That is true. She has come a long way since she found out she was a witch."

Jordi nodded and punched in Harriet's number then waited rocking side to side, her teeth chewing her bottom lip. The longer I waited the more my right leg shook. I gripped my thigh, and it stopped.

"Hi, Harriet," Jordi said, in her most cheerful voice.

Like she won't be able to see straight through that hello.

Jordi kept her eyes glued to mine. "We're at Salty Snips." She paused and rolled her eyes, listening to Harriet ramble on. Then her back shot ramrod straight. "What do you mean make you another appointment?"

My forehead tightened, and I tilted my head.

Make another appointment? But I thought she already had one.

"Hang on a minute, I'm just going to put you on speakerphone." Jordi paused and clicked the button holding the phone between us. She continued. "I thought you had an appointment already for today?"

"I did," Harriet said. "But just as I got home, I had a missed call from Misty and a message cancelling my appointment. I tried to call back, but there was no answer, and you know how I hate to leave messages. Is Evelyn there with you?"

"Yes, Harriet I'm here," I said, my throat clogging up.

"What are you both doing at Salty Snips?" she asked, a sliver of trepidation coming across in her tone.

I looked at Jordi, nodded at her and pursed my lips. If evil glares could kill, the way Jordi was staring at me, I would have been incinerated on the spot.

"Um, Harriet there's something we need to tell you," Jordi said, keeping her gaze glued to mine. "It's Misty."

Harriet sighed. "What about Misty?"

"There's a situation at the salon." Jordi paused, and Harriet's heaving breathing tightened my gut. She maintained silence at the other end of the phone as though she were waiting for a pin to drop. I waved my hand at Jordi to tell her to hurry up and spill the beans.

"Misty is dead. Ashlyn found her body after she came back from lunch with Blair."

The silence extended, and the tension in my body doubled. "Harriet, are you still there?"

"Yes," she said in a barely audible whisper.

"Are you okay?" Jordan asked.

"I'm not sure."

I glanced at Jordi, and she frowned. "What do you mean?"

"I think I knew it was going to be bad news when you rang. Something deep in my gut told me to brace myself. I just never thought it would be Misty. Oh, well, I'm sure everything will turn out okay in the end."

Oh, well? What kind of response is that?

Jordi's lip turned up, her brows joined in the middle, and she frowned at me. She covered the mouthpiece of the phone and whispered, "Did we hear the same thing?" I nodded and Jordi continued. "Something is not right here, not right at all. Her last sentence almost sounded happy."

"I know," I mouthed.

"Um, Harriet, are you feeling okay?" I asked.

"Of course, why wouldn't I be?" She snapped down the line. "I'm pretty busy, so if there is nothing else, I have to go."

Jordi covered the mouthpiece once more. "She took that way too well. I'm worried."

"Me too," I mouthed.

"Sure." Jordi paused and shook her head glancing at the clock on the wall above the counter. "Harriet, do you mind a visitor? Evelyn's going to be off on her date with Tyler soon, and I've a pretty boring evening planned. I could definitely use some company. I was thinking about heading over to your place for a while. Would that be, okay?"

I smiled and sucked in a lungful of air, releasing the tension as I blew it out. *Thank goodness for Jordi.*

"I suppose so," Harriet said, her voice plain and without emotion. "Have a great night, Evelyn."

"I will, and make sure Jordi doesn't eat all the food in your fridge," I said winking at Jordi. "Bye."

"Bye, Evelyn."

"See you soon, Harriet," Jordi said and pressed *end call* and slipped her phone back into her pocket. "She took the news better than I expected. Maybe it hasn't sunk in yet?"

"Maybe. Thanks for taking the time to go see her, I would go—"

Jordi butted in and rolled her eyes. "I wouldn't let you go. You have a birthday dinner with your man, and you're not going to miss it under any circumstances. If I can't have a love life, I'm going to live vicariously through yours."

I threw my arms around Jordi and squeezed. My heart was on overload. "I love you. You know that, don't you?"

She nodded and returned the hug. "I sure do, and I'm never going to let you forget it." She pulled back and headed towards the door. "Have fun tonight. Don't do anything I wouldn't do. Don't forget. Harriet and I want all the juicy details."

I tutted and shook my head. "Maybe they won't be fit for your innocent ears." I shooed her out. "Get going before I change my mind and keep it all to myself."

Jordi nodded and bolted from the salon. I couldn't help smiling as her raven hair vanished past the shop's front window and down the street.

"Evelyn?"

I spun at the sound of Detective Huxton's voice and came face to face with the man a foot apart. Stumbling, his hands shot out and caught my shoulders just as my body pitched forward.

"Easy there," he said in a warm tone. "I'm sorry. I didn't mean to frighten you."

Heat bled into my cheeks, and my eyes stung under his constant stare. I cleared my throat and stepped back brushing my sweaty palms down my thighs. "Sorry about that."

"Are you all right?" he asked.

"Of course, you just caught me off guard, that's all." I hiked my handbag up on my shoulder and eased myself backwards a step or two. "If we're done, I'm going to head off."

"Of course," he said, pausing and rapping his fingers against his thigh.

He had a tightness around his eyes and between his rapid blinking and rubbing his neck I knew the conversation was far from over. "Was there something else you wanted to say?"

"Um, I just wanted to say if I don't see you, happy birthday for Wednesday," he said, then turned back and headed towards Misty's body.

Strange man.

CHAPTER FOUR

I leaned my head against my hand and pushed the last mouthful of meatloaf around my plate. My gaze was focused on the food in front of me, but my mind was a gazillion miles away.

Who would want Misty dead? What did she do that was so bad it would cause someone to murder her? And how did the Licarbre fern fit into the picture?

"...half-naked..." Tyler's voice murmured in the back of my mind with that one word breaking through the haze.

Wait...half-naked? Who's half-naked?

I looked up. "What?"

Tyler was watching me from under his lashes. "I said, 'I think I'm going to run through the main streets of Saltwater Cove half-naked wearing nothing but my Tweety boxer shorts'."

My back stiffened and my arm dropped to the table. My brain hurt from trying to make sense of his words. "What are you talking about?"

He sighed, placed his knife and fork together on his plate and pushed it to the centre of the table. Tyler's face dropped, and his shoulders slumped. "I'm sorry. I was just trying to get your attention by lightening the mood, but it seems all I've done is confuse you."

"Now I feel bad for letting my mind wander and not paying attention to you," I said my chest tightening with each word. "It's just that I keep going back and asking myself why. Why would someone want to kill Misty?"

His hand slid along the pristine white tablecloth and found mine. The smooth skin on his fingers rubbed back and forth, easing the built-up tension. "I know," he said. "I was asking myself the same question, but I think Misty would want you to have a good time rather than harp on about her death, don't you?"

"I suppose you're right." Under the circumstances, I shuffled in my seat and gifted him the best smile I could muster. "Thank you for my birthday dinner. It was nice of Mercer to make sure we had a table away from all the other diners and he even arranged Marlana to be our private server for the night."

Mercer owned The Four Brothers Bar and Grill, and it was always a hive of excitement, especially on the weekends.

Tyler wiped the corners of his lips with his serviette then folded it neatly, placing it on the table in front of him. "I must confess, I had a little to do with the organisation. I know this place is one of the most popular locations in Saltwater Cove, and the idea of having your birthday dinner in amongst a bunch of revelling partygoers from the bar didn't impress me and…" He paused and held his arms out open and winked. "Voila! Our own semi-private dining room."

My breath caught in my throat. His gorgeous blue eyes drew me in with each twinkle.

Gosh, I love this man.

"Thank you, it's perfect. A perfect birthday dinner with the perfect man." My pulse raced and all I wanted to do was jump up, throw my arms around his neck, and kiss those sexy lips until the early hours of the morning. He held up a finger, and my thoughts paused.

"It's not perfect yet," he said, with a cheeky glint in his eye.

"It's not?"

He turned around and fiddled with his jacket on the back of the chair, and my chest seized. Was he reaching for an engagement ring? Heat ran up my neck to my cheeks, and my heart pounded inside my chest.

Oh, no, is this the moment? Is he going to propose?

Butterflies exploded inside my belly, and I clenched every muscle to calm my nerves. There was no question what my answer would be, and now that it might happen, I wanted nothing more than to be Mrs Tyler Broderick.

He turned back and placed his hands in his lap, out of sight under the tabletop. I bit the inside of my cheek and sat as casually as I could ignoring the fact that my heart was beating so fast it was about to jump right out of my body.

Tyler's gorgeous blue eyes smiled at me from across the table. "Evelyn, this has been a long time coming. I think I knew from the first time you arrived in Saltwater Cove all those years ago that we were going to be great friends, and as we grew closer over our senior year at school, I knew my feelings for you were more, but I never quite knew if you felt the same about me. You had your witch schooling to contend with as well as normal school, and the last thing I wanted to be was a burden."

"Tyler, you could never be a burden," I said, emotion clogging my voice.

He held up his hand. "Please, let me finish. When I left for my travels after graduation, I played the tough guy, determined to get by without giving in to the feelings I'd pushed deep down. It wasn't until I hit Nepal and started really looking at myself inside and out that I realised I loved you and didn't want to go a day without seeing you or talking to you. I missed you. Nepal changed me. My heart woke to the possibilities of what we could have together if only I took the plunge. I wanted to be the man you could love, the man who would take care of you and love you to the moon and back."

Tears clouded my vision, and I blinked at the ringing in my ears. I sat unable to move, waiting for the inevitable, my heart pounding away.

"But."

But? No, no, no, no buts, just ask the darn question.

Tyler licked his lips and continued. "But I've just started my new private investigation business, and I know how important being a witch is to you, and I know what graduating to full witch status will mean to you, and the last thing I want to do is stand in your way."

"What are you trying to say, Tyler?" I asked, my heart and my head fighting a losing battle.

He lowered his gaze and shook his head. "I'm not doing a very good job of this."

"You're doing fine, but if you got to the point, it would make both of us feel a lot better," I said, hoping to lighten the mood. A noisy commotion just outside the entrance to the dining room distracted me, but I pushed it aside and focused on my man.

He looked at me, and his lips parted. "You always know the right things to say. That's why I love you. Okay, like I said I've just started my private investigation business and—"

"And I'm about to graduate to full witch status," I said, my mind determined to hurry up the process before I spontaneously combust in my chair.

"Exactly." He reached out and grabbed my hand. It trembled in his. "Even though I know in my heart I want to spend the rest of my life with you, what's important now is that you focus on what you are going to do after you graduate to a full witch, and I'll focus on getting my business off the ground. In the meantime…" He paused and pulled out a little square black box and held it in the palm of his hands in front of me. He flipped the lid open, and I gasped. "Evelyn, please accept this promise ring as a token of my love for you knowing that when the time is right, I will be swapping it for an engagement ring."

My jaw almost hit the floor. A high-pitched gasp hit my ears as I flattened my hands against my chest. "Oh, Tyler, it's beautiful." I blinked back tears. "Of course, I will accept your promise ring."

His shoulders relaxed, and a slow smile spread across his face. "I love you, Evie Girl."

"I love you too," I said through tears.

My heart overflowed with love. I sniffled and wiped my eyes with the backs of my hands and plastered on a grin from ear to ear.

He took the gorgeous blue sapphire and diamond rose gold teardrop ring out of the box and picked up my right hand and held the ring over the tip of my ring finger.

Tyler sucked in a deep breath, and his face turned serious. "Evelyn, I make this promise to you. I promise to love you forever, no matter what witch adventures we stumble across. I promise to protect you, care for you, and love you to the moon and back."

"Oh, Tyler, I love it, and yes, I'll accept your promise, and although I have no ring for you, you get my promise in return." I held my hand up to see the sparkling gems shine against the fluorescent lights. It sparkled as bright as the twinkle in Tyler's eyes. I clasped my hands together and held them close to my racing heart. "It may be my birthday dinner, but I know in my heart that had you popped the actual question, I think you would have been very pleased with my response."

His eyebrows shot up. "Oh, really?"

I nodded and glanced once more at the exquisite ring glistening under the lights and an electric buzz warmed me from the inside out. I might not be engaged, but this was as good as, if not better. "This is the best birthday dinner ever."

Tyler picked up the dessert menu and cheekily glance over the top. "Oh, sweetheart, the night is far from over."

A shiver danced up my spine, and his cheeky grin had my belly doing somersaults.

Cheque, please. I know what I want for dessert.

"Get out of my way." A snappy woman's voice rang out from outside the dining area.

Tyler grimaced and glanced toward the commotion. "What is going on?"

I cringed and shook my head. "I have no idea, but I wish they would keep it down."

"Tiffany…no," Marlana yelled.

Tiffany? What is she doing here?

I looked up and straight into the green eyes of Saltwater Cove's most deceitful fae. *There goes my night.* The energy drained from my body within seconds as I took in the snarky expression on her face. She stood there with her hands on her hips, her gaze rocking back and forth between Tyler and me.

"Thank goodness, I found you," she said, breathlessly, her focus now solely on Tyler.

His brows drew together, and he dropped the dessert menu down onto the table. "This is a private dinner, Tiffany."

Marlana threw her arms in the air and huffed. "That's what I tried to tell her, but she insisted on seeing you immediately. She wouldn't take no for an answer."

Tiffany turned and glared at Marlana. "You wouldn't understand. It's imperative I talk to Tyler. It's a life-and-death situation. My life to be exact."

Tyler held up his hand. "It's okay, Marlana. She's here now; she may as well stay." He pointed his finger directly at Tiffany. "But only as long as it takes to explain this interruption, and then you're going. Understand?"

Tiffany nodded, and Marlana tutted and spun on her heel prancing out muttering an array of expletives under her breath.

"Thank you," Tiffany said.

"Don't thank me, just tell me what you're doing interrupting Evelyn's birthday dinner," Tyler said, leaning back in his chair and folding his arms.

Her gaze shot to mine, and she forced a half smile. "That's right, it's your birthday on Wednesday. I guess I should wish you a happy birthday."

My gut turned, and I swallowed back the lump in my throat. "Thanks, but I know you didn't come here to wish me a happy birthday. Get to the point, Tiffany."

The expression on her face turned dark, and her eyes glazed over as though a tidal wave of fear had taken over her body—an expression I would never have associated with Saltwater Cove's most cunning fae.

"I think I'm in trouble, and I need your help," she blurted, looking at Tyler.

Tyler's jaw dropped, and his eyebrows shot up.

"Excuse me?" I said my gut clenching at the prospect. Tiffany has been the bane of my existence since I moved in with Aunt Edie. Tiffany along with best friend and my arch nemesis, Prudence McAvoy, who incidentally was murdered and is now a ghost attached to the pond at The Melting Pot, made my life hell. Come to think of it, I hadn't seen that unfriendly spirit in months. Maybe she'd moved on.

I should be so lucky.

Tiffany stood twisting her hands in front of her chest. "Tyler Broderick, I would like to hire you."

Tyler stared at me with wide eyes. "Hire me?"

Tiffany nodded. "Yes. I heard you're a private investigator now, and I'd like to hire you to prove my innocence. Prove that I didn't kill Misty."

What the…? This conversation just got a whole lot more interesting.

Tyler rubbed his creased forehead. "I'm confused, and obviously I'm missing some vital information. I have no idea what you are talking about, Tiffany."

"Geez, how much plainer can I be," she snapped. Bending down to his level, she spoke with animated arms. "I want to hire *you* to prove that I did not kill Misty. Do you understand?"

"No need to be condescending," I said, folding my arms across my chest. "I think we both understand exactly what you're saying."

"Well, it sure as hell doesn't sound like it." Tiffany grabbed the chair from the other side of the room and plonked it at the end of our table.

Make yourself at home…Not. This night is going from great to awful in a blink of an eye.

I sent her my best evil glare. "The question is why would we help you? You haven't exactly instilled a lot of trust in us lately."

Tyler added, "And if I remember rightly, you once said we weren't friends."

Tiffany feigned hurt and stuck her bottom lip out, flattening her hands to her chest.

Oh, please.

"Tiffany," Tyler said, tapping his fingernail on the table, "just get to the point, and tell us what is going on."

"Okay, okay. I had an unexpected house call from Detective Huxton today, and he told me about Misty's murder. He also said that I'm a suspect in her murder. Me, for goodness' sake. Just because I've been seen hanging out at the salon with the ladies. I may have had a few altercations with Misty, that's because she screwed up my haircut once or twice. I would never kill anyone over a bad haircut."

"So why do you need me?" Tyler asked, his lips set in a permanent grimace.

"I'm getting to that." She paused and wiped her brow. "Detective Huxton told me she was struck down with her first-place trophy. The problem is, when I was in the salon the other day, Misty was rearranging. She asked me to hold her trophy so it wouldn't get damaged when she moved her desk, and I did."

"I think I can see where this is going?" I said, looking at Tyler.

"Oh, thank goodness," she said placing her hand over her heart. "I thought I was going to have to explain every second of it."

"You do if you want my help," Tyler muttered.

Tiffany gasped and her jaw dropped. "Fine. Misty was killed with her trophy, and it has my fingerprints all over it. I'll be the number one suspect in her murder. But I didn't do it. I swear. He told me

I'm not to leave town and has put a block on my magic."

"If you didn't do it, then you'll have no problem proving it. I'm sure Ashlyn and Blair will vouch for you." I lifted my glass to sip my wine and winked at Tyler.

"No," she said bolting from her chair and pacing the room. "I don't know if they will or not. We're not exactly friends, more like business acquaintances. I don't trust them."

"And you trust us?" I asked. My insides were rumbling like a slow stream of burning lava.

"I may not have shown it in the past, but yes, I trust you." She turned her pleading eyes on Tyler. "Will you help me? I can pay."

"I don't know, Tiffany," Tyler said, his eyes narrowing, his fingers drumming on the white tablecloth. "I don't know how I could possibly take your case knowing the way you treated Nicolas and Nerissa. You manipulated them with your magic, almost destroying their chance at happiness. That is not someone I want to work for."

"That was not me, it was Prudence." She held her fingers to the sides of her temples and pressed them against her skin. "She blackmailed me. I told you, she made me do it."

"What?" I asked. "Blackmail? What on earth could Prudence have had against you that she could use to blackmail you?"

Tiffany paled and paused a few meters from the table. "I can't tell you. You're going to have to trust me."

I ground my teeth together and lifted my jaw. "Trust you? That's rich coming from the most deceitful fae in town." I pursed my lips into a thin line and glared at Tyler, my eyes stinging from staring so hard.

I could use a disappearing spell on the woman, but that would go against the number one witch law of using magic to satisfy your own need. I was sure half the townsfolk of Saltwater Cove would thank me and give me the key to the town for getting rid of her.

Tyler stood, pulled his jacket from the back of the chair, headed around the table and stood behind my chair. "I think this conversation is over. You've wasted enough of our time, Tiffany. If you wouldn't mind, I'd like to salvage whatever's left of my evening with Evelyn."

Tiffany's face paled, and her jaw dropped to make a round O. Her head shook back and forth in little jarring movements. "No, you can't go. I need your help. I don't have a solid alibi for Misty's murder, and I just know that all the evidence will point to me, but I'm innocent."

My body ached from holding in my annoyance at this woman. "Tiffany enough is enough. If you're serious, tell us one truth that we don't know about you. Just one."

Silence met my words. Tiffany's eyes thinned, and she thrust her hands on her hips. "Fine. I'll give you two. My real name is Sabrina, and I had to leave my homeland of Savanna Woodlands because I killed a man."

CHAPTER FIVE

*K*illed a man? That's one hell of a secret to keep—*if it's true.*

Tiffany huffed and flopped down in the chair, dropping her head in her hands. "Happy now the cat's out of the bag?"

Tyler's wide eyes looked at me, and he shrugged, mouthing, "What do we do now?"

I returned a shrug and looked at a crushed Tiffany sitting deflated in the chair opposite. I held up my hand and paused Tyler. "Back in a sec. I think this conversation calls for a strong coffee or two." Moving to the edge of the dining area, I haled Marlana, ordered a cafetière for three and headed back in to see Tyler sitting in silence staring at Tiffany. The eeriness hanging in the air sent a cascade of shivers down my spine.

I sat down, and his spine stiffened. "Tiffany, I think you have some explaining to do."

"I've ordered a cafetière of coffee. Take your time," I said, my jittery insides desperate to know who she killed.

Tiffany's head snapped up, and there was an edge in her gaze that had my heart breaking for the woman. "I'm not a murderer if that's what you're thinking. There were extenuating circumstances."

Tyler fake-coughed. His gaze caught mine, and he tilted his head toward the entrance just as Marlana walked in. I smiled and nodded as she placed the tray of coffee on the table.

"Will there be anything else?" she asked, looking at each of us in turn.

"No thanks," Tyler said. "But if there is, we'll let you know."

She raised her eyebrows and looked him up and down. My gut tightened. If Tiffany weren't about to spill her guts, I'd put Marlana in her place.

Tyler handed Tiffany a cup of steaming coffee. "Unless I'm mistaken, you said you killed a guy. Maybe that would be the best place to start."

I pressed my hand to my twitching stomach and waited while Tiffany sipped her coffee.

Oh, come on, the anticipation is killing me. Jordi and Harriet are not going to believe this. Who did you kill?

She slid her coffee cup across the table and sighed. "No, the best place to start would be the beginning."

"I agree," I said.

"Like I said, my real name is Sabrina, and my sister and I used to live with my parents in the Savanna Woodlands. My sister, Johanna, is the kindest, most beautiful soul." A light shone from Tiffany as she spoke of her sister.

Tiffany has a sister…who knew?

She continued. "Johanna fell in love with and married Dane. Unbeknown to us, Dane was a demon werewolf. A witch had put a spell on him when he was younger, and the only way to break it was to get someone to fall in love with him and stay married to him forever. The witch was convinced due to his horrible and violent nature, no one would ever love him, let alone marry him."

Tiffany shot up and paced the small area behind her chair, twisting her fingers in tighter knots with each step. A heavy weight pulled at my chest, and I sucked in a deep breath knowing the story was going to get worse before it got better.

"He charmed Johanna with all sorts of love and affection. She was smitten with him, and even though he wasn't fae, my parents accepted him for Johanna. As soon as she confessed her love for him, he waited no time at all until they were married, and the spell was broken."

"What happened?" Tyler asked, sitting on the edge of his seat.

Tiffany stopped pacing, and her drained expression was clouded only by the depth of pain radiating from her eyes. "As if you can't guess. The spell was broken, and my trusting gorgeous sister was stuck in a violent marriage with a demon werewolf who used and abused her, punishing her for the simplest of actions."

"I'm sorry." A cold shudder ran through my body as I looked into her make-up-smudged eyes. "That must have been terrible to watch. I remember when Harriet was tied up and at the mercy of a madman—that almost killed me. I can't imagine how you must have been feeling."

"You cannot possibly understand." Tears ran freely down her cheeks, and she wiped them away with the back of her hand. "Johanna tried to leave so many times, and he always caught her. The punishments worse each time until the final one"— she paused and swallowed as though bracing herself— "when he killed our parents just to spite her."

Oh, God, no.

Tiffany continued. "She's a strong woman, but there is only so much one fae can take. On hearing he'd killed our parents, she retaliated and used her magic which angered him even more. He made sure no one would recognise her by disfiguring her face."

"Oh, my goodness, what did you do?" I blurted, the hairs on my neck standing to attention.

A blank expression crossed Tiffany's face, and she looked deadpan. "What any sister would do. I killed him with his own sword."

"Yes!" Tyler fist-pumped in the air, and a splash of coffee jumped the edge of his cup, landing on the white tablecloth. "Good for you."

"I saved my sister, but it was still a crime that had to be punished. One of my wings was torn, and they sent me to the Forsaken Forest Penitentiary." She stood tall and rolled her shoulders back. "After everything my sister went through, I was happy to take the punishment. I got out early because I caught the warden of the jail abusing his power."

Oh my gosh, this is better than any soap opera.

"Wait a minute," Tyler said, rubbing the creases on his forehead. "When you came to Saltwater Cove, you joined the same year as us. How can that be? You must be way older than we are."

Tiffany shook her head. "I am older, but not by that much. You see, once I served my time, I returned to Savannah Woodlands, but it was never the same. Everyone knew what I had done, and Johanna was so disfigured she wouldn't even leave the house. But word had gotten out, and she was granted one wish by the town sorcerer for the injustice done to her."

"Did she get her face fixed?" I asked, wiping my sweaty palms on my serviette.

Tiffany took a sip of her coffee, and her cheeks glowed a warm pink. "No, she asked for my powers to be restored and my wing fixed. But under fae law, one's powers cannot be restored if they were taken through an act deemed punishable by the Fae Council, and taking a life, no matter the circumstances meant most of my powers were gone and would stay that way forever. Johanna then asked for the next best thing."

"Which was?" My head was pounding, but it wasn't going to stop me from knowing the end of the story.

"Since she was always going to be recognisable, she asked for her appearance to be changed and a new life for us somewhere far away where we wouldn't be recognised, where we could live or lives out together."

Tyler snapped his fingers. "And that's how you ended up in Saltwater Cove?" Tiffany nodded. "I guess that's why you look younger and blend in so well with our year group."

"On the upside, Johanna will always be provided for, and with the name change it means she will be protected forever."

"I thought you lived with some distant relatives or something like that. Then again, I wouldn't know, you rarely give us the time of day. I've never even been past the foyer of your house."

"No, it's just Johanna and me." Tiffany's eyes thinned, and she held her gaze squarely on me. "Do you think it's been easy for me, knowing what I did, and that Johanna will have to pay for the rest of her life? Prison wasn't exactly a walk in the park. But it made me tough. If I was rude and mean, then people would stay out of my business and leave us alone. I did and said things I'm not proud of."

"I'm guessing you had to, to survive," I said, clutching my hands together.

"I don't trust easily," Tiffany snapped. "And now you know why."

"Yet, you trusted Prudence?" Tyler said, puffing out his chest and folding his arms. "How do you explain that?"

Tiffany's expression turned cold, and a grayness settled in her cheeks. "I had all the best intentions of flying under the radar when we moved to Saltwater Cove, of keeping my nose clean and staying out of trouble. Then Prudence turns up on my doorstep wanting to be 'best friends.' I don't know how, but she must have found out about Johanna because she threatened to expose her and her disfigurement to the whole town if I didn't become her best friend and do all she asked. Being her friend was the least I could do if it meant keeping Johanna's secret safe."

Tyler sniggered. "Yeah, that sounds like Prudence."

She continued. "I know I shouldn't speak ill of the dead, but that woman deserved everything she got."

"You could have fooled me, Tiffany." My blood began to boil. "You were the first to accuse Jordi of Prudence's death. If you didn't like her, why accuse one of my best friends?"

She stared at me, blinking rapidly while the colour drained from her face. "Did I? I guess I was thrown by her death and still worried that somehow she'd get to me from the grave. When she wants something bad enough, Prudence is the kind of woman that wouldn't let death stand in her way."

Looks like I'm going to have to have a chat with our resident Melting Pot Café ghost. It's time Prudence comes clean about how she found out about Johanna.

Tiffany turned her pleading eyes to Tyler. "Now that you know, back to my original question, can I hire you to prove my innocence?"

Tyler looked at me, and it was as though his decision lay with me. I tilted my head and shrugged. "It's your business, Tyler. The choice is yours."

"I appreciate you coming clean, Tiffany, but—"

She shook her head as though anticipating a rejection. "Tyler, if all the evidence points to me and I go to jail, there will be no one to look after Johanna, and that's just something I cannot even contemplate. I have never let anyone get close to us before, and I'm super protective of her, but if it will help, come over tomorrow and meet her. You'll see why I need your help."

"Come to your house?" Tyler said, as though she'd just asked him to walk the plank.

She nodded. "If it will help you take my case."

An electric buzz blasted through my system, and my belly ignited with a burst of energy

Hell, yes, I so want to see inside your place and meet your sister.

"And me? Can I come and meet Johanna too? I'm working in the afternoon, but free in the morning," I asked, a tingle running through my fingers. "Tyler and I often work as a team, so if he agrees to take your case, you're going to want my help too."

Tiffany rolled her eyes. "If you have to, but can we keep it between the three of us?"

"Of course," Tyler said, sending me a cheeky well-done-you grin. "If that is all, I'd really like to finish my evening with Evelyn. We'll see you tomorrow around tenish."

Tiffany pulled back and stopped still at Tyler's abrupt brush-off. "Oh, okay. Ten sounds good."

I watched her turn and walk out of the room pausing by the entrance to glance over her shoulder. "In case I forget to say it, thank you." And she was gone.

Tyler's jaw dropped, and his eyebrows shot up. "Did that really just happen?"

I licked my dry lips. "Well, if it didn't, we're both having the same dream…or nightmare."

CHAPTER SIX

Snuggled under the doona, the corners of my lips turned up as my fingers danced over the sapphire and diamond ring on my right ring finger. Heat crept up my chest and neck and settled in my cheeks. "Tyler Broderick, you certainly know how to woo a woman."

"It sounds like someone had a great night last night." The sassy voice of Miss Saffron sailed from the doorway.

Startled, I sprang upright in my bed just in time to catch my furry familiar as she jumped up on the bed next to me. She plonked herself down beside my thigh and let out a sullen purr until I rubbed under her chin and behind her ears. "Is that what you want, hey?"

"You know it," she said in her cheekiest voice. Her eyes widened, and her whiskers twitched as she flung her paw right on top of Tyler's ring. "Um, I think you have it on the wrong hand. Doesn't an engagement ring go on the left-hand ring finger?"

"An engagement ring would, if indeed this were an engagement ring, but it's a promise ring."

Miss Saffron sniggered. "A promise ring? What a cheapskate. I bet he was Scrooge in a past life."

"Ooh, you are so cheeky this morning." I scooped her up in my arms, and she snuggled in under my chin, her fur tickling my cheeks and nose. "But I love you all the same."

Miss Saffron's paw circled her head. She arched her back and ran her tongue up the side of my cheek, leaving a trail of wetness in its wake. "Must you?"

Wiping the fresh dampness from my cheek I pushed the doona down. "Okay, that will be enough sucking up from you. I can hear the coffee machine calling."

Miss Saffron stretched her legs and jumped from my arms onto the lump of doona clumped in the middle of the bed. "I'm assuming your date with Tyler went well?"

Threading my hands into the armholes of my dressing gown, I tied it around my waist and stood looking at Miss Saffron as she circled first one way and then the other before settling in a curled position on my bed.

"Oh no you don't," I said, lifting her off the bed and onto my warm shoulder. "If I'm up, then so are you."

My lips drooled at the seductive scent of coffee wafting up from the kitchen. "Looks like Aunt Edie is up nice and early," I muttered running my hand up and down Miss Saffron's spine. Turning the corner into the kitchen, I froze, clamping my jaw tightly closed. A rush of burning heat invaded my neck and cheeks, and I blinked at the sight before me.

Detective Huxton stood by the coffee machine decked out in Aunt Edie's pink and purple fluffy dressing gown. It wasn't the first time he'd stayed over, but it was definitely the first time parading around in Aunt Edie's dressing gown. I cringed. I didn't want to think about what led to his decision. I glared down at Miss Saffron and pursed my lips in a thin line while my thoughts screamed from my mind to hers.

You cheeky little familiar, you knew all along he was here, and you didn't tell me? I bet you knew he was up too.

Miss Saffron ducked her head underneath my arm.

"Oops," she mumbled as quiet as she could inside my head, but I still heard it.

Oops? Oops, is that all you can say? This is not over by a long shot, my furry friend.

I held my breath and edged myself back the way I came, taking each step as slowly as I could, rolling through every part of my foot. Zero noise was the objective, anything not to gain his attention.

Miss Saffron whispered as clear as day in my mind. "You're going to need to get used to him being here. Where else do you think he's going to live after he and Edith get married?"

I guess I hadn't thought of that.

Am I going to come downstairs every morning and find the image of Detective Huxton in Aunt Edie's dressing gown? Why is he even in her dressing gown? On second thought, I don't want to know. What will he be dressed in next? I scrunched my eyes shut and wiped any image of them together.

Maybe it was time I moved out. Harriet had a spare room; I could stay with her.

"Evelyn?" Detective Huxton's voice rang out. "Are you okay?"

I lifted my eyelids one at a time to see him holding a tray with two coffees and a plate of pancakes. "Um, yeah, sure. My eyes are still adjusting to the image of you in Aunt Edie's dressing gown."

He looked down at his attire, and his cheeks glowed crimson red. "I see. Yes, I can see how this would be a frightful sight. In all honesty, I hadn't expected to run into you this morning, and as for the dressing gown, I spilled a glass of red wine on my clothes last night. Edith washed them, but they're still in the dryer. I wanted to surprise her with breakfast, so I grabbed whatever I could."

"You don't have to explain, and pink really does look good on you," I said, unable to keep my lips from turning up into a grin and the laughter silent in my belly. "It brings out the warmth in your cheeks. I wish I had my phone with me, I could have captured this moment in history. I could have used it as bribery material at a later date."

He grinned smugly. "Ha-ha, very funny. I suppose I was asking for that. Point taken; don't wear Edith's dressing gown again."

I covered my lips with my fingers and swallowed back the new round of giggles that threatened to seep out past my fingers. "I'm sorry. It's not my place to judge."

Please change the subject.

I walked toward Miss Saffron's basket in the corner of the kitchen and placed her down, her golden almond eyes looking straight at me. "You'll keep," I whispered.

She huffed, circled her bed, and snuggled down with a breath of air into a tight furball.

I made a beeline for the coffee, my insides screaming for an infusion of the brown liquid to kickstart my body into full motion. My hands moved automatically, making my coffee, and my thoughts drifted to the planned adventure later that morning to Tiffany's house—or was it Sabrina now? We all knew her as Tiffany, so unless she said otherwise, Tiffany it is.

"Evelyn?"

I jumped at the raised intonation in Detective Huxton's voice.

"Sorry, I was off with the fairies." One fae in particular. I leaned against the edge of the kitchen bench and folded my arms across my chest. "Was there something else you wanted?"

"Not really. Just to remind you of our two-way street," he said.

"I remember. I want this murder solved as quickly as possible too, you know." The bubbling scent of rich caramel mixed with chocolate wafted up from behind me. I spun and quickly had the milk blended with my coffee, and I sipped, my insides jumping for joy as the hot liquid inched its way down my throat.

The skin on my forehead tightened. "I thought Aunt Edie was opening The Melting Pot this morning?"

"She was, and then she changed her mind and arranged for Keelin to open up for her. Give us a little more time together before I have to get back to the investigation."

Ah, Heaven.

"I know it's early, but do you have any leads yet?" I asked, looking at him over the top of my steaming cup.

"The investigation is still in its early stages, but all I can tell you is that I'll know more when I get the results back from the trophy. The fingerprints should give us a clear suspect or two. Then they'll be some interviewing I expect."

My stomach tensed. "Okay, but maybe you shouldn't just rely on the fingerprints. I'm sure there is more to this than meets the eye."

"What makes you so sure?" he asked, in his usual suspicious policeman tone.

I shrugged. "We live in Saltwater Cove, a town full of magical beings. Since when is murder as clean-cut as it seems?"

"True. Anyway, I better get this coffee up to Edith." He headed toward the staircase pausing by the entrance. "You'll let me know if you hear anything?"

I nodded and forced my lips into a smile. "Of course."

Heat blasted my neck as he paused a moment longer staring straight at me before he turned and left the room.

I wasn't lying, I didn't know anything, at least not yet. Tiffany had better have been telling the truth last night. I moistened my dry mouth with another shot of coffee and movement from the corner of the room caught my eye. Miss Saffron sat up, her ears standing upright, and her fur spiked. "What's got your attention?"

She issued a low growl from her belly, pounced up onto a chair and then onto the kitchen bench. She paused then slinked her way to the window. "As I suspected."

"Excuse me?"

"Looks like our resident ghost has decided to pay us an early morning visit." Miss Saffron paused. "No wonder my caution radar was screaming out."

I joined her at the window and recoiled at the image of Prudence's ghost standing by our pond in her pink New Year's Eve dress. Nausea welled in the base of my stomach at the thought of interacting with the woman. Finding out that our parents were best friends before we were born was gut-wrenching, and now it appeared she was stuck in our pond. Banish the thought. It was bad enough dealing with her when she was alive, but knowing she was going to haunt me from beyond the grave was too much.

I turned my back on the woman and stood, my built-up anger festering until my body was as tense as an elastic band ready to snap. Why did she have to turn up two days before my birthday? "I am not going to let that woman get to me." Closing my eyes, I took several calculated breaths calming my seething insides. "There, that's better."

"Evelyn, surely you must wonder," Miss Saffron said.

"Wonder what?"

"Why she's still here." Miss Saffron withdrew her gaze from Prudence, slinked to the end of the counter and sat facing me eye to eye. "I've been a familiar long enough to know something or someone is keeping her here. She wouldn't be stuck in your pond if she didn't have unfinished business."

Her words hung deep in my heart. Unfinished business, what unfinished business could she have? "Please don't tell me she has to make amends to everyone she's wronged? There aren't that many hours in a day. If that's the case, she'll be stuck in the pond for all eternity."

"Really, Evelyn. It's my job to guide you to be the best witch you can be, and I think it's time to have another chat with Prudence to see what you can do about releasing her spirit."

I glanced over my shoulder at the lost soul by the pond.

I'm not sure about releasing her spirit, but I did want to know why she had blackmailed Tiffany into doing her dirty work.

I grabbed Miss Saffron's head between my hands and rubbed noses with her then smacked a great big kiss on the top of her head. "If you say so, oh great one."

"You're not funny, you know," she said, pulling her head from my grip, leaping onto the floor, and prancing over to her bed, her head held high.

Pulling my dressing gown tight around my waist I pushed the door open and headed down to the pond, my chest tightening with each step.

Prudence's head snapped up, and a huge smile spread across her face. "Evelyn, it's so good to see you again." She stood hands clasped together at her waist.

There was no malice behind her tone as far as I could tell, but I didn't trust her as far as I can throw her.

That is the most ridiculous thing to say, as if you can throw a ghost.

"Hi, Prudence, it's nice to see you again too. What brings you back this time?" I asked, hoping she knew the answer.

She looked at the pond water and frowned; the ceases wrinkled her forehead. "I'm not sure. My memories are all jumbled, but I'm pretty sure I was supposed to tell you something important."

"Can you remember what it was?"

She shook her head.

"Who it was from?" I asked, more eager this time.

She shook her head again, and I had the urge to grab her by the shoulders and shake it out of her, but that was not an option with a ghost. "Try to remember; it could be vital. Maybe it's why we're still house buddies and your spirit's stuck here."

I paused and then tackled the reason for my visit. "I was talking to Tiffany last night. You remember her, your best friend?" I watched Prudence's face go through a myriad of expressions coming to rest on one with pursed lips and eyes that looked straight through me.

Prudence crossed her arms and huffed. "Why should I care who you have been talking to?"

There's the Prudence we know and love to hate.

"I would think you'd be interested since she was your best friend."

She shrugged as though what I said meant nothing. "Best friend is a loose term. We were friends, yes, but our friendship had its moments."

"I cannot believe you said that." I stood with my hands on my hips and glared at the woman. "You and she were best friends for as long as I can remember. I'm pretty sure she was the only one who put up with your nonsense, and now that I know the full story, you were lucky you had her at all."

Prudence's jaw dropped. "What do you mean, 'the real story'?"

Talking to this woman had my head throbbing, and I pressed my fingers to my temple. "She told me how you blackmailed her into being your best friend. That is the lowest of lows if I ever heard one."

Prudence stood stock still as though she were a statue, her eyes turning glassy. The way she didn't move was freaky. Pulling my gaze from her, I paced and shook out the tingles in my fingertips. "It's time to come clean, Prudence. Why did you do it?"

She finally broke her statue-like appearance and turned her back on me. "Like you would understand."

"Try me," I said, my temperature rising. "I'm a pretty good listener."

"Fine. I was sick of everyone leaving me for other friends."

"Excuse me?" My breathing sped up, and I was seeing red. "Let me get this right. You blackmailed her so she would be stuck being your friend forever?"

Prudence nodded, still with her back to me. "Yes."

"Oh, my goodness. I cannot believe our parents were even friends. You are...were despicable. You don't keep friends by blackmailing them, Prudence." I was fuming, my whole body ready to explode. "You were your own worst enemy. When we first met, you were one of the nicest people, so loving after finding out my parents had died. Then you decided popularity was better no matter who you trod on in the process, and you turned into Prune face."

Prudence spun and glared daggers at me. "You take that back right now."

"You can't take something back that's ground in Saltwater Cove history. You'll forever be known as Prune face, and that's on you. I didn't make the name up."

"No, it can't be." Prudence's body shot backwards as though she'd been hit with a clenched fist. She hunched over and grabbed her knees, her breath breathing heavy.

I gasped and watched stunned by the sudden force that pushed her body backward.

"What just happened?" she asked, straightening her body upright.

I shook my head and shrugged. "I have no idea. You realised the consequences of your actions from your real life, and it was as though someone punched you. Your body took the brunt of the force, flinging you backwards. Maybe it's karma? They always say what goes around, comes around—or something like that."

"I don't care what the hell it was, I don't ever want to experience it again," she said, rubbing her chest.

"Perhaps you're stuck here to make amends to all those you hurt when you were alive." As soon as the words left my lips, a cold shiver raced through my body cementing itself in my chest.

Oh, please no, she'll never leave if that's the case.

"I have better things to do than to stay here all day. Maybe you should give a good strong go at working out why you're still here." I turned on my heel and marched towards the house looking over my shoulder long enough to see her disintegrate into thin air.

"Maybe that will keep you thinking until we meet again."

CHAPTER SEVEN

By the time Tyler pulled up outside I'd gone over my conversation with Prudence in my head so many times I'd made myself nauseous just thinking about it. "Will that woman ever understand there are consequences for one's actions?"

"Why the grumpy face?" Tyler asked as I closed the car door behind me.

Looking over at him, my thoughts halted, and my breath caught in my throat. How is it that he grew more handsome each day? I was the luckiest witch in Saltwater Cove. "Good morning," I said leaning over and planting a kiss on his soft lips. I lingered, delighting in their delicious taste.

Mm, I could kiss these lips forever, and I plan to do just that.

The spicy scent of his aftershave accosted my nostrils, and I pulled away to see the glint in his eye as he ran his tongue over his bottom lip. "And a good morning to you too."

I picked up his hand and threaded my fingers in his. Pulling it up to my mouth I kissed his hand and his lips parted.

Nice to know I can have an effect on him.

"If I ever start the day grumpy, I want you to remind me that I'm the luckiest witch in the world to have you by my side."

He returned the kiss shooting a tingle down my arm.

"You have a deal as long as you remind me what a lucky man I am to have you in my life."

I squeezed his hand. "Deal. Should we get this show on the road? I, for one, can't wait to meet Tiffany's sister."

Tyler pulled away from the curb, and his face lit up. "I know me neither. I can't imagine what they must have gone through—first, to live through such a nightmare, and then move here not knowing if their past would follow them."

I huffed and shook my head. "Yeah, only to be blackmailed by the town snob."

He continued. "I was curious. It's not that I didn't believe Tiffany. I mean it's almost impossible for a fae to lie, but I just wanted to be sure what we were stepping into. I used my super 'computer powers' as you would say and did a bit of digging into her story. Turns out, there really is a Forsaken Forest

Penitentiary, and there is a record of a Sabrina having been released on good behaviour."

"No way," I said, the words coming out breathier than I anticipated. "It's true then, everything she said? I wasn't sure if I'd believe her until I saw Johanna with my own two eyes, but now that you've done the snooping, it kind of makes it all very real."

My heart shattered for the two women. The memory of my parents' deaths floated back into my thoughts. Losing them in the car accident was horrific, but I couldn't imagine I would even have survived if they'd been murdered at the hands of a deranged werewolf.

"It almost makes you see why Tiffany behaved the way she did for so many years," Tyler said, turning down Tiffany's Street.

I looked at him, my forehead creasing, and I pressed my lips together. "Mmm, doesn't excuse it though. She said and did some pretty awful stuff."

"I know, but how about we look at the present situation for what it is? She wants to hire me to prove she didn't kill Misty, and that's what we should be focusing on, not the past."

I glanced at him and smiled, and my stomach fluttered as we pulled into Tiffany's driveway.

"What?" he asked, innocently.

"I love the way you see things so cut and dried. You're right, we should be looking at the situation at hand."

"Good, then let's do this, Evie Girl?"

I nodded and jumped out of the car, waiting at Tiffany's gate for Tyler. Clasping my hands at my chest, my thumbs circled each other until I felt the soft touch of Tyler's hand on my lower back. "Is it me, or do you see this house differently now that you know it's a protective haven for Johanna?"

Tyler tilted his head to the side and looked at the limestone house before us. The drapes were dark, dreary, and drawn closed. The house sat alone in the middle of a large block of land which made sense considering their story and wanting to keep Johanna a secret.

"It looks the same to me." A shiver ran through him, and his body did a little shake. "Whoa, someone must have walked over my grave."

"Come on." I opened the gate and headed down the path with Tyler hot on my tail. "The sooner we get this over and done with, the sooner I can get back to The Melting Pot for my afternoon shift."

Tyler rang the doorbell, and the surrounding air thickened. My stomach was turning in circles, like a washing machine on a spin cycle. I wiped my sweaty palms across the back of my butt and scrunched my hands into fists.

Why am I so nervous? We hold all the cards in this interaction.

The door flung open, and Tiffany stood in a pair of black dress pants and a bright pink off-the-shoulder sweater. Her skin was ashen white against the brightness of the jumper. It took a moment to put my finger on what was different. Then it jumped out at me like a jack-in-the-box—she wasn't wearing any make-up. How unlike Tiffany. The grimness of her expression portrayed a woman carrying the weight of the world on her shoulders.

"You came," she said, her gaze roaming between the two of us. "I wasn't sure if you would after I wrecked your birthday dinner last night."

"We said we would, and we're here," Tyler said, clearing his throat. "Mind if we come in?"

Tiffany nodded and stepped to the side. The foyer had the same daunting sterile atmosphere as it had when we were here trying to prove Jordi's innocence.

"Wait," Tiffany said, closing the door with a thud. "This is all new for Johanna. She's willing to meet you. All I ask is you try not to stare; it makes her uncomfortable. She's still vulnerable and now and then the nightmares return, especially on the anniversary."

"We'll try our best, Tiffany, but there are no promises here." Tyler stepped closer and withdrew his notepad from his pocket. "If we're to help you, everything must be above board and transparent for all to see."

"I understand." The lump in Tiffany's neck moved up and down as she swallowed. She turned and headed in short jerky movements towards the room at the end of the foyer. "This way."

I licked my lips and looked at Tyler's wide eyes staring back at me. He held his arm open for me to go first. Stepping off, my gaze roamed the bland room, and it was only then that I noticed there were no pictures or family decorations of any kind in sight. No way of identifying who lived here.

Now I know why.

Tiffany paused, and her right arm snapped up like a stop sign halting Tyler and me dead in our tracks. "Johanna?" Tiffany called in a strained tone. "Can we come in?"

"Yes, Tiffany it's okay." A petite voice sailed across the room.

Tiffany sucked in a deep breath, and I held mine and followed her into what looked like a dimly lit lounge room. In the corner, a woman with long wavy blonde hair sat at the end of the couch reading a book, her legs curled underneath her. I edged myself closer, and my chest burned from lack of oxygen.

This is it. No turning back now.

"Johanna, this is Evelyn and Tyler. They're the two I was telling you about yesterday," Tiffany said, easing down on the couch beside her.

Johanna closed the book and looked up; our gazes met. My lips pressed together, and the tension drained from my body. The scars, although visible, were nothing as I'd envisioned.

She smiled, and she was beautiful. I was expecting a horror version of Frankenstein's daughter or a patchwork quilt, but the woman in front of me was nothing of the kind. It was true, she had around five incredible scars down one side of her face all different lengths, but she still looked like a woman, one who had been in a terrible accident. They'd healed the best they could, but people would still cross the street if they saw her coming.

"It's lovely to meet you," she said, brushing the stray strands of hair behind her ears.

Tyler was the first to speak. "It's lovely to meet you too, Johanna. Do you mind if we sit down?" he asked pointing to the sofa catty-cornered to where she was sitting. She nodded.

I made haste and joined Tyler. "I'm pleased to meet you, Johanna. Do you know why Tiffany has asked us here today to meet you?"

Johanna pursed her lips together and squinted her eyes in Tiffany's direction. They had an inner glow lined with a twinkle of mischief. "Yes, she asked you here because my sister is an overprotective worry-wart."

The image of Tiffany as an overgrown wart popped into my head, and an eruption of giggles threatened to escape. I pressed my lips together, the tightest they've ever been and pasted on a neutral expression.

"Johanna, that's not exactly right, now, is it?" Tiffany asked, clasping her hands together in her lap.

"No, I guess not." She paused and looked at Tyler, then at me. "Sorry. You're here to see if I'm real or a figment of Tiffany's imagination and if the story she told you was real."

"Pretty much." The heaviness in my chest was hanging around like a lost deer unable to find its way back to the herd. "After Tiffany told us your story, I think deep down I was hoping it wasn't true. It must have been horrible to go through what you did and live your life out in hiding here in Saltwater Cove."

Johanna shrugged. "It's not that bad. I'm alive and thankful every day I'm still breathing and that I have my sister by my side. She's the one who does all the worrying. She has always insisted I stay inside for fear of what the vultures outside these walls would say when they saw my disfigured face. It's the least I can do after what she did for me." She reached over and squeezed her sister's hand and a lone tear trickled from Tiffany's eye. She ducked her head hiding her weakness from our view.

I pinched the inside of my cheek between my teeth. It was the first time I'd seen Tiffany show any real emotion. It was odd, to say the least. The heaviness in my stomach returned, and I sat still, taking in the display of unspoken love between the sisters.

"Forgive me for asking," I said, cringing at the question about to seep from my lips. "But why haven't you tried plastic surgery?"

"We want her to," Tiffany said, looking over at her sister.

"But it was too dangerous due to the depth and location of the wounds." Johanna twisted and pulled at the hem of her shirt, a classic nervous signal if I ever saw one. "So we decided against it."

A stillness fell over the room, and a brush of anxious tension settled between us.

Tyler cleared his throat. Both ladies turned their heads and looked at him with matching questioning gazes. "I'm curious. You said you had your wing torn as punishment."

"Yes."

"Can I see it?" he asked, an eagerness to his tone I'd not seen in a while.

Tiffany shook her head. "No."

Tyler leaned forward and rested his elbows against his knees. "Then how do you explain your disappearance last year at the annual show when we followed you from the judges' arena?"

Tiffany pulled back, and her posture stiffened. Her eyes narrowed, and she squinted at him. "You followed me?"

"Of course, we did," I said, my body angling away from her. "You had just left the judging arena, no one was supposed to be in there. But you were...why? What were you doing?"

Johanna's head turned toward her sister, and her brow wrinkled. "Tiffany, why were you there?"

"I...um." She paused, her troubled gaze looking between the three of us.

Adrenaline pumped through my veins, and I forged ahead. "You do realise a secret room was found in the arena underneath the grandstand? It was the first sighting of the Licarbre fern in Saltwater Cove?"

"What?" Johanna paled.

I nodded. "Yes, that's when we realised black magic had appeared and with it the illegal sale of contraband on the black market."

Johanna's blanched expression turned to her sister. "Do you know anything about that, Tiffany? Please tell me you had nothing to do with it?"

An awkward silence had my stomach knotting.

Tiffany's skin flushed, and she rolled her eyes. "I believe that's my business. Not everything I do is newsworthy, Evelyn."

"No, but if it has—"

Johanna's words were interrupted by several sharp knocks at the front door. Her back stiffened, and she gripped the edge of the lounge, her veins popping against her skin. Her eyes were wide enough to see the whites around the pupil. "Oh, no."

Tiffany bolted from her position and ushered Johanna out through a door leading to the back of the house. "You know what to do?

Johanna nodded, wrapped her arms around her sister and squeezed her eyes shut. "I love you."

"I love you too, baby girl. Now go, I'll come to get you as soon as the coast is clear," she said, pulling away and patting her on the backside. Johanna was off like a bolt of lightning. Once she was fully gone, Tiffany spun on her heel and looked straight at me. Another succession of knocks had her flinching backward. "Who can that be at my door? I don't get many visitors, except you two."

"It could be a number of people, but I'm leaning toward the police," Tyler said, checking his watch.

"The police?" she said, the veins in her neck pushing against her skin. "This is not good, not good at all. If it's the police, it means the fingerprint results are probably back and they point straight to me."

"You don't know that." A shiver walked across my shoulders.

"Don't I?" Tiffany snapped. "I was home with Johanna when Misty was killed."

Tyler stood and sighed. "Then you have an alibi. Why not tell the police?"

Tiffany paced the room shaking her head and twisting her fingers together. "No, absolutely not. Johanna's existence stays a secret, I'll not have her ridiculed and made the laughing joke of the town. Promise me you won't tell anyone about her? Promise me?"

I held my hands up in a placating manner. "Okay, okay, calm down. We won't tell anyone about her. Will we, Tyler?" I glanced his way, and he nodded.

A louder more persistent knock echoed through the house, and Tiffany paused her step. "Okay, let's get this over with." She rolled her shoulders back and stuck her nose in the air as she walked toward the door.

Tyler and I followed, keeping sure to stay back and let Tiffany take the lead.

Pausing, she took in a lungful of air and pulled it open. Detective Huxton's gaze found mine. Officer Cameron Martins stood close behind him, his gaze just as intent as Huxton's.

Oh no, how am I going to explain this visit?

Detective Huxton stepped back, and his Mediterranean blue eyes widened. He stared straight at me. "Evelyn? What are you doing here?"

My mouth dried, and I swallowed back the knot forming in my throat. "Oh, you know, Tyler and I were in the neighbourhood."

His gaze moved to Tiffany. "And you thought you'd pop in and see Tiffany? I was under the impression you and she weren't friends."

I shrugged. "Friends is a very loose term, don't you think?"

"We're not friends," Tiffany snapped. "They're here on business."

His eyebrows shot up. "Business? What sort of business?"

Well, I guess that clears that up. Friends we are not. No news to me.

Tiffany stepped forward and put her hands on her hips, her glare piercing his. "That's none of your business, now is it, Detective Huxton? Why they're here is no concern of yours. What brings you by?"

Detective Huxton's lips thinned, and his cheeks reddened.

You are not going to win any battles with that attitude, Tiffany.

He cleared his throat and moved up to the next step, doubling the tension simmering between them. "I have a few questions regarding Misty's murder."

"I had nothing to do with her murder," Tiffany spat, her shoulders raising and lowering with each sharp breath she took.

Cameron Martins huffed. "That's not the way it looks from our end."

Detective Huxton glanced over his shoulder, his eyebrows raised, and lips pursed together. Cameron's back stiffened, and he dropped his chin stepping back out of Detective Huxton's personal space.

What is that all about?

"Tiffany, I'd appreciate it if you would accompany us to the station for questioning," he said, his gaze drilling her to the spot.

Tiffany's skin turned ashen under his formidable stare. "What? Why? I was nowhere near the salon when it went down. Ashlyn and Blair can tell you. I was in there to see them earlier in the day but not Misty."

"Interesting." He paused and flipped his notepad open and checked over his notes "Nope. According to Ashlyn, you came in to see Misty."

Tiffany's draw dropped. "No, that's not true. They're lying."

"Why would they lie?" Cameron asked, a single brow raised in a crooked line.

I looked at Tiffany and a streak of doubt had my belly doing topsy-turvy backflips.

That's a very good question. Maybe it's time I paid them a visit.

Tiffany shrugged, and her hands raised and flopped down by her thighs. "I have no idea, but they are. I swear to you that I had nothing to do with Misty's murder."

Detective Huxton cleared his throat or was he hiding a giggle? "You'll forgive me if I don't believe you at this point. Your track record isn't exactly sound."

Tiffany's hand grabbed my forearm and squeezed. I gasped as her nails dug in, sending pain shooting up my arm. Her haunted gaze looked from me to Tyler and back again, and tears glazed over her eyes.

"Evelyn, Tyler, you have to help me," she pleaded.

I peeled her fingers away from my skin, the blood in my arm began circulating again and a rush of tingles flooded my fingertips. "I think it's best to go with the detective, Tiffany, and be honest and answer his questions. The truth is always the best path to follow."

"That's sound advice." Detective Huxton put away his notepad and pen and nodded. "Let's go."

He stepped aside and held his arm out towards the waiting patrol car.

"Very well then, but you'll see I am innocent." She rolled her shoulders back and stuck her chin out, turning to look at me one last time. "I know this is all a mistake, but if things drag on, promise me you'll look after the precious situation we were discussing?"

"I…um." The words were stuck in the back of my throat like a lump of peanut butter.

"Promise me, Evelyn," she said, her voice soft and her eyes wide. She sucked in a steady breath and held my gaze, waiting.

"Let's just say I'll keep regular tabs on the situation and make sure all is okay."

She let out a breath and nodded clasping my hand in hers. "Thank you."

Tyler threaded my hand in his as we watched Detective Huxton escort Tiffany down to the waiting police car. "Do you think she's telling the truth?" I asked.

He nodded. "I do, and don't ask me how I know because I couldn't tell you."

"Sounds like you're taking the case," I said, raising my gaze to see his intently focused on the back of Tiffany as Officer Martins opened the back door for her.

"It appears so."

CHAPTER EIGHT

"Tiffany?"

The startled voice of Johanna caught me by surprise, and I spun to see the woman standing there frozen to the spot. The haunted emotions conveyed in her expression clawed at my heart.

"Where's Tiffany?" she asked, her fingers twisting in knots at her waist. "Who was at the door? Why didn't she tell me where she was going? She always tells me where she's going."

Tyler closed the door as I headed towards the woman, my pulse racing.

Great, how am I going to explain this one?

I cleared my throat. "Um, there was an incident yesterday at Salty Snips."

The scars on her cheek wrinkled and doubled as she frowned. "What do you mean? 'Incident'?"

"Come and sit down." We headed back to the couches we occupied earlier, I sat opposite Johanna, and Tyler sat by my side. His close presence calmed my racing heart. "Yesterday, Misty Sinclair, the owner was found murdered in the back of the salon."

Johanna gasped and pulled back. Tears welled in her eyes, and she stared at me as though she were asking what it had to do with Tiffany.

"There's no easy way to say this, so I'm just going to come straight out with it. Tiffany asked us to come meet you today because she knew there was a possibility she would be accused of Misty's murder."

Johanna sat stunned; her hand gripped the edge of the couch.

I nodded. "Unfortunately, Tiffany's fingerprints were found on the murder weapon, and it looks like she has become Detective Huxton's number one suspect."

"No," Johanna said, shaking her head from side to side in sharp movements. "That is a lie, it's just not true. Tiffany would never kill anyone."

"But she did," Tyler said, leaning forward and placing his elbows on his knees. "She killed for you, remember? What's to say she wouldn't do it again?"

Johanna bolted from her seat and headed to the other side of the room. She paced the carpet, a frown dented on her forehead. "No, you've got it all wrong. She only killed in self-defence to save me. She would never take another life on purpose. Everything she has done has been to protect me from the outside world."

"Who knows, maybe Misty threatened your life and Tiffany retaliated?" Tyler took on the role of devil's advocate.

Pain bled through my chest, but I ignored it and pushed on, needing answers. "Johanna, I understand how you feel."

She spun around, and there was a tightness in her eyes that held me at bay. My body tensed as I watched the woman transform into a defensive sibling before my eyes.

"Do you? Do you really understand how I feel? Do you have an innocent sister being accused of murder?"

My jaw stiffened, and my body itched to jump up and scream, yes, I do. I tensed and stood, moving over to where she was standing. "Johanna, I may not have a blood sister, but I have three best friends who are my entire world, and they've been in enough life-threatening situations to scare me half to death. I could not imagine a day without them.

"When Harriet was tied to a kitchen table in an old, abandoned hotel, a deranged witch standing above her pointing a carving knife straight at her heart, what I felt in that moment was very real—and it had nothing to do with the fact that she isn't my blood sister. She is as much my sister as Tiffany is yours. I understand how important it is to protect those we love."

"I'm sorry." Her chin lowered, and a lone tear trickled down her cheek. "I've been telling Tiffany for a while now that I'm finally okay with the way I look, and she doesn't have to protect me anymore. She's given up so much for me. All I want is for her to start living her life and not worry about me for the rest of it. I know she hasn't always done the right thing, but her heart is in the right place."

"It's not as easy as that, Johanna," Tyler said, rubbing his fingers over his bottom lip. "Over the years, Tiffany has done some questionable acts. She's not the most popular fae in Saltwater Cove. I'm afraid that doesn't leave her in good stead with the police."

Johanna paled and grabbed Tyler's hands in hers and squeezed. "You have to help her, please. I know in my heart she didn't do this terrible thing. I'll do anything to help her."

"It all depends on the evidence. They have her fingerprints on the murder weapon, and she was at the salon yesterday. Add it all up, and it's not looking good."

"Wait," Johanna said, her eyes lighting up like a sparkler. "What time did this all happen?"

Tyler looked at me, and I shrugged. "I guess it was sometime during their lunchbreak. Ashlyn found her body after she returned from lunch with Blair."

A smile broke out across Johanna's face and my heart skipped a beat. For a moment, her scars seemed to disappear, and a beautiful striking woman sat in her place. "Tiffany couldn't have done it. She was home here with me from around eleven onwards."

"That's not much of an alibi. You forget that no one but Tiffany, Evelyn and I know you exist." Tyler sat back in his chair and breathed a sigh under his breath. "By the sound of it, since arriving in Saltwater Cove, Tiffany has spent her entire life protecting you and keeping you a secret from the outside world."

"Even befriending the town snob," I added.

Tyler continued. "If you come forward, it could unleash a whole set of new questions she may not be prepared to answer. Questions about your past." He paused and pulled at his collar. "Last night, Tiffany wanted to hire me to prove her innocence. I told her I wanted to meet you first and then I would think about it. I'm willing to take her case, but you have to promise me you'll stay here behind doors and let us take care of it. I'll keep you updated every step of the way, and I'll leave you our contact details. I'll be in touch as soon as I have news."

Johanna clasped her hands together at her chest and squealed. "Thank you, thank you, thank you. I'll do whatever you say—just get my sister out of jail."

I glanced at Tyler and pressed my lips together. *Easier said than done.*

***

Pushing through the door of Salty Snips with Tyler, I was taken aback by the buzzing hive of activity. Misty had been dead just over twenty-four hours, yet the hairdressers appeared busier than ever.

Two customers were getting shampoos at the basins in the back. A pretty blonde was in front of a mirror having her hair straightened by an employee I'd never seen before. Ashlyn was involved in an animated discussion with a woman while she cut her hair, and Blair was standing at the products by showing an array of items to Marlana Hass, from The Four Brothers.

Vivienne Delany, Aunt Edie's best friend, sat waiting in front of a mirror, her nose stuck in a copy of *Witch Weekly*, the trashiest gossip magazine ever produced for the supernatural.

"I'm surprised to see you here," I said, moving over to stand behind Vivienne.

She glanced up into the mirror and smiled at my reflection. "Evelyn. Sorry, I didn't see you come in. I was engrossed in the latest saga about the sexy Elliott Malone. He's such a honey."

A grimace screwed up Tyler's face. "Elliott Malone…The movie actor? Isn't he a witch?"

"A-huh." She closed the magazine, placed it in her lap and swivelled in her chair to face us. Vivienne's eyes lit up like gemstones. "Witch or not. He's my favourite actor. Did you know that he is down to the final two location choices for his next movie? You'll never guess where they are."

An instant flashback hit me, and my mind wandered to the half-naked body of Elliott Malone with a sheet wrapped around his lower half in a love scene from his last movie *Take It or Leave It*. Damn, that man has the body of a model, complete with a six-pack of abs.

I cleared my throat and heat warmed my neck. "I can't say I've heard. *Witch Weekly* isn't on my top ten list of reading material, Vivienne."

She continued. "Well, it should be. Ever since Edith lent me a copy last summer, I can't stop reading it. I may not be a witch, but it can't hurt a girl to dream. It has all the latest news, not to mention some great visuals, if you get my drift."

Oh no, Vivienne did not just wink at me, did she?

"I just love Elliot's movies, you can't go past, *Love on the Rocks*. I'd give anything to be his co-star in that movie. I bet I could teach him a thing or two between the sheets."

"Vivienne!" I said an octave higher than I expected.

"What? I'm not that old you know, and I have been known to turn a head or two in my younger days. He's choosing between Saltwater Cove and Seacliff Sands for his next movie. Isn't that just the best? Can you imagine how exciting it would be to have Elliott Malone right here in Saltwater Cove?"

Elliott Malone in Saltwater Cove? That could be fun.

"Anyway, what brings you two by?" she asked.

Tyler nodded towards the girls. "We're here to see Ashlyn and Blair. I'm actually surprised they're open so soon after what happened to Misty."

"I know, me too. I was surprised when Ashlyn called and said my appointment was back on. I thought they'd be more upset with what happened to Misty, but as she said, they still have to earn a living and they can't do that if they keep the salon closed."

"I suppose not," Tyler said, popping his phone out of his pocket and snapping a few shots of the goings-on. "Who is that woman down there?" he asked, pointing to the lady straightening hair.

Vivienne followed his gaze and shrugged. "Oh, that's the new hair stylist. I know Ashlyn mentioned last time I was here that they were looking at hiring as business had picked up. What a day to start work."

"Tyler...Evelyn. What a surprise." A nasal woman's voice echoed behind me.

I turned to see Ashlyn staring down at me, her hazel-green eyes speaking volumes to her sudden control and power at the salon. My gaze dropped to her temporary made-up badge.

"Manager?" I said, my gossip radar was well and truly spiked. "That didn't take long. Misty's body is barely cold, and you've taken over the reins already."

The corners of her lips turned down, and she shrugged. "Someone has to, and there is no one else as qualified as I am. I was Misty's second-in-command, so it's only natural I assume the manager's role."

"I'm surprised this place is still not deemed a crime scene," Tyler said, picking up an odd triangular-shaped object from a trolley and twisting it in his hands.

Ashlyn's arm shot out and swiped the object from Tyler's hands, placing it on a trolly behind her. "It took some doing, but it was cleared early this morning. It's what Misty would have wanted, to see her legacy continue and thrive. We'll always remember her. In fact, I'm going to get a new trophy made up dedicated to her commitment to this salon. She will be missed, but as they say, the show must go on."

Ashlyn's words distressed me to no end, but I couldn't work out why. She had every right to take over, I guess—that is until the will was read. "That's kind of you; Misty would be impressed. And it doesn't hurt to assume the role of manager, at least until the will is read and the new owners of the salon decide what they are going to do with the place."

Ashlyn's face dropped, and her cheeks turned as white as a bowl of flour. It was obvious I'd struck a sore point. She swallowed and then brushed the hair from her face. "I'm sure Misty will do right by me. Besides, I don't see how it is any business of yours."

And with that, she flicked her ginger red locks over her shoulder and stormed toward the room at the back of the salon.

"I think someone's hit a nerve," Vivienne whispered.

"I believe you may be right." I smiled at Vivienne and grabbed Tyler's hand. "Please excuse us."

She smiled. "Of course." And spun her chair around to face the mirror, planting her nose back in her trashy gossip magazine.

My stomach tensed as I moved toward Ashlyn. I whispered to Tyler, "Is it me, or does it seem as if Ashlyn was under the impression she was going to get the salon after Misty's death?"

"Sure sounded that way to me," he said, keeping in time with my step. "They've been working together for years, and it was common knowledge Misty had no relatives. Maybe she assumed she would get it— maybe she will." He paused and rubbed his nose blinking his eyes open and shut several times. "For now, can we get back to the reason for our visit? All these sweet scents from the lotions and sprays are playing havoc with my senses."

I stopped and pulled him up short of where Ashlyn was sitting in the back office. "Oh, my poor sweet, Tyler," I said, placing my hand on his warm cheek. "allergic to the scent of women." A giggle bellowed up from my chest, and I smothered it with my hand.

"Oh, ha-ha, very funny." He smirked then leaned and whispered against my ear, his hot breath skimming my earlobe and sending goose bumps down my neck. "There's one woman I'm not allergic to. In fact, I could spend every second of every day with her and still be thirsty for more."

Yes, please.

I swallowed and squeezed my thighs together squashing the instant desire that flared within me. "Down boy, there will be plenty of time for us later. I've got your lifetime commitment right here." I waggled my right hand at him, the gemstone of my beautiful ring glittering in the overhead light. "Remember?"

He nodded. "I do." His lips found mine, and he pressed against them. He pulled away, and my breath hitched wanting more. "I'd love to kiss you more but standing in the middle of Salty Snips is not my idea of romantic."

A rush of heat bolted up my neck and cheeks, and I stepped back to see most of the women in the salon either staring or giving me a thumbs up. "Of course. But I'll take a raincheck?"

He winked and the heat in my cheeks doubled. "You're on. Time to find out if Tiffany was telling the truth."

I followed Tyler to the counter where Blair stood having bid her customer farewell. "Blair, I was just saying to Ashlyn that I'm surprised you two have opened up today considering Misty was killed right here in this salon only twenty-four hours ago."

Blair's gaze shot up, and she froze, her hands resting on the half-closed drawer of the cash register. "Um." She dropped her gaze and closed the cash drawer. She turned and began to stacking product on the shelves behind the counter, and my stomach turned over at her effort to ignore us.

Not on my watch.

"Anyone would think you two have something to hide getting back to work so quickly," I said, baiting her for a reaction.

"What?" She spun on her heel; a bottle of conditioner slipped from her hands, crashing to the floor. Drawing her darkened gaze away, she bent to retrieve the bottle. "Sorry about that, slipped from my hand."

Ashlyn suddenly appeared beside Blair. "Is there something I can help you with? As you can see, we're rather busy."

My gut was telling me Blair had been spooked by our questions. "We'll come straight to the point."

I looked at Tyler, and he took over asking the questions. "Tiffany claims she was in here yesterday before Misty's murder to see you two ladies, yet when the police questioned you, you indicated that was incorrect and she was here to see Misty. Care to clean up the confusion for us?"

Blair stood stock still while Ashlyn rolled her eyes and tutted loud enough that she caught the attention of certain ladies in the salon. "She may have come to see us, I can't remember."

"What do you mean, 'you can't remember?'" Tyler asked, his forehead creasing. "It was only yesterday for goodness' sake."

Blair opened her mouth to speak, but it was Ashlyn's snarky voice that answered. "Exactly, yesterday was crazy, we had a full day of customers and then poor Misty was murdered while we were at lunch together down at the Esplanade Café. You can't imagine what a shock it was coming back to find this place a crime scene. Yes, Tiffany came in early in the day, we chatted, and she talked to Misty too."

"So, she did come in to see you?" Tyler asked, his tone short.

"Yes, she did." Blair's shaky voice didn't go unmissed.

"And then she spoke to Misty." Ashlyn was quick to add. "I don't see what the big deal is?"

I folded my arms across my chest and gritted my teeth, my gaze firmly on Ashlyn. "It's a big deal for Tiffany who, at this moment is down at the police station under suspicion of murder."

Both women gasped in unison, but it was Blair who paled and faltered in a step backward. "What are you talking about?" she asked.

"It appears her fingerprints were on the murder weapon along with Misty's and another unidentified set."

"What?" Blair's pitch raised two octaves and her eyebrows shot towards the ceiling. "How do you know that?"

"You forget it's not what you know, but who," I said with an air of cheeky confidence. "And I happen to be pretty close with Detective Huxton. We're practically family."

As soon as the word slipped past my lips, my stomach dropped, and a cold shiver rocketed through me.

Family? He's going to be my new uncle once they are married. Talk about Awkward with a capital A.

"The murder weapon? The police said they found Misty's trophy next to her body. Is that what killed her?"

"I'd say it was from the massive blow on the back of her head, but sure, the trophy played a part in it." The sarcasm dripped off my tongue like liquid chocolate.

"Oh, my goodness, that's terrible," Blair said, her hand covering her mouth.

"Not as terrible as professing your innocence and not being believed which is the predicament Tiffany now faces." Tyler's lips turned down, and he stood his ground. "Tiffany maintains her innocence. She said she didn't do it."

"Pfft," Ashlyn said, rolling her eyes. "Of course, she would say that. You're talking about a devious, deceitful fae here, and one who hasn't always followed the rules. Let's not forget how she put a love spell on Nicholas and made him fall in love with Prudence then lied about it. How can you believe anything she says? The words falling from her lips are tainted with darkness, hatred and lies."

Ashlyn had a point. My stomach recoiled at the memory of poor Nerissa, heartbroken after Nicholas dumped her—both manipulated by Tiffany's lies. But if I'm to believe Tiffany's story about Prudence blackmailing her, what choice did she have?

I rubbed my forehead to alleviate the stabbing pain shooting back and forth behind my eyes. Tyler's stern voice brought my thoughts back to the present.

"Tell me, why didn't they find either of your fingerprints on the trophy?"

Ashlyn glanced sideways at Blair, and they exchanged looks as though to confirm they were on the same page. I swear the air between the two of them was getting thicker by the second. My witch-confession radar was on high alert, and I knew Blair was close to cracking, but how to push her over the edge was the question.

"It's a well-known fact to those who work here or are regular customers that no one is permitted to touch Misty's trophy. It's the only one she has ever won. That is…was her pride and joy," Ashlyn said leaning into the counter.

"It's true," Blair said. "Once I pulled it down to dust around it, and she went ballistic."

"Seriously?" Tyler asked. They both nodded.

Time to take this conversation to the next level. I cleared my throat and smiled. "While we're on the topic of Misty…Ashlyn, since you found the body, do you think Tyler might be able to pop down, and you can tell him exactly how the crime scene looked when you found it? He was just saying before we came in that he never gets to see enough and practice his observation skills." I turned to Tyler, dipped my head to the side and plastered on my best fake smile. "Isn't that right sweetie?"

Please pick up on my lead, Tyler.

It took mere seconds before he whipped his head around to Ashlyn and smiled. "Yes, that's right. You'd be doing me the biggest favour, Ashlyn. The more training, I have, the better private investigator I'll be."

Ashlyn's lips pursed, and she folded her arms across her chest. "There's nothing to see. It's not even a crime scene anymore."

Tyler took a step closer, and my chest tightened as he gave Ashlyn one of his flirty smiles. "Maybe not, but I know you'll understand how important it is to do what it takes to rise to the top of one's field. I mean, just look at you."

A crimson blush worked its way up her cheeks, and her gaze dropped. Giggling she swatted Tyler across the shoulder. "You're right. I know what it takes to be number one."

Oh please, don't make me throw up in my mouth.

I bit the inside of my lip and ignored the bubble of annoyance growing in my belly.

"So, is that a yes?" Tyler asked, adding a cheeky wink for good measure.

Ashlyn's eyes sparkled. She gave him a nod and returned a sassy grin. "Why not? It's not like you'll be able to see much, but I can explain what I saw when I found Misty's body."

"That would be a great help." Tyler slapped his hands together and looked at me, turning his back to the ladies. "You don't mind waiting here, do you? I promise I won't be long."

How could I begrudge him when he was only following my lead? I pushed down the jealousy bug simmering inside and offered up a comforting smile. "Of course not. Go do your thing."

He nodded and winked then turned back and gifted Ashlyn a smile. "Shall we?" he asked, holding his arm open for her to lead the way.

A high-pitched giggle assaulted my ears, and it was as though Barbie were standing next to me. Ashlyn covered her mouth with her hand and blinked in rapid succession. She headed towards the back of the salon chatting and laughing with Tyler.

"Typical," Blair said so quietly I barely heard.

"Blair, I couldn't help but notice—and please let me know if I am stepping over the line here," I said, placing my hand on her forearm, "but it seems Ashlyn has taken to the manager's job a little too well."

Blair licked her lips and paused. She looked over her shoulder at where Ashlyn and Tyler were animatedly talking. "I guess."

"You know, if you need someone to talk to, you can always count on me." I looked her square in the eye and felt her arm tense below my hand. "You know me, the good Samaritan."

Blair frowned, her hand fidgeting with the bracelet on her wrist. She kept glancing over her shoulder as though checking if they were coming back, but Tyler had Ashlyn deep in conversation.

I pressed my lips together and shook my head with a sigh. "I hope you haven't done anything stupid, Blair."

She whipped her head back to me and the wrinkle in her forehead had doubled. "What do you mean?"

"I would hate to see you end up like Misty, that's all." I paused for dramatic effect. Judging by the large gulp Blair took, I figured my ploy was working. "I can tell Ashlyn isn't her normal self anymore. It's like she's taken the job of manager to a whole new level. It's all power and control for her now."

Blair blinked and licked her lips. "You have no idea."

Adrenaline burned through me, and I pushed for more. "How is that good for you, Blair? I'm not an idiot, I can see how uncomfortable you are around her. Let me help you."

Blair shook her head. "No, no you can't I'm in way too deep. I couldn't get out now even if I wanted to."

Too deep in what?

"Blair, look at me," I said, commanding her focus, and she obeyed. "Tyler and I are here for you, and if you're in trouble, we can help you. I promise to use all my witch powers to do whatever I can to help you out of whatever predicament you're in. Just tell me what it is."

Blair let out a huge breath and closed her eyes for a moment. "I don't know what to do. Ashlyn is out of control. Tiffany and I are just pawns in her power game."

Bingo.

A single tear streamed down Blair's cheek. "Evelyn, you might be my only hope."

CHAPTER NINE

Nervous jitterbugs jumped around inside my stomach. Blair was on the verge of spilling her guts, and I was going to be the first to hear about it. A sudden intrusion of high-pitched laughter stiffened Blair's spine, and she stepped back from the counter, brushing the wrinkles out of her blouse. "I promise to let you know when the product you're after comes back into stock, Evelyn."

Talk about an unwanted brush-off. I could have strangled Tyler at that moment. Two more minutes would have been all it took, and Blair would have been eating out of the palm of my hand.

"You ready to go, sweetie?" Tyler looked at me with a smile.

I wanted to scream "No, I am not," but I knew he'd done the best he could to keep Ashlyn away.

"Sure." I pulled two of Tyler's business cards from his pocket and handed one to each of the ladies. "If you think of anything that could help us, you have my number, and this is Tyler's new business number. You can call either of us."

"Anytime," Tyler said with a nod.

"Thanks," Ashlyn said, staring straight through me. "But as far as I'm concerned Tiffany deserves everything she gets. Now, if you'll excuse us, I think you've wasted enough of our time. I'm sure you can show yourselves out."

I forced a smile and nodded. Turning on my heel, I headed for the door, my blood pressure rising with each step.

Safely outside and heading for the car, I let rip. "I cannot believe that woman dismissed us like that. Misty would be turning in her grave if she knew how she spoke to us."

"My thoughts exactly," Tyler said as he pulled away and into the line of traffic. My shoulders slumped against the chair, and my head lulled to the side relaxing on the headrest. "Thanks for the warning, by the way. Next time you want me to sneak off with another woman, give me the heads up so I can make sure I have plans. That woman did not shut up, and she barely said anything I didn't already know."

I flinched at the tension embedded in Tyler's expression. "Yeah, sorry about that, I had to think quickly. I could see Blair was about to break."

Tyler glanced my way. "Please tell me you got something, and my time stuck with that woman wasn't wasted?"

My cheekbones pushed up, and the skin tightened around my eyes. "Oh, it was worth it, all right. Two minutes longer would have been better, but Blair did confirm that the power has indeed gone to Ashlyn's head, and Blair really looked afraid of her. Whatever Blair's involved in, she's in way too deep and it's freaking her out. She was ready to spill when you guys came back."

Tyler pulled up outside The Melting Pot and killed the engine. "That's great. If she was that close, then she will be again. I think there's more to it with those two. Maybe it's something for my super computer powers to look at. I'll see what I can dig up on them."

"Agreed," I said. The closer I drew to the door of The Melting Pot Café, the more my tastebuds drooled over the decadent scents wafting from the kitchen. "Keelin has outdone herself today. This place smells divine."

"I couldn't agree more." Tyler patted his tight abdominal muscles. "None, for me though if I'm going to keep this Greek-god-looking body you keep raving about."

I swatted him on the shoulder then reached up and planted a kiss on his warm cheek. "You're *my* Greek god though, and that's all that matters."

He winked and blew me a kiss, and my heart skipped a beat. I would never get tired of those kisses or the real ones for that matter.

Pushing through the door I reveled in the comforting homey atmosphere Aunt Edie had created with the renovations to the café. I loved that I was a witch working in a café designed like a witch's cave. The new ultra-modern decor brought it up to date with the rest of the world. Any stranger walking in would think it was all make-believe—Saltwater Cove residents knew better.

We made it halfway to the kitchen when an uproar bellowed from the back. Male and female voices vied for top position in the shouting match. I looked at Tyler, and he shrugged. The customers sitting closest to the kitchen looked at me with questioning glances and my stomach dropped. The voices continued, and the steam was slowly boiling inside my ears.

What is going on back there?

"That voice sounds familiar," Tyler said as we moved behind the counter and through the doorway to the kitchen.

I froze, as did Tyler behind me, both of us staring at the chaotic scene before us.

Eli? My protector sent to ensure black magic stays well away from me has finally returned.

I tried to speak, but my mouth went dry, and the words faded away.

"I don't care if you say you worked here. You haven't since I've been here, so get your bony little butt out of my kitchen," Kellin yelled, standing tall in front of Eli, her hands on her hips.

"Bony little…how dare you," he said, recoiling back as though he'd been punched in the stomach. "Do you even know who I am?"

Keelin folded her arms across her chest, pushing her shoulders out. "If you don't mind waiting out in the main area until she gets back, I'm sure she'll sort it all out."

Eli's cheeks turned bright red, his hands shook by his sides and veins popped out against his skin.

She shook her head and stood her ground. Good on Keelin for defending The Melting Pot; Aunt Edie would be proud. But I wasn't sure Keelin was ready to go head-to-head with my protector. This place had only just finished being renovated; I'd hate to have to explain the damage if Eli let his powers get the better of him.

A rigidness set in my bones, and the hair lifted on the back of my neck almost as though an icy wind had brushed past.

I shivered then snapped, "Eli!"

His gaze turned, and he immediately drew back from Keelin, putting some much-needed space between them. He lifted his chin and stood a moment before his shoulders and torso loosened slightly.

It was only a moment before his eyes softened and his smile resembled the old Eli. "Evelyn, thank goodness you're here. This woman wouldn't—"

He stormed at me, babbling. I jabbed my arm straight out with my hand flat and my fingers pointing to the heavens. "Hold it right there, bucko."

His lips ceased moving. His shoes skidded across the floor, and a high-pitched screech echoed through the kitchen as he stopped inches short of my hand colliding with his chest.

"What gives you the right to barge in here and assume everything is the same as when you left?"

"What are you talking about?" he said, his arms open and eyes squinted.

"This is Eli?" Keelin asked, pointing at him, her gaze looking him up and down. "Wow, by the way you were all talking about him being your protector and all, I expected someone with a little more muscle."

Eli's nostrils flared, and he pushed up his sleeves. "Who knew I'd be replaced with an obnoxious know-it-all woman who can't keep her nose out of other people's business?"

"Eli, that's enough," Tyler said, stepping forward and placing his hand on my lower back. "Back off. Things are not the same around here as before you left, which I might add was a good eight or so months ago."

The engorged vein in his neck started to disappear. He turned my way, and my gut knotted at the hurt rooted in his expression. "Didn't you get my letter?"

"Oh, I got your letter all right." Shoving my hands on my hips. "It didn't say much, only that you would be back for my birthday and you would explain the life and death situation when you got back."

"Voila." He grinned a cheeky grin and spun in a circle. "Here I am back for your birthday."

I ground my teeth together, and my jaw stiffened. "Don't laugh it off, Eli. I needed you, and you weren't there for me, and neither was your supposed replacement."

His expression dropped. "No one came in my spot?"

I shook my head. "No."

Tyler huffed and glared right at Eli. If his eyes shot laser beams, Eli would have gone up in flames in seconds. "We were counting on you, man. We had a deal, remember? We'd both work together doing whatever was necessary to keep Evelyn safe.

"What happened?" Tyler asked. "She could have used your help in Australia, where were you?"

"I can't save Evelyn or anyone for that matter if I've had my powers stripped or I've been banished, can I?" Eli paced the confines of the kitchen, his expression one of devastation. "How long is Edith going to be? I'd rather not have to repeat the story if I can help it."

I looked at Keelin, and she shrugged. "She went to the main house for some lunch, but I know she was feeling tired. Maybe she took a nap."

"I'll find her." I turned to Tyler and smiled. "Can you do the introductions while I have a chat with Aunt Edie?"

"Of course," he said, with a smile then moved off to stand between Keelin and Eli. I ignored his voice and concentrated on reaching my aunt.

Aunt Edie, can you hear me?

I waited to hear her chirpy voice resonate in my head, but nothing.

I know you're not far away, please answer me. We have a situation in the kitchen at The Melting Pot that needs your immediate attention.

I waited…and waited. *Why isn't she answering me?* My chest seized. *What's going on?* I could hear Tyler, Eli and Keelin's voices animatedly chatting in the background, but where was Aunt Edie?

Aunt Edie, where are you? This is the last telepathic phone call I'm making. Look out if I have to walk into the house to find you.

A grumble of a stirring registered in my mind, and I knew I'd made contact.

Aunt Edie?

Evelyn, is that you? I must have dozed off on the couch during my lunch break.

I'd say you were out like a light. I tried to call you a few times. What is wrong? Are you okay?

Of course, love, just tired from the morning work at The Melting Pot, that's all. My body isn't as young as it used to be, dear.

Nonsense. You're only as old as you feel. Right now, I need you in the kitchen of The Melting Pot. Eli is back, and he hasn't exactly gotten a warm welcome from Keelin.

Say no more, I'm on my way.

I turned back to see Tyler and Eli deep in conversation while Keelin had done a vanishing act. "Please don't tell me you vanquished Keelin while my back was turned."

Light laughter assaulted my ears. "She wishes," Eli said with a giggle. "She's out front. I have to say she's on the ball out there."

"Of course, she is. You don't think Aunt Edie would have replaced you with someone who couldn't keep up, do you?"

Eli paled, and his eyes widened. "Replace me?"

"No one knew when you were coming back," I said, cocking my head to the side and shaking it.

"What was I doing, Eli?" Aunt Edie's annoyed tone rang out from the doorway, and we all turned to see her standing by the kitchen entrance. Miss Saffron sat in her arms, her pesky expression directed at Eli.

Wow, that was quick. Pays to be a master witch. What I wouldn't give to be able to do the transportation spell like she can. One day.

She continued. "You left me no choice. I had no idea when you were coming back."

"I know I left in a hurry." He paused and rubbed his chin.

"Keelin was keen to cut her shifts down over at The Four Brothers—something to do with Mercer's nephew, Slade. She said he arrived just before Christmas, but they didn't get on. So, I offered her a job here to help out while you were away."

"And I'll be forever grateful," Keelin said as she slid past Aunt Edie and dropped a pile of dirty dishes in the sink. "Thank goodness that lunch rush is over. Slade is a rotten egg of the monumental kind. If I'd had to work with the pathetic bozo on one more shift, I was going to drop him like a lead weight."

My eyebrows shot up into my hairline, and I smiled at the tough image of Keelin sitting at the forefront of my mind.

"I'm sorry about earlier," Keelin said in Eli's direction. "But I had no idea who you were, and I'm on strict rules from Aunt E, that no one but family and employees is allowed behind the counter and in the kitchen."

Aunt E? Even I don't call her Aunt E, and she's my flesh and blood aunt.

Eli continued. "I understand. I said I would be back as soon as I could. It's not like I was on vacation galivanting around the world, I was dealing with a life and death situation."

I planted my hands on the island bench in between a pile of dishes and a variety of salad bowls. "Enough with the life and death talk already. Just get to the explanation before I turn another year older."

Judging by the collection of chuckles and giggles that followed, the irony of my comment was not lost on them. "If it weren't so serious, I'd be laughing too."

Mis Saffron jumped out of the comfort of Aunt Edie's arms and landed on all four paws on the kitchen bench. Slinking toward me, she said, "Let the man speak." As clear as day inside my head.

Aunt Edie looked at Eli, stuck her hand up and pointed to the ceiling. "Hold that thought." She turned to Keelin and patted her arm. "Keelin, honey do you mind holding the fort down out front when the afternoon café and cake hunters come in? Until I can be sure what is going to transpire here, I think it's best if we keep it between family."

"No problem on my part," Keelin said, holding up her hands. "The less I know about it, the better. I may live in a town occupied by witches and shapeshifters and other supernatural beings, but I'm happy to go about my business and leave the nasty stuff to you guys."

"You may not have magical blood running through your veins, but that doesn't stop you from being an important member of our community and The Melting Pot Café family."

Keelin nodded and her gaze lowered. She cleared her throat. "I'll be outside manning the floor if anyone needs me." And she was gone.

Aunt Edie pulled a stool from behind the counter and made herself comfortable. "All right, Eli, let's hear it."

Pale-faced, Eli stood. His gaze moved from Aunt Edie to Tyler then Miss Saffron and came to settle on me once more. My body tensed at his apologetic expression, and a wave of nausea rolled around in my stomach.

"Evelyn, I know I could have handled things better. I should have been here to protect you if you needed it, but they say your past mistakes always come back to haunt you. Mine came back tenfold. It makes me a lousy protector I know, but when the clock is running out on your life and you have to choose between being stripped of your powers and doing jail time or trying to prove your innocence, I'm sure you would agree with me when I say that proving my innocence was all I was concerned with at the time."

"Oh dear," Aunt Edie said, her hand rubbing her neckline.

"Eli, I had no idea." A wave of dizziness hit me all at once, and I sucked in a slow, deep breath. "Stripped of your powers and jail time?"

He nodded.

"What did you do?" I asked, bracing myself for the worst.

Eli dropped his head and leaned against the edge of the island bench. "It all happened so quick I was barely able to follow it myself."

"But you did do something?" Tyler asked.

Eli shook his head vehemently, his eyes widening to show the white surrounds. "No, I didn't; that's the issue. I take my job as protector very seriously, as Evelyn would know. While on a previous assignment, we were caught in a terrible situation."

"We?" I asked.

"My charge and me." He rubbed his forehead. "I'd rather not relive the nightmare again, so I'll just say I pulled out every stop I knew in an impossible situation, and it still wasn't enough."

I held my breath, knowing there was worse to come.

"All my efforts were in vain. I couldn't protect her even with my powers. She died in my arms." He paused, his body swaying as the words left his lips. He squeezed his watery eyes together.

Oh no, poor Eli.

Pain shot through my chest, and I realised I was holding my breath. My heart tore into pieces, breaking for what he must have gone through, and here I'd been thinking he'd ditched me for a better offer.

"Wait, hold up," Tyler said stepping forward. "I'm confused. If you did all you could, then why were you going to be stripped of your powers and thrown in jail?"

Good question.

"Because, after all this time her parents decided to sue me. I don't know why, but they blamed me for her death. It took longer than I expected, but I had to find the evidence I needed to exonerate myself in the eyes of the law."

A deathly silence settled in the room, and it was Aunt Edie's sweet forgiving voice that broke the tension.

"Eli, you have a good heart. I can't imagine you not doing everything in your power to save her. Can I assume now that you are back, you have it all sorted?"

He nodded and swallowed, dipping his head. "I have, but not without destroying the heart and soul of a family in the process."

"How so?" I asked.

Eli stared at me, and my entire chest caved as I watched him shuffle backward, his face drawn. He dropped his jaw to answer, but in that second, his voice had vanished. His shoulders rose and fell. It wasn't hard to tell he was struggling with the emotional turmoil of the situation. Who wouldn't? I'd be a babbling mess by now. "It's okay, Eli, you don't have to tell us if it's too painful."

The whip of chilled air circled the kitchen launching a string of tingles down my arms. Eli sucked in an audible lungful of air and shook his hands. Looking over his shoulder, he forced a smile. "It's better if it comes out now and you hear it from me instead of some twisted version from someone else at a later date."

Eli paused before turning around to face us head-on, his gaze hollow and without feeling. He licked his lips. "It gets me every time I think about it, it takes a moment to prepare myself. I've never known hatred to be so all-consuming it can take over one's entire reason for living, rule their entire life until there is nothing left but to live in a bitter world of loathing and self-destruction."

Aunt Edie's spine stiffened, and she sucked in a gasp of breath. My pulse picked up.

Aunt Edie, are you all right?

Yes, love. Eli's words dredged up an old haunting memory I'd rather have stayed hidden.

Oh. Is there anything I can do?

No, love. She patted my arm and smiled. *Let's hear the rest of the story. We owe him that much.*

"After she died, I was relieved of my protector duties until a full investigation had taken place. I was cleared of any wrongdoing, reinstated, and given a new charge to protect. I will never forget her or what happened, but I thought that was the end of it. Unbeknown to me, her parents wouldn't let it rest, they kept investigating, trying to find new evidence to locate and convict her murderer."

"Sounds pretty full-on," Tyler said, folding his arms and leaning back against the kitchen bench.

"I was surprised when I found out, but even more surprised to find out all the evidence pointed to her sister."

"No," Aunt Edie said, in a shaky disbelieving voice.

Tyler stood frozen, staring at Eli, not even blinking. A clamp tightened around my windpipe, and my breathing sped. I forced out the words I was looking for. "Her sister's hatred of her was strong."

He nodded. "Yes, she loathed the very ground she walked on."

"Good heavens, why?" Aunt Edie asked.

"Casula was bequeathed to Prince Amaurri since birth. Since conception actually. It was planned that way. The joining of their kingdoms would have meant great power for both families. Then Quinteth was born, an unexpected child, one conceived in love, not a necessity, and one who would steal the heart of many a man."

"Let me guess," I said shaking my head. "Prince Amaurri fell in love with her too."

"Bingo. As soon as his gaze fell upon Quinteth, they were mated, destined to be together forever, which didn't bode well for Casula. She not only lost the love of her life, but her parents doted on Quinteth as did everyone who met her. An attempt was made on her life which was where I came into the picture. I had no idea Casula's hatred of her sister had grown so fierce she planned every meticulous detail of her demise. It was only when her parents drew closer to the truth, she planted enough evidence to point to me as the killer."

He paused, and the vile taste of bile rose to the back of my throat.

"They'd already lost one daughter, and proving my innocence meant I had to expose their other daughter as a murderer." Tears freely ran down Eli's cheeks, and he wiped them away with the back of his hand. "It rips my heart out knowing I couldn't save either of them."

"I'm so sorry, Eli. I should have known you wouldn't have left me unless it was important."

"Thanks, Evelyn."

Aunt Edie pushed up from her chair and walked toward Eli. She threaded her arms around him and just held him. She oozed calm, and he stood there soaking it in.

A knotted twinge bit at the inside of my stomach, and my cheeks warmed—a senseless murder stemming from jealousy and revenge.

My own loving parents rose to the forefront of my thoughts—murdered because they wanted to keep the one item that can control all magical worlds, the Sphere, a secret and from falling into the wrong hands.

I've heard it said that revenge is a plate best served cold. I can't wait to find out.

The soothing hand of Tyler rubbed up and down my back, and my insides relaxed. Looking into his gorgeous blue eyes, a sense of belonging washed over me, and I knew I was exactly where I was supposed to be.

Aunt Edie stepped away from Eli and I watched a smile light up her eyes. Her gaze scanned the room, and she cleared her throat. "I have an announcement to make."

What announcement? You never said anything about an announcement.

My voice must have registered in her mind because she turned and pointed straight at me. "That's because I haven't made it yet." She cleared her throat and continued, "I think it's time I retired."

"What?" My body froze to the chair as though I were paralysed.

"You can't retire," Eli said, shaking his head.

Tyler added, "Retiring is for old people and you're far from old."

Keelin entered just at the moment and plonked a bunch of dirty dished in the sink. "What all the commotion?"

"Aunt Edie's retiring."

Keelin's back stiffened, and her brows pulled together while her gaze immediately went to the woman in question. "What are you talking about?"

Aunt Edie took a deep breath, her gaze looking around the room at everyone's shocked reactions. A warm smile crossed her face. "I am honoured that you all value me so highly, but time is too valuable to waste, and I've wasted enough when it comes to Micah. There comes a time in a witch's life when she must decide. Evelyn, love, I'm not getting any younger, and I'm getting married soon. I don't want to waste any more time. I have all of you including Harriet to look after The Melting Pot."

A burst of energy rocketed through my chest. I threw my arms around her and squeezed, soaking up her love. "I guess I always knew this day would come, but I hadn't thought it would be so soon."

She giggled. "Okay, maybe I can semi-retire, take a back seat so to speak. Now that we have enough staff, I can take time off knowing The Melting Pot is in good hands."

"Hell yes, it is," Keelin said, following up with a sharp slap on the bench.

"I second that," Tyler said, fist-bumping Eli and then Keelin.

"It's settled then." She pulled away and grabbed at the sides of her head. "I can't believe I just did that."

"Well, believe it, and I, for one, am thrilled for you," Keelin said, holding her fist out toward Aunt Edie, who reciprocated the fist bump, followed by a laugh. "Evelyn and I can talk details later, but for now can we keep this between us? I want a chance to tell Micah myself before he finds out from someone else."

"Sound fair," I said, beaming at my aunt.

I'm so proud of you.

Thank you, sweetheart.

A sharp succession of claps echoed from across the room, and all eyes turned to Eli. "Right, now I've caught you all up, and I've been privy to Aunt Edie's bit of news. I'm sure Evelyn and Tyler can pass on my story to Jordi and Harriet. My number one priority is to find out the Saltwater Cove town gossip."

I looked at Tyler, and the cringing expression on his face said it all. "Fine, I'll tell him."

"Tell me what?" Eli asked all eager-like.

I was surprised he hadn't heard already. Hot gossip in this town spread like honey. "Where do you want to start?"

"We can cross off new employees at The Melting Pot, I think we've covered that for now."

Keelin headed toward the door. "I'm sure you can handle this one without me. I've got to do the final touches of cleaning and sorting out in the main area." She gave Eli a wink over her shoulder. "Next time, maybe come bearing gifts. It will get you a lot further." Then she was gone.

I watched her leave and wondered.

Did Keelin just flirt with my protector?

The unexpected intrusion of Aunt Edie's voice in my head caught me off guard.

I think you're right. They would make a cute couple.

Cute couple? Are you serious? Eli's only gotten back from a harrowing ordeal, and you're match-making him up already? Can we let him settle back in and let the cards fall where they may?

Yes, you're right as always.

Eli folded his arms. "That's one thing I haven't missed."

"What?" I asked.

He nodded toward me and then toward Aunt Edie. "You two having your internal conversations. I see things haven't changed much on that front."

I poked him in the belly, and he cringed, swiping my hand away. "You'll keep. Now, where do you want to start?"

"Good to have you back, Eli." Aunt Edie pointed over her shoulder. "I'm going to give Keelin a hand."

I nodded and turned back to Eli. "So...?"

"How about working backwards from the most recent events to what happened in Australia."

"I've heard it all before." Tyler reached over and planted a peck on the side of my cheek. "If it's all right with you, I'm going to head off to follow up on that other case I have at the moment."

"Other case?" Eli asked, leaning forward, and resting his elbows on the bench. "Anything I can help you with?"

Tyler shook his head. "Not at the moment, but if I need your help, you'll be the first to know."

I squeezed Tyler's hand and watched the sexy sway of his derriere as he vanished from sight.

"You two still have it bad for each other," Eli said, giggling. "I'm glad to see it." He paused, then grabbed my hands in his and looked intently into my eyes.

My breath caught in my throat, and I bit my top lip. His cool touch flattened the searing heat discharging from my palms.

"Evelyn, I want you to know you mean the world to me and there was no way I would have left you unprotected unless I knew you would be looked after.

I had no idea my replacement didn't turn up. I'm so sorry, I'll be following up on it; you can count on that."

"It's okay, Eli." I gave his hands one strong squeeze and then slid mine out. "I know you wouldn't have left me if it wasn't important. I do trust you with my life."

He cleared his throat and brushed his hands together as though he were clearing them of dirt. "I have to ask…that gorgeous sapphire and diamond ring on your finger, is it an engagement ring?"

Oh darn, I thought he'd missed that altogether.

I shook my head. "No, it's a promise ring from Tyler for my birthday. It will be an engagement ring one day. Does that bother you?"

His eyebrows furrowed and then released. "Hell no, I think it's fantastic. I know he loves you more than life itself and would do whatever is needed to protect you. It's good to know he's going to be around for a long time."

"Forever," I said with a genuine smile.

He nodded and smiled then shoved his hands in his pockets. I took his actions as a green light to go ahead. "While you've been away my life has been anything but boring. There will be plenty of time to catch up on all the events, but for now I guess the most important news to tell you is that of Misty Sinclair."

"The hairdresser?"

"Yes, she was found murdered yesterday afternoon. Killed with her own trophy. It looks like Tiffany is the prime suspect, although she maintains her innocence." Saying the words left a vile taste in my mouth. After everything that woman has done, I still find it hard to believe she had nothing to do with Misty's death.

"I'm not surprised. She's a piece of work that fae." He wrinkled his nose. "Was there any magical funny business with this murder?"

"Detective Huxton doesn't think so."

But I do.

"I didn't ask what others thought. I was asking if you thought magic was involved."

I nodded. "Yes."

He grabbed a bag I hadn't noticed from the ground and hiked it over his shoulder. "Sounds like the police have it all in hand. I'm going to get going if that's okay with you. I'm beat, and I haven't had a good night's sleep since..." He paused, tilted his head to the side and raised his eyes in a classic thinking pose. "Since I left Saltwater Cove."

My jaw dropped. "That was months ago. The rest of my gossip can wait. Off you go and get some sleep. You'll probably be out of it for a week. We'll catch up soon."

"Thanks, Evelyn." He held his hand up flat in front of me. "We good?" he asked.

I gave him his high five and then some. I smiled. "Yeah, we're good. Now get out of here and get some sleep."

He winked, and I watched him go. Guess he wasn't too interested in the goings-on of Saltwater Cove after all. Hmm. So much was happening, I was almost glad to have been left alone to soak up the afternoon happenings in silence.

Aunt Edie walked in with another handful of dirty dishes and placed them beside the dishwasher. "Evelyn, love, you shouldn't be doing that, you're not rostered till later this afternoon."

"It's all good, I don't mind helping out a bit." The rattle and clatter of the dishes struggling to fit into the dishwasher pounded in my temples, but I put every piece in. I stood with my hands on my hips, the satisfaction of a job completed. "There, done."

Aunt Edie sat on a stool and patted the one next to her. "Evelyn, come sit with me a minute."

I looked at her, and the skin on my forehead creased. "Should I be worried?" I said, joining her.

"Of course not." Aunt Edie brushed the hair behind my ear letting her hand come to rest on my cheek. "You are so beautiful, just like your mother."

My murdered mother.

She continued, a combination of pain and pride beaming in her eyes. "I am so proud of you. And it should be your mother here telling you this, but I take pride in the witch you have become and like to think I've had a hand in it."

"You've had every hand in it. If it weren't for you taking me in after Mom and Dad died, I don't know where I would be today. I love you." My heart hammered against my chest and a comfortable warm flush crept over me. "You are the reason I am who I am."

She smiled, and her eyes teared up. "Oh, stop it or you'll have both of us blubbering messes."

I laughed and blinked black my tears, as did she.

"While we have a moment alone, I wanted to talk to you about your birthday in two days."

I shook my head. "No, I haven't changed my mind. I am not having a party."

She pulled back, and her body perked up. "What?" Realisation hit, and she shook her head. "No, you misunderstand. I want to talk to you about your graduation to a full witch."

My stomach dropped. "Oh."

"Don't look so terrified, it's a simple process really."

I huffed. "I have learned that nothing is ever simple when it comes to being a witch."

"I'm hearing you, but this shouldn't be too painful."

I shuffled in my seat. "Go ahead, I'm listening."

"The final step in gaining your licence is an interview with a member of the High Council," she said, as though it were as simple as making her strawberry shortcake. She continued. "On Wednesday morning at ten, a member of the High

Council will descend and meet with you to give their decision. They have the final say whether you will be issued with your full magic license or a probationary license."

"What?" My blood pressure skyrocketed into the heavens. "Probationary? I see why you waited until two days before my birthday to tell me this news."

She patted my knee and smiled. "I'm sure you will be fine, but I wouldn't keep them waiting if I were you. I have faith that you have met all the requirements and proven yourself worthy of the full title."

Unable to sit still a second longer, I paced the kitchen, shaking the cold tingles from my fingers. "I can't believe this. The High Council will decide the rest of my future. This is unbelievable."

"It's not that bad, Evelyn. Just a formality, really."

I stopped and looked her straight in the eye. "Who is it? Who's coming down?"

She shrugged. "I have no idea, and I'm not permitted to butt into the process."

My hands fisted at my sides. "What good is being a master witch if you can't use your powers to find out this one little thing?"

She pursed her lips and sat back in her chair folding her arms across her chest. "Evelyn Brianna Greyson, are you asking me to break the one law we all must live by—to use my powers for my own personal gain, ignoring the disastrous consequences that may follow?"

When you put it like that…I guess not.

"No, of course not." I slumped into my chair and ran my hand through my blue-streaked hair.

"Just be yourself, love, and you'll be fine."

"Easy for you to say," I huffed.

"Change of subject is in order," she said jumping off her chair and clasping her hands together in front of her breastbone. "I know you don't want a party, but—"

"No, no, no. I said no parties." I glared straight at her.

"Snappy, snappy." She held her hands up in a stop sign action. "If you had let me finish, I was going to suggest that with an unsolved murder hanging about town it wouldn't be wise to throw a party, but neither is missing the chance to celebrate this milestone with those who love you. I was going to suggest we close The Melting Pot Wednesday afternoon from about four-on and have our own private dinner. You, me, Detective Huxton, Tyler, Jordi, Harriet, and Eli. Just those who mean the most to you."

"I don't know. Can I think about it and get back to you?"

"Of course. I won't say a word until you give me the go-ahead."

Another year older and another birthday without my parents. Another year without knowing the truth about their deaths. This will be the last. I promise.

CHAPTER TEN

I stood barefoot and searched the barren land surrounding me. As the wind picked up pace. dust and dirt spiked my feet and shins like needles.

Where am I? Why don't I know this place?

Pushing through the tempestuous wind, I dragged my feet towards the old run-down building in the distance.

"Hello," I called out. The whistle of the wind drowned out the echo as it circled me.

I searched right, then left and spun in a circle, my gaze coming to rest on the weatherworn building standing alone in front of me. The green paint was peeling off in spades, and the dirty smudged windows had seen better days. Ripped red and white curtains hung behind the smudges, while a half-attached broken awning was left hanging to the veranda by a thread. I gagged at the nose-tickling stench of wet straw hanging thickly in the air. Drawing nearer to the building, the rustle of hay crushed underfoot. Used horse blankets lay strewn on the ground leading to the open door. It was a used barn, but whose?

"Hello? Is anyone here?" The shake in my voice caught me off guard. I tensed and held my breath as I walked over the blankets and through the doorway. Dark, empty spaces greeted me, and a cascade of shivers ran through my body, each as though it had its own harrowing story to tell.

A dim light shone under a door at the end of the corridor, the only source of light in the entire place. My feet moved on autopilot as though I were in a spell, and the light itself was drawing me in like a moth to a flame.

I stopped outside the door. My racing heartbeat pounded my temples, and a swirl of nausea rolled around in my belly. The silence was interrupted by the soft murmurings of what sounded like two women behind the door. My breath hiccupped. Placing my hand over the cool metal door handle, I turned it and pushed the door open, my widened eyes eager to see the interior.

I blinked repeatedly conditioning my eyes to the bright light shining from inside the room. In the distance a consistent buzzing sound getting louder by the second. I rubbed my eyes and stared into the room where two women stood, their backs to me. One somewhat familiar, one unknown to me.

I dropped my head in my hands, pressing them against my temples. Quiet, that's all I wanted. The buzzing became an increasing crescendo until I thought my head might explode from the pressure.

"Evelyn?" A sweet, soft woman's voice echoed from the other side of the room.

My head snapped up to see my mother, an expression of pure fear embedded on her face. The other woman I'd not met before. She had a short blonde pixie haircut, big blue eyes, and wore a burgundy cape. I never knew many of my mom's friends.

"Mom?" The word, so gentle it was barely audible, competing with the constant buzzing inside my head. "What are you doing here?"

"Evelyn," my mother said, "you shouldn't be here. Go back to sleep."

Sleep?

Heat pulverised my neck and cheeks, and I could barely think straight against the increasing noise.

"Mom…Mom? Don't go."

I stretched my arm out to grab onto her, and she shook her head, her eyes wide and unwelcoming.

My head thrashed from side to side on the pillow, and the blast of a horn pierced my skull. I bolted upright in my bed, gasping for air, my shoulders hiked up around my ears. The buzzing sound screamed from my bedside table, and I bolted upright in my bed slamming my hand down on the alarm button, silencing the harrowing sound.

"What the hell was that?" I pressed and rubbed the heel of my palm against my heavy chest. "Damn dreams. Why can't I dream of happy thoughts, like lying on a beach with a private butler who serves me nothing but Expresso Martinis and chocolate while I watch the sun set over the water? No, I dream of old rundown barns that smell of rotten hay and used horse blankets."

Kicking the quilt off, I threw my legs over the edge of the bed and glanced at the clock. "Five forty-five, are you serious? I can't even set the time right on my alarm" My lethargic body flopped back on the bed, and I stared at the ceiling, my mind going a hundred miles an hour.

Who was that woman with my mother? A friend. A fellow witch.

It wasn't unusual to dream about my mother but having a conversation with her—that was new. I couldn't wait to tell Aunt Edie about this dream. "It's not like I'm going to get back to sleep. Time to clear my head," I said, making a beeline for the shower.

By the time I returned, my rejuvenated body thanked me for spending those extra minutes letting the hot water run down my back and the steam clear my head. Dressed in my work outfit complete with my trendy black and orange horizontal striped stockings and my feet comfortably housed in my pink bunny slippers, I pulled the towel from the top of my head, dropped it on the end of the bed and jumped when it moved by itself in circles.

"Do you mind?" Miss Saffron said, wriggling and squirming until her head popped out from underneath the towel. "About time you got back."

"Why?" I asked, ruffling the fur on the top of her head. "Did I forget something?"

Miss Saffron's paw wiped her eye, and she licked her whiskers before arching her back and settling down in a small flurry lump "No, but I know everything is not right with you, so spill."

Taking the brush to my wet tangled hair, I cringed as it detangled each knot. "I'm okay, just another dream about my mother."

"That explains it then," she said, pushing her paws out into a stretch.

"Explains what?" I stopped and put my right hand on my hip, the brush secure in my hand.

"Why you're up so early." Miss Saffron sprang off the bed and circled herself around my legs in a figure eight rubbing her fur against my shins each time she passed. "It's not like you to be up showering before six am." She stopped and stretched her neck, gifting me a look at her beautiful golden oval-shaped eyes. "Is there anything I can do?"

I shook my head, then bent down and scooped her up in my arms rubbing my nose against the silky fur under her chin. "No, but aren't you the cutest for asking?"

A high-pitched succession of dings rang out from my phone, and I dropped Miss Saffron on the bed and picked it up.

My gut tightened as I saw Blair's name flash up on the screen.

Evelyn, I need to see you as soon as possible.

"What kind of message is that?" I pinched the bridge of my nose and rested my eyelids a moment. "Well, that doesn't tell me much, does it?." I clicked on the next message.

Evelyn. I'm so scared, and I don't know what to do. I'm pretty sure Tiffany is innocent, and I can prove it.

"Yes!" I fist-pumped the air and ruffled Miss Saffron's fur on her belly. "That's what we want to hear. Tyler will be happy." Next message.

Can you meet me outside the church by the front steps?

"This is gold." My fingers moved double time typing a response while my heart raced ahead.

Hi, Blair, yes, I can meet you at the steps to the church. How can you prove Tiffany's innocence? When do you want to meet?

Settling the phone beside me on the bed, I slipped my size seven feet into a pair of black lace-up Doc Martens ankle boots and fumbled with the laces a few times before finally tying them in knots. I picked up my phone at the same time the new message came through.

OMG. Thank you, Evelyn. Can you meet me in twenty minutes? Ashlyn has lost it. I don't even know if I can trust her anymore, and I know she lied to me. She said she was going to the toilet at lunch the other day and was gone for about thirty minutes. Plenty of time to go back to the salon and kill Misty.

"What the...? My head was spinning with this new information.

Calm down Blair and take some deep breaths. I'll meet you at Christian McAvoy's statue in twenty minutes.

No sooner had I pressed *send* than a ding came back, vibrating the phone in my hand.

No, it must be the church. I'm not a religious person, but I'm so scared I'll take any help I can get. Meet you outside the front steps of the church in twenty minutes.

Okay, deal. See you in twenty.

"Ahem, aren't you forgetting something?" Miss Saffron asked, her head stretching above the pillow.

My forehead tightened, and I tilted my head, waiting.

Miss Saffron rolled her eyes. "You're opening up The Melting Pot this morning."

"Oh, yeah." My shoulders slumped as I sat brooding in my stupidity. I slapped my forehead. "What was I thinking? Wait." I bolted upright and gave Miss Saffron my best hero smile. "I've got it. I'll ring Eli, and we can swap shifts, and then Tyler can meet me at the church."

Sounds like a plan.

I ruffled Miss Saffron on the head again, grabbed my jacket and threw the strap of my handbag over my head to my shoulder. Taking the steps two at a time, I breezed into the kitchen and headed straight for the coffee machine. "I may have to meet her in twenty minutes, but this brain does not work without at least one shot of coffee in the morning."

Thank goodness there's no Detective Huxton in Aunt Edie's pink, fluffy dressing gown this morning.

I hit speed-dial number six, put the phone to my ear and held it in place with my shoulder. "Come on, Eli, where are you?"

"Hello." A grouchy grumble answered.

"Good morning to you too," I said, pouring the milk into my Nespresso.

He cleared his throat, and his tone was far more cheerful the next time he spoke. "Evelyn, sorry about that. I didn't get much sleep last night."

Join the club.

"I'm sorry to hear that." I took a quick sip of coffee letting the warm caramel scent coat the back of my throat and indies. "Listen, I need a favour. I'm supposed to open up The Melting Pot this morning, but something urgent has come up, and I need you to cover for me. Can we swap shifts, and I'll do yours this afternoon?"

"What?" he said, as though I'd asked him for a kidney. "I was hoping to sleep in before I got back into the swing of things."

"Oh, come on, Eli. I need your help, please," I asked in my best persuasive tone. "You know I wouldn't ask if it wasn't important."

"What about Harriet or Jordi? Can't they fill in?" he asked, in a whiny tone.

I picked at the mini balls of lint on the wrist of my jacket, his voice droning on inside my head.

"No, they're too far away. I need someone closer who can be there in ten minutes."

"Ten minutes. Geez, Evelyn, way to welcome me back into the fold."

My heart just about jumped into my throat. "Is that a yes?"

He sighed, grumbling, "Yes, I guess so."

"Thank you. I can't thank you enough." I grabbed my car keys out of my bag and high-tailed it towards the door. "You still have your keys to open up?"

"Sure do, anyway, what was so urgent that you couldn't open?" he asked.

"I can't get into it right now, but I promise I'll fill you in when I can. Thanks again. I gotta go. Bye." Before he could get another word in, I hung up and quickly hit speed-dial one for Tyler. It felt like ages before he picked up. My anxieties were creeping off the charts.

"Tyler, where have you been?" My body was on high alert as I headed to my car, the keys tight in my hand.

"There is something called a 'shower' normal people have in the mornings to freshen up." Tyler's sarcastic tone made me smile.

"Ha-ha, very funny." A gurgling giggle tossed around in my belly. "Glad you've had your shower. It will make it faster for you to meet me at the steps of the church by the mausoleum in ten minutes."

"The church? Why am I meeting you at the church?" he asked but didn't argue with the request.

"Because of Blair. She messaged me this morning and said she has proof that Tiffany is innocent, and she wants to meet me in twenty minutes on the steps to the church. I couldn't turn her down."

"That's wonderful. If it all pans out, we should have Tiffany cleared by the end of the day. I'll see you in ten. Bye."

"Bye," I said and rang off.

***

"Where are you, Blair?" I muttered under my breath, tapping my phone against the palm of my hand. Standing on the steps, I could smell the faint scent of burning incense coming from inside the church. I rubbed the bottom of my itchy nose and glanced at the car park in search of Tyler or Blair. The sickly smell of incense liked to play havoc with my hayfever. Today was no different.

"Evelyn."

I heard my name being called out from a distance, and I turned to see Tyler waving above several cars in the car park. I smiled and let out a sigh, pressing my hands against my tense stomach. I watched as he strutted toward me.

"Gee, you didn't waste any time, did you?" he said weaving his arm around my waist and yanking my body close to his. Tyler's lips descended on mine so soft and silky smooth.

I gasped, opening my lips, and our tongues entwined together in a dance of love. Warmth overflowed inside my chest, and I pulled away gasping for air. My cheeks bones rose as a smile spread across my face. "Good morning to you too."

He gifted me a gorgeous smile followed by a cheeky wink. "Any sign of Blair yet?"

I shook my head and scanned the area by the cars, cemetery, and mausoleum. Turning back to Tyler, I reached up and brushed stray hair behind his ears, my fingers tingling as they skimmed down his cheek. "Nothing yet."

Mere seconds later, an almighty bang roared from inside the church like five sets of drum kits had been dropped from a great height. My hand shot out and grabbed Tyler's forearm; my fingers tensed, nails digging into his skin. "What was that?"

Tyler peeled my fingers off one by one. "Whatever it was came from inside the church."

"Blair?" I said, my thoughts going to the worst possible scenario. Without another thought, I took off sprinting up the stairs toward the entrance, Tyler hot on my heels, his voice calling from behind.

"Evelyn? Stop. Evelyn? Evelyn, wait…wait for me." A strong hand grabbed my shoulder and pulled me back to a halt a meter from the door. "Would you slow down?"

I clenched my hands by my sides, the tension riding up my arms. I looked him straight in the eye and said, "What is your problem? Did you not just hear that?"

His brows lowered in a frown as he looked down at me. "Yes, I heard it, and I also know that you shouldn't go running into buildings including a church without assessing the situation first. You have no idea what or who could be in there and with what weapon. It could be a trap. Blair might be setting you up for all you know."

"Setting me up? I seriously doubt that." I folded my arms across my chest aware of my rapid heart rate.

"But can you be a hundred per cent sure?" he asked, staring me down like a mother would a cheeky child.

My face grew hot under his stare, and I knew he was right, but I also knew if we waited it could cost someone their life. I put my hands on his arms, gripping his strong biceps. "We've been here before. You know that the longer we wait the less time we have to help whoever may be injured inside and the more chance there is of the culprit getting away. We can take it slow and stay in the shadows, but I am going inside that church to find out what that noise was. You can come with me or stay behind. Your choice, Tyler."

He pressed his lips together and shook his head. "Evelyn, I swear one day you're going to give me a heart attack, but I get it." He grabbed my hand and pulled me along behind him. "Come on. Stay behind me."

We headed inside the church. The spooky whine of the opening door rattled my bones. I swallowed and squinted, letting my eyes adjust to the darkened interior. Scanning for the source of the commotion, I caught movement near the altar, and my pulse raced.

"There," I said, pointing past Tyler at someone moving hastily around the altar toward the side exit. "They're getting away."

"I'm on it," Tyler said, taking off after the mysterious figure. Looking over his shoulder, he called, "Stay here."

I hesitated, the eeriness of the empty church pausing my next step. I stood watching as he approached the halfway point of the aisle. A sudden explosion of smoke and light at the altar picked Tyler's body up and threw it backward down the aisle as though it were a feather, sending him skidding across the wooden floorboards like a bowling ball landing against the rounded edge of one of the wooden pews.

"Tyler," I screamed at the top of my voice, my heart seizing in my chest. Green-tinged smoke billowed from the altar, evaporating as quickly as it appeared. My mind focused on Tyler's still form as I ran toward him. Dropping to my knees, my trembling fingers felt his neck, and a wash of dizziness swept through me as his carotid pulse beat against my fingertips

"Oh, thank goodness. Tyler…Tyler can you hear me?" I patted my hands over his body looking for blood or injuries. I let out a big exhale when I couldn't find any visible sign of injuries. He started to come around.

A muffled grunting moan sounded as he twisted to a sitting position. "What the hell was that?" he asked, the strain of the fall plastered on his face.

"I have no idea." I glanced towards the altar. There was nothing there. Turning back, I caught the wince on Tyler's face as he pushed himself up off the ground. "Maybe you should take it easy."

"I'm fine," he grumbled and proceeded to brush the debris off his clothes. "You stay here. I'm going to see if there's anyone outside."

I ran my hand through my hair and shook my head. "Are you sure you're, okay?"

"Yes, I'm sure," he snapped, moving off toward the side exit.

Watching him disappear out of sight sent chills down my spine. I made a promise to myself then and there—*Tyler will not be without a protection spell from now on.*

I swept my gaze around the church, but it was empty. There was a stillness about it that creeped the heck out of me. Time was wasting standing here doing nothing. "This is going to get me nowhere." I made my way down towards the altar, holding my breath at the point where Tyler was when he was violently thrown down. Nothing.

I edged closer to the altar, the air around me thick as molasses, my breath catching with the sweet honey and lavender scent drifting from the altar's flower arrangements. The upturned baptism font caught my attention, and I bent to check the debris. Nothing but spilled water and smashed marble. This destruction, a senseless act, or was it? I had no idea what transpired here before I heard the crash. I stood, rubbing my forehead. "So many unexplained occurrences happening all at once. This cannot be good. I have to know what happened."

I bit my bottom lip

"Dare I try to find out my way? But what do I touch first? The baptism font, the altar, the pew, the communion table?"

Why do my powers only work when I'm touching the object in question?

Maybe things would change after I graduated and got my full witch qualifications, but for now, this was the only way I knew to find the answers.

I looked around to check if the coast was clear, my belly jumping like nervous butterflies. *It's now or never.* My stomach bottomed out as I placed my hand on a piece of debris from the baptism font, closed my eyes and whispered, "With this spell bring forth to see, what time has taken and hidden from me. That last half hour I wish replayed, show me all without delay."

An intense burning sensation ran through my fingers, followed by a multitude of tingles, but I kept them stuck to the debris. My vision blurred, and I blinked a few times as the scene before me transformed. It was like I was watching a re-run of a television show. I gripped the piece of debris hard, and the vision suddenly cleared in my mind.

"Oh, no, Blair," I whispered. The blood ran cold in my veins. Pain shot through my chest, and my shoulders hunched. A hooded man stood at the front of the church in the centre of the aisle in front of the communion table, his arm stretched in front of him. A green beam shot from his hand, wrapping around Blair's neck holding her two meters from the ground.

"I...I..." Blair gasped, and her body shook, her legs waving around frantically. Her cheeks reddened, and her hands grabbed at the green stream crushing her neck as though there were an imaginary pair of hands choking the air from her body.

"I'll ask one more time," the man demanded in a gruff tone. "Where are they?"

Where is who? Are you the one dealing black market goods? Are you Salis van der Kolt?

It would make sense. How else would you insert yourself in Saltwater Cove to look for the Sphere as an undercover black-market dealer?

A woman wearing a black cape stood by the baptism font, the cape's hood covering her face. Her gaze moved back and forth from the man to Blair continually as though she didn't agree with his actions.

If he's Salis, then who are you?

He shook Blair, and her body trembled. "I should never have trusted a word that came out of your mouth."

"Enough," the woman yelled. "You're going to kill her."

"Silence!" he screamed. His arm whipped out, and a bolt of lightning shot from his fingertips connecting with the woman's chest, sending her screaming to the ground writhing in pain.

My body shuddered at all the woman endured.

He returned his focus to Blair. "You've wasted enough of my time. I'm done with you."

The woman dragged herself up from the ground and staggered towards the baptism font. She placed her hands flat against the side, they illuminated bright yellow and then she pushed in his direction. Water from the font splashed across his face and arms, and he shrieked away as though it had scarred his skin.

"Ahh!" He screamed and covered his face with his hands breaking the connection. Blair's limp lifeless body slipped to the ground. An explosion of electrified smoke filled the front of the church.

Gasping, my hand disengaged from the font, and I fell backwards against the floor, my limbs shaking and my racing heartbeat sending a stabbing ache in my chest. "Did I just witness Blair's murder? Blair,

Blair." There was no body where she fell. Did she survive?

Hiking mine off the wooden floorboards, I stumbled toward the place she fell.

An unnerving silence sent shivers down my spine. Searching, I moved to the other side of the communion table and froze at the sight of Blair's body slumped over in a heap on the floor. There was no sign of the other woman. The blood ran ice cold in my veins, and I raced towards her, bent, and checked her neck for a pulse.

"Blair...Blair." My fingers sat stagnant against her skin. My stomach hardened, and my breathing sped. The walls of the church caved in around me, and I started hyperventilating. I was too late. Blair's dead body lay in front of me, killed by the hand of a magical madman. A madman I was yet to identify.

A noise to the left startled me, and I shot to my feet. "Tyler?" I called, looking for the source. Silence met my words.

Blair, how could you get mixed up with black magic?

I looked down at the mangled body, my thoughts all jumbled. "Oh Blair," I said moving around to the area for what, I had no idea.

"What the?" I said, my forehead tightening. A brown paper package wrapped in string sat three-quarters hidden by her body. Crouching down I eased it out and a sharp pain thrust into my head like a butcher's knife had been stabbed into my skull. "Ah."

Shaking the pain away, I reached for the package, and a wave of nausea so extreme washed over me that I swayed and gasped for air. The scent of the package was familiar. Stabbing pain bled through my stomach, and I doubled over in excruciating pain, the scent wiped from my thoughts replaced with instant panic. "What is going on?"

I grabbed the sides of my head squeezing, but the throbbing overwhelmed every inch of me. My legs wobbled and turned to jelly. "Something's wrong."

My body was like a lead weight, and I couldn't hold it up any longer. "Help…someone…Tyler."

"Evelyn?"

My eyes rolled back into my head, my legs gave way and I slid into a black abyss.

CHAPTER ELEVEN

The pounding beat of my heart echoed in my ears like a timpani drum. Weightless, my arms drifted away from my body as though I were floating in space with my extremities in a world of their own. I stretched my hand out in front of my face and sparkles glistened off my skin like crystals. Beautiful.

Where am I?

My eyelids flickered, struggling to open against the pull of my surroundings. Floating upward, my body spun in circles, and I sucked in a breath expanding my lungs to their fullest.

"Evelyn…Evelyn, can you hear me?"

In the distance, a familiar male voice called, but the voice and I were worlds apart.

My eyelids finally pushed against the pressure holding them down, and for the first time, I could see where I was. But it wasn't anywhere I'd been before. It was black and void of life except mine.

"Evelyn, wake up."

The same voice called out to me again. I twisted and turned, looking for the source. I tried to get up, and a fist-like object slammed into my chest crashing my body downward and knocking the air out of my chest. I gasped, heaving for breath.

"Why is she not waking up?"

Tyler?

"Damn it, Evelyn. Wake the hell up," his gruff voice demanded.

Another punch slammed into my chest. My eyelids snapped open, and I gasped. Coughing and sputtering, my lungs heaved, starving for air. The rough outline of a man's face and upper body appeared in front of me, and my hands flew out grabbing onto his arms. I squeezed, my knuckles whitening under my grip. The heaviness in my chest made it almost impossible to breathe.

"You're all right, Evelyn. Just breathe. Take long, deep breaths."

"Eli?" I pushed the one word past my blocked throat.

"Yeah, it's me. Looks like I came back just in time."

"Thank goodness, Evie girl, you came back," Tyler said, brushing the hair from my forehead.

"What…"

"Easy, Evelyn. Don't try to talk, just get your breath back," Eli said.

I licked my lips and squinted in the bright sunlight. I was lying on the lawn outside the church. "Why does my chest feel like a piano has been dropped on it, like my heart is about to shatter inside my chest?" I asked, rubbing my palm against my sternum.

"How else was I going to keep you alive when you weren't breathing except to perform CPR?" Eli snapped. "Why the hell would you put yourself in danger, Evelyn? You know the risks."

I looked at him like he was speaking gibberish. "I…I don't know what you are talking about."

"The package, Evelyn. Do you remember the package by Blair's body?" Tyler asked.

I pressed my fingers on my forehead and dropped my gaze. "The package, yes."

Tyler continued. "It was filled with freshly mulched Licarbre fern."

I shook my head. "No."

"You could have been killed. I'm damn lucky I heard your call for help," Eli said. "I materialized just in time to catch you before you hit the ground. Then I got you the hell out of there. Tyler called the police. They should be here any minute."

Licarbre fern? Blair dead.

I looked up into Tyler's eyes, still rubbing the pain in my chest. "Why would Blair have a package of Licarbre fern?"

He shrugged. "I have no idea."

His words were interrupted by the vibration of my phone against my backside. I closed my eyes and lay back down on the grass. "Of all the times for my phone to ring." My muscles were so lethargic and heavy that I had no idea if they were moving or if it was just in my imagination until I saw Harriet's smiling face staring in front of me from my hand.

"Hello, Harriet."

"Evelyn, please tell me you're, okay?" she asked, her voice quivering.

"Yes, I'm okay, thanks to Eli and Tyler. Why do you ask?"

"I saw you, Evelyn." The emotion in her voice clogged my throat. "I saw you and you weren't breathing. Your body was not responsive. What happened? And don't lie to me."

"Harriet, I'm..." I paused and consciously slowed my breathing so I could speak. I needn't have bothered. Eli swiped the phone from my hand and gave it to Tyler, then mouthed the word *rest*.

You'll get no argument from me.

"Harriet...it's Tyler. Okay, if you slow down, I'll explain everything."

He paused and smirked, probably at some smart remark from Harriet.

"She's fine, there was an incident in the church. She happened to stumble upon a package that contained freshly mulched Licarbre fern. E—"

He rolled his eyes, and the corner of his lip turned up.

Poor Tyler.

"Harriet, I'm going to hang up if you don't zip your lips and let me speak."

I smiled. A giggle erupted in my belly, and I tensed against the wash of pain that ran over me. I slapped Tyler on the arm and whispered, "Don't make me laugh; it hurts."

He nodded, and his expression turned serious. "Harriet, Evelyn is fine. Your vision was a good warning, and I'm sure she will take it on board. For now, Eli and I will monitor her and keep you up to date."

I pushed up onto my elbow and mouthed, *tell her about Blair.*

He nodded. "Also, before you hear it on the town grapevine, all this went down after Evelyn and I heard an explosion in the church and Evelyn discovered Blair's body near the communion table."

Tyler pulled the phone away from his ear and cringed, looking at the picture of Harriet on the front. "Man, has that woman got some vocal cords on her."

"Wrap it up," I said, using every ouch of strength to push my body off the ground.

He replaced the phone to his ear. "Harriet...Harriet. We haven't any idea how she died, but I'm sure Evelyn will keep you posted on every detail. I've got to go now. Bye. Far out, when that woman gets on a roll there's no way of stopping her," Tyler said. He stood by my side and Eli on the other.

"What are you doing, Evelyn?" Eli asked. "I hope you're going to be heading home after what's happened."

"I may be sore, but I'm not dead yet. I'm perfectly capable of going in and checking out the body before the police get here."

"What?" both men said in unison.

I slumped and placed a hand on each of their shoulders. "Guys, I have you two here, what can happen with you two close by my side?"

They glanced at each other.

Then Tyler snapped his fingers at me. "A protection spell. Do a protection spell like you did on me that time you were worried about me."

"A protection spell? Mmm." That could work.

"Tyler has a point," Eli said. "Both of us know there's no use trying to talk you out of things once you've made up your mind. But a protection spell would put both our minds at ease."

I nodded. "Okay."

"Okay?" Tyler's brows wrinkled, and he shot a suspicious look at Eli. "You're not going to fight us on it?"

I shook my head. "Nope. I'm not keen on walking into something that has the power to destroy me."

I searched my surroundings for something useful. I spotted a shiny flat rock on the ground and bent to pick it up. A cascade of pins and needles ran through my aching body, and I gasped in pain.

"Ahh." I closed my eyes and sucked in a few deep breaths. Pressing my hand to my chest I waited for the pain to subside.

"Is this what you're after?" Eli asked, holding the rock flat in his palm.

My eyelids slowly opened, and I nodded, smiling. "Yes, thank you. I guess I forgot I was still a little tender from my earlier ordeal."

I held the rock flat in my hand and shooed the guys a few steps back. Enclosing it in my palm, I took a breath and recited the words to the spell. "With this spell, I cast away the dark forces that have come to play. Protect the one who holds this near and save them from a life of fear."

"That's it?" Tyler asked.

I opened my eyes and pushed the stone into my front pocket. "That's it. Easy, huh?"

He nodded. "For a witch. Still, take it easy and stay away from the Licarbre fern even with the protection spell activated."

"I will, now let's get in there before the police get there before us."

***

"I don't know about you guys, but it looks like a pretty straightforward crime, nothing suspicious at all," Eli said, standing at the foot of Blair's body.

"I might have agreed with you if Tyler and I hadn't seen an explosion of smoke with our own eyes just before Tyler was picked up and thrown down the aisle. Or it could have been the vision I saw of a hooded man holding Blair by the neck, squeezing the life out of her with nothing but a green stream of energy. I'd say that this has magic written all over it." I bent to examine the strangulation marks on her neck.

"What vision?" Tyler asked. "You never said anything about a vision."

"I'll explain later." I pulled out my phone and started snapping photos. "I think it's crucial we take note of everything before the police rock up and kick us out."

I'm so sorry, Blair. I wish you had met me by the statue instead of here.

I moved around the other side of her body, and my gut tensed at the sight of the package still half-hidden beneath her. I waited for a reappearance of the same triggers I experienced earlier, but nothing happened. A sigh escaped my lips.

"I think the police are going to find this a very interesting situation," Tyler said, rubbing his chin.

A voice came from behind us. "And why would that be?"

Is that who I think it is?

I froze as still as a statue, not wanting to turn and have my suspicions confirmed, but curiosity got the better of me. There was Wade Antonio, standing by the communion table looking as rugged and unkempt as ever with Constable Cameron Martins a few steps behind him.

"Evelyn, good to see you again," he said, dipping his head forward.

Heat raged up my neck and cheeks, and I pressed my lips together. *Who does he think he is? First, he breaks my best friend's heart and then waltzes back into town as though nothing has changed. I've a good mind to teach him a lesson of two.*

"Wade Antonio." Tyler cleared his throat and stuck his hand out to greet the man. "Good to see you. You too, Officer Martins. Wade, it's been a while since we've seen you around town. Good to have you back."

"Thank you, it's good to be back in Saltwater Cove," Wade said, moving up and standing next to Tyler.

My fingers tensed, and I balled them into fists and hid them behind my back.

Does Jordi know he's back in town? Oh no, how is she going to react when she sees him? She's still got it bad for him.

"What do we have here?" Wade asked, taking a walk around the body. He crouched down and lifted several strands of hair from Blair's face with a pencil. "Poor girl."

"Yes, poor Blair. She didn't deserve this. No one deserved something like this," I said, my gaze following his as he examined the body.

"When did you get back into town?" Tyler asked, shoving his hands in his pockets.

Wade glanced at him a moment before returning his focus to Blair. "Just this morning."

"And you're back at work already?"

Wade nodded. "I've been away on assignment, just a different sort of assignment."

"I'll say." Martins paused from taking the crime scene photos. "Some assignment. I wish I had an assignment where I met the woman of my dreams and came back with a fiancée."

"Fiancée?" The word exploded from my lips in a screech. "You're engaged to be married?"

Wade glared at Martins, and he gave back as good as he got. "Shouldn't you be taking photos and collecting evidence from the crime scene or something?"

Martins paused, half nodded and then returned to his duties.

I glanced at Tyler, and he shrugged, wide-eyed. *This news will devastate Jordi.* "Wade." I waited for him to return his focus to me. "You're engaged? How can you be engaged? What about Jordi?"

His brows pulled together in the centre of his forehead. "What about Jordi? We're friends. I'm sure she'll be happy for me."

"Happy for you?" The sarcastic tone in my voice could not be missed.

"How is Jordan?" he asked. "I hope she's doing well."

My nostrils flared, and I wanted to reach out and throttle the man. "I guess that depends on how you look at things, doesn't it?"

"Meaning?"

"Well, how can one really be doing well when your parents go missing on the other side of the world in Australia, and the man you figure will be by your side helping you find them vanishes into thin air and then comes back months later engaged to another woman?"

My voice roared in my ears. Heat blazed through my chest, and I ground my teeth together.

"Her parents went missing?" he asked, tilting his head, and holding my gaze. "Are they all right now? Evelyn, I would have helped if I could have, but circumstances prevented it."

"Yes, they're fine now," I said.

Eli piped up from my right. "We all understand circumstances come into play in every situation, don't they, Evelyn? I'm sure Wade's special assignment is no different from others who had to leave at short notice."

There was an awkward and strained silence that hung around even after Wade began moving around Blair's body, taking notes, and examining the scene. Eli, Tyler, and I stepped back and let them work.

He was about to pick up the package when I stepped forward. "Watch out, it's dangerous. It's full of mulched Licarbre fern, extremely deadly to a witch and possibly other magical beings."

He nodded and clicked his fingers at Martins and pointed to the package, indicating its contents. Turning back, he looked at me and squinted. "You don't look affected by it, why is that?"

"Because of this." I pulled the flat rock out of my pocket and opened my fingers, holding it out to Wade.

"A rock? Seriously? Am I missing something?" he asked with a smirk.

"No, it's not just a rock," Eli snapped. "She put a protection spell on it. Do you really think we'd let her come back in here with freshly mulched Licarbre fern?"

Wade's lip turned up, and he stared at Eli. The testosterone challenge between the men was doing my head in.

"Why are the three of you in here, anyway?" Wade asked, flipping his notebook open. "And why are you so interested in Blair's body?"

I stepped forward and took the lead on this one. "Blair contacted me this morning and asked me to meet her here. She said she had evidence that would prove Tyler's client innocent of Misty's murder. When we got here, she was already dead."

Wade focused on the notes he was scribbling.

"She was scared, and in one of her text messages she said she thought Ashlyn had lost it. She didn't even know if she could trust her anymore. Blair said she'd been lying to her and wondered if she was the one who killed Misty."

"I see," Wade said, tapping the end of his pencil on his notepad. He headed to the front of the altar and examined the shattered baptism font taking copious amounts of notes, then looked back to me.

"There's more to the story, isn't there, Evelyn? You know what happened to this font, don't you?"

I nodded. The conviction of his words called to me like a pied piper calling his followers. I stumbled to join him in the exact spot where I witnessed the attack on Blair. A cold shiver ran up my spine, leaving me jumpy and nervous at the slightest sound.

"Can you elaborate on what happened here?"

Sure, I've nothing to hide.

I pressed my teeth into my bottom lip and sighed. "I did a spell, and all I can tell you is that there were two of them, one more powerful than the other. One was a man, and one was a woman. I couldn't see their faces; they were covered by hoods. The more powerful one could be Salis van der Kolt." Behind me, I heard Tyler and Eli's shocked muttering to each other. "I'm not a hundred per cent sure, but Blair was freaked out about something, and I'm sure Ashlyn is connected somehow. He had some sort of magic stream wrapped around her neck squeezing."

"And the package?" Wade asked, his expression softer.

I glanced over to where the package lay to see Constable Martins snapping photos of it from all angles. "I didn't touch it, where it is now is exactly where it was when I found the body."

"But you knew it was Licarbre fern?"

"Yes, because it nearly killed me. If it weren't for Eli, I'd be dead right now." I crossed my arms and clutched my elbows.

"Or…" Wade paused lifting his gaze and searing it into me. "Maybe the whole thing was a setup, and the package was intended for you in the first place. Maybe Blair was just collateral damage."

My lungs seized, and his words darted around in my mind like lost souls.

The package was intended for you in the first place. Why would it be for me? Who would want me dead?

My jaw dropped and made an O shape while my hands pressed against my chest.

Tyler moved up to stand beside me and placed his hand softly on my lower back. "I think a more plausible option is that Blair was mixed up in it with Ashlyn, was dealing or supplying illegal goods, was in the wrong place at the wrong time and paid the ultimate price for it."

"Either way." Wade paused and flicked his notebook closed, depositing it in his jacket pocket. "It looks like Ashlyn may have some answers, and that's as good a place as any to start."

CHAPTER TWELVE

"Martins, when you're done processing the crime scene, can you organise to have Ashlyn come into the station for a chat?"

Martins nodded, void of emotion, then resumed his work.

"Wade, do you mind if we have a private chat?" Tyler asked, his serious expression almost had me laughing...on the inside.

"Sure," Wade said, puffing his chest out.

Here comes another testosterone challenge. I looked at Tyler and my forehead tensed. "Is that really necessary?"

He leaned down and gave me a kiss on my temple. "Afraid so. Better to tell him about the runaway we saw now. Full disclosure and all," he said, his lips still connected with my skin. "I won't be long, promise, and then we can head on home."

"Okay, I'll wait over with Eli." I gifted Wade one more I'm-going-to-make-you-pay-for-hurting-my-best-friend look before I left. They say actions speak louder than words. I turned on my heel, flicked my chestnut-blue hair over my shoulder and trotted off towards Eli, leaving the two to chat.

The sooner this day was over the better. I moved around Cameron Martins while he worked. His camera sat beside him on an evidence bag. He must have completed all his photos and had now moved on to gathering evidence. He half-rolled Blair's body, and I slowed to a virtual stop. The book splayed open on the floor underneath her was surely a Bible, but it was the angle of Blair's body that caught my attention.

My breathing accelerated. There was no way that Bible got there by accident, Blair must have grabbed it before death finally consumed her. The question was why. Her finger was sitting in an awkward position, but clearly pointing directly at the Bible.

Could it be a message? Why else would she have concealed it from view?

Angling my body away from Cameron Martins, I held my breath while I whipped out my phone and snapped several pictures of Blair and the Bible. Tyler was still chatting with Wade but had turned them around so that Wade's back was to me. Heat worked its way up my neck as though the entire universe was looking at me. I stopped to see Eli staring at me. I put my finger to my lips in a shushing action, and he nodded his understanding. I kept snapping. Martins turned away to fiddle with something from his case, and I seized the moment to stretch my arm out over the top of him and snapped one last photo then pretended to check my emails.

"That's great, thank you," Wade said, leading Tyler back to where Eli and I were standing. "You've been very helpful, but Martins and I can take it from here."

"Glad we could be of assistance," I said. Threading my arm in Tyler's, I looked up into his eyes and smiled. "Let's head back to The Melting Pot for a bite to eat before my shift starts."

Tyler nodded, and we stepped down from the altar, heading down the aisle. "I'd love to."

The image of the two of us walking arm in arm down the aisle of the town church popped into my head and a continuous stream of emotions bombarded my heart. Scared...happy...afraid...nervous...in love.

Would this be what it will feel like when we get married? Am I supposed to feel any different after we say, 'I do'?

Eli cleared his throat behind us. I dropped my arm and glanced over my shoulder, having forgotten he was still there.

Tyler pushed the oak doors open, and we exited straight into the blinding rays of sunlight shooting from the radiant blue sky. "Well, this is a change, I thought the sun was going to keep away today."

"Guess not," Eli said, moving past both of us. "Do you want to tell me what was going on back there?"

Tyler's brows dipped, and he glanced from Eli to me. "What's he on about?"

My belly fluttering, I explained my find. "While you were telling Wade about the intruder—"

Eli butted in, his eyes wide. "Wait…what intruder?"

Tyler told Eli about the stranger dressed in black. "I nearly caught him down by Christian McAvoy's statue, but I lost him." He turned and glanced down at me, laying his hand across his breastbone. "I would have been there for you otherwise."

"I know." I squeezed his hand and pushed up on my tippy-toes planting a peck on his cheek.

"Back to the photos. What did you find?" Eli stood with his arms folded across his chest, waiting.

"I'm not sure yet. As Martins lifted Blair's body, I saw she was lying on a Bible. Strange place to have a Bible, don't you think? Open? Underneath a dead body? Anyway, it looked like she was pointing to a particular section, sort of like she was trying to tell us something. I have no idea if I'm right or not. It could be something, or it could be nothing, but it's worth investigating."

"Agreed. Are you sure you're going to be okay now?" Eli asked.

"Yes, Eli. I'll be fine." I reached out and squeezed his hand. "Thank you for being here for me and saving me."

He shrugged. "I'm your guardian. That's what I'm here for, to protect you." He moved off and picked up the pace, waving goodbye. "I've a few errands to run, so I'll see you back at The Melting Pot."

I nodded, and he was gone.

Tyler and I walked hand in hand towards the carpark where our cars sat side by side. "You still up for a bite to eat before your shift?"

I shook my head and ignored my sluggish heartbeat. "Would it be okay if we skip it, head back to your place and take a look at the photos of Blair's body I snapped while you were talking to Wade?"

"Of course. You mean use my computer superpower?" Tyler said, a sly grin turning the corner of his lips up.

"Yes, sweetheart, use your superpower. You know you are a whiz when it comes to computers, better than I will ever be."

"Why don't we leave your car here, shoot back to my office and work on the photos? Then we can pick it up on the way back to The Melting Pot before your shift."

I nodded and before long we were sitting in his warm car heading east towards his house. I glanced at the town as it zoomed past my window. The giant illuminated P above the police station sent my heart sinking through the floor. "I can't believe Wade is engaged. I could have sworn he felt something for Jordi. I know it wasn't my imagination. How could he just go off and get engaged like it's no big deal?"

Tyler shrugged. "You can't control who you fall in love with, Evie girl. Take me for example."

I pulled back and my eyebrows creased, pulling the skin on my forehead tight. "Excuse me?"

He chuckled and patted my knee. "All I meant was, I tried for years to block my feelings for you, pretending they didn't exist. All it did was make me miserable. Then when I hit Nepal and stopped to take a good look at myself, it was like a lightbulb had switched on. I knew my heart belonged to you, and I had to man up and come home and make you see we were meant to be together."

I folded my arms across my chest and patted my elbows with my hands. "Right, just like that, huh?"

Tyler nodded and grinned. "Still, it's going to be a shock to Jordi when she finds out. It will be better coming from you than having her find out on the town gossip vice."

"Good point. Mind if I ask her to join us at your place?"

"Not at all, go for it. I'll be working on the pictures, anyway."

I pulled out my phone and clicked on her programmed number, my guts twisting in knots as each dial tone rang out.

"Hey, Evelyn, what's up?" Her monotone voice masked her emotions. "I hear there was some commotion down at the church this morning."

"What the...how did you find out?" I asked, shaking my head.

"Oh, come on, Evelyn. You forget we live in the number-one town full of gossips. There isn't much they don't about."

"So, you know about Blair?" I asked, holding my breath.

But do you know about Wade?

"I'm pretty sure the whole town knows about Blair by now. Marlana Hass was on her way to work at The Four Brothers and stumbled across the scene. Looks like Tiffany has been hard at work again."

"I don't think Tiffany did it. But I could use a sounding board. Any chance you're free and can come hang out with Tyler and me at his place?"

"I suppose. I mean I have nothing planned," she said.

"Great, see you in twenty minutes or thereabouts." I hung up not giving her a chance to object.

"Smooth, real smooth," Tyler said.

Tyler took the corner, and my stomach swirled and dropped. "I thought it would be better face-to-face than over the phone."

He reached over and grabbed my sweaty palm. "Whatever works for you, Evie girl."

***

It hadn't taken long to get to Tyler's office and begin downloading the photos, but the niggling sensation in the base of my neck would not go away. The news of Wade's engagement was going to break my best friend's heart.

Sitting cross-legged on the chair in the corner of Tyler's office, I took a moment to admire my man at work. He really was a whiz on the computer. Between the fastness of his fingers moving across the keypad and the number of screens in front of him all displaying different information, there was no way I could keep up. More to the point, I didn't want to. One computer whiz was enough for this relationship. "It's so great your mom and dad let you start your private investigation business from home."

"I know," Tyler said, keeping his eyes glued to the screens in front of him. "Rent-free. And it has its own entrance separate from the house, which is great. My clients appreciate the privacy away from others. I know we're waiting for Jordi, but what do you say we get the coffee started?" He paused then swivelled around in his chair and leaned his elbows on his knees "Earth to Evelyn, come in Evelyn."

My eyelashes flicked several times, and I refocused to see Tyler waving to draw me out of my thoughts and back to the present. "Sorry, what were you saying?"

"Where were you? Off with the fairies, or maybe one fae in particular? I mentioned coffee and that maybe it would be good to have one." He leaned back against the chair and faked being exhausted. "All this computer stuff can be draining, even for someone with supercomputer powers like me."

I stuck my bottom lip out and gave him my best cheeky pout. "Aw, is my computer super nerd fading? Does he need some liquid medicine to keep him going?"

His back stiffened. "Hey, what's with the super nerd title? I thought I dropped that one when I came back from Nepal."

"Yes, you sure did." The memory of him walking off that plane looking like a Greek god will never grow old. How I never noticed him before he left, I'll never know.

Regardless, he was mine now, and look out anyone who thinks otherwise. I threw my legs over the edge of the chair and rose. "One coffee coming up," I said, heading towards the kitchen.

The chime of the doorbell rang out, and I paused, looking over my shoulder. "I'll get it. It will most probably be Jordi, anyway."

"No problem," he called.

I flung the front door open, and my chest tightened at the smile on Jordi's face. "Come in. You're just in time for coffee."

Jordi's shoulders dropped, and she let out a sigh. "That would be a massive yes. Hit me with a double shot of caffeine please."

"Hey, Jordi," Tyler called from his office.

"Hi, Tyler," she yelled back and continued to follow me.

I walked down towards the kitchen, my guts churning faster with each step. Maybe she's already heard the news about Wade. "What's been happening with you this morning?"

Jordi pulled out a kitchen chair and sank into it. She rested her elbows on the table and her chin on her hands. "I think my mom's going through a mid-'shifter'-life crisis or something. She's driving me insane."

I flittered around the kitchen making the coffees while Jordi filled me in on her day. "How so?"

"Ever since we came back from Australia, she's been so clingy, always wanting to hang out as if it will be the last time I see her. She quit her job, changed her hairstyle, brought a new car, actually two—one for her and one for Dad."

"Gee, she has been going all out." I handed her a steaming cup of coffee and joined her at the table. "I guess you can understand it in a way. She almost died in Australia, and now she doesn't want to waste another second without letting you know how much you mean to her."

Jordi stuck out her bottom lip, and her brows pulled together. "Gee, when you put it like that I feel like the worst daughter in the world. But it just gets a bit much sometimes."

"No one's saying it won't so why not talk to her? Be honest and tell her how you feel. Honesty is the best policy." My head throbbed. I felt like the biggest hypocrite. I held up my hand. "Hold that thought. Let me run this coffee down to Tyler, and I'll be back."

When I returned to the kitchen, Jordi was sipping her coffee, and my guts were fast becoming an internal tsunami.

"What's Tyler working on?" she asked, her gaze inquisitive.

I slapped my forehead. "How stupid can I be? I forgot you don't know."

I was too worried about how she would react to the news about Wade I forgot to tell her about Blair.

Her cup slowly lowered to the table, and she stared at me through darkened eyes. "Give it to me straight. What's happened? Is it Harriet?"

"Gosh, no, Harriet is fine." I wrapped my hands around my steaming mug to keep them from shaking. "It's Blair from Salty Snips."

The corner of her lip rose as did one of her eyebrows. "Blair?"

I nodded. "I found her body this morning in the church. She's been murdered."

Jordi gasped, and her hand covered her gaping mouth. She sat frozen, staring at me for a long time. "Murdered? Are you sure?"

I opened my mouth to confirm, and she huffed and dropped her hand slapping it on the table startling me.

"Look who I'm asking. If Evelyn Grayson says someone is dead, then, of course, they're dead." She edged forward on her seat and looked at me, her eyes wide and inviting. "What happened?"

"I'll cut to the chase. She was strangled by a magic force but that's not the most interesting thing that happened."

Here goes.

"You mean there's something more interesting than murder by magic? Do tell."

"As usual the police turned up at the scene." I licked my lips and jumped into the deep end. "It was Wade—he's back in Saltwater Cove."

Jordi's face dropped, and she sat frozen to the chair, her coffee cup paused in mid-air. "He's back?"

I nodded, and my insides were as tight as an elastic band stretched to the maximum. "There's more."

"Go on." She sat so despondently, her expression hard as though he meant nothing to her. And we both knew that wasn't true.

"He's engaged to be married."

CHAPTER THIRTEEN

"What?" she said in a whisper, her cup descending to the table as though in slow motion. "Engaged?"

Jordi sat looking straight through me, her gaze plagued with hurt and anger. My heart broke for my best friend. The once delicious-smelling coffee had now lost its appeal. I pushed the cup out of the way and grabbed Jordi's hand. "Are you okay? Talk to me, don't just sit there. Throw something, whatever makes you feel better."

"I'm not going to throw anything, Evelyn." She took a sip of her coffee, but I could see the hurt beaming through her glazed focus. "Did he say anything else? Maybe who or why?"

"No. I'm pretty sure he was annoyed that Cameron Martins brought it up. Maybe he intended to keep it a secret."

Jordi rolled her eyes and cringed. "Yeah, keep a secret like that in Saltwater Cove? Like that could ever happen."

"Maybe I can find out more information on the new bride and why she's thrown the ball and chain around the neck of our necromancing policeman."

"Just leave it, Evelyn." She took another sip of her coffee and held it in front of her lips. "Obviously, they were meant to be. Otherwise, why would he marry her?"

I shrugged. "I haven't the foggiest, but I think it's bad form on his part to lead a woman on like he did you and then dump her the first moment another offer comes along."

A sharp startling, "Eureka!" boomed from the direction of the office, and I jumped in my seat, coffee sloshing over the brim of my cup and onto my hand.

"Aw, what the hell?" Grabbing the hand towel I wiped the hot coffee away, but it didn't stop the skin on my wrist from going all red and blotchy where the hot liquid had made contact—plus, now my hand stunk of coffee.

I shot up from my chair. "Tyler? What's wrong?" Leaving the coffee behind, I hightailed it down the hallway to his office, holding the towel against my wrist. I stopped at the entrance, but Jordi came up behind me barrelling me into the room. Righting myself, I saw Tyler rummaging through his filing cabinet, his eyes bulging as though he'd seen a ghost and his lips muttering at full speed.

"Tyler?" I said, my gaze fixated on his mouth moving with zero audibility. "Tyler, what is going on?"

He paused long enough to look up, his face alight with energy. "I found it."

"Found what?" Jordi asked.

He continued searching through the documents on the top shelf and then pulled a manilla file out of the top drawer and began flicking through it.

I walked over to where he'd paused halfway across the room, his eyes glued to the contents of the manilla folder all the while still mumbling under his breath.

"What are you saying? I can barely hear you," Jordi said, pulling up to my side.

His lips suddenly stopped, and he looked up to see Jordi beside me. "Jordi, welcome."

"What's with all the jibber-jabber, Tyler? You know talking to yourself is the first sign of madness," Jordi said, easing into my corner chair.

"Very funny." He grimaced sarcastically. "I'm pretty sure I found the message Blair was trying to send."

Jordi frowned. "Message? What message are you talking about?"

My back straightened, and my hands clenched together at my waist. "I never got around to sharing that piece of news." I quickly brought Jordi up to speed on Blair's message. Her interest piqued instantly. "This was the first morsel of hope we'd had so far."

I turned to Tyler. "What's the message?"

Tyler returned to his desk and scattered the contents of his file. I stood behind him on one side, and Jordi shot up from the couch, joining his other side.

He cleared his throat. "First, from the photos, it looks like Blair was pointing at the Gospel of Mark, chapter fourteen."

"What's so special about Mark, chapter fourteen?" Jordi asked before I could get a word in.

"Verses twenty-two to twenty-six to be precise," he added.

I stared blankly at Jordi, and she shrugged.

He glanced at her and returned his focus to the papers. "I've kind of been researching the Cup of Acronus." He turned and grabbed my hand, rubbing his thumb over my palm and sending tingling sensations up my arm. "Spoiler alert. I was looking into it as one of your presents for your birthday, but if it's what I think it is, I'm sure you won't mind me telling you now."

Warmth radiated through my body. "Another birthday present for me? How sweet."

Jordi rolled her eyes and cleared her throat. "We all know you're the perfect boyfriend, and we all love you for it, but can you get to the point and tell us what Blair's clue has to do with the Cup of Acansis?"

He tutted. "It's the Cup of Acronus, not Acansis."

"Oops." Jordi shrugged. "My bad."

"Go on, Tyler," I said, squinting and giving Jordi my best shut-up-and-let-the-man-speak look.

He flattened his hands on the pages and sighed. "Right. The passage that she was pointing to, Mark fourteen verses twenty-two through twenty-six, is the part in a communion service where the priest says—" He paused and shuffled his papers before finding the correct one. "Here. I'm starting at verse twenty-two." He began to read. "*While they were eating, Jesus took bread, and when he had given thanks, he broke it and gave it to his disciples, saying, 'Take it; this is my body.' Then he took a* **cup**, *and when he had given thanks, he gave it to them, and they all drank from it. 'This is my blood of the covenant, which is poured out for many.' He said to them, 'Truly I tell you, I will not drink again from the fruit of the vine until that day when I drink it new in the kingdom of God.' When they had sung a hymn, they went out to the* **Mount of Olives**."

"So, how does that help us find Misty or Blair's murderer?" Jordi asked folding her arms across her chest, her brow pulling tight.

"Let me finish," he said, his tone apprehensive. "In my research on the cup, I've found out it was used by some of the first witches and not very nice ones at that. It was used for evil not good, and that's why it has been hidden all these years for fear that evil will resurface. Problem is that evil's resurfaced, and black magic is playing havoc in Saltwater Cove. It's rumoured to have great power, and I believe it is somewhere in Saltwater Cove. I also believe that's why the power of the cup has been awakened, and Blair knew the cup was linked to black magic and that's what she was trying to tell us. I could be wrong, but it all seems to fit."

"Wait a minute." My hand flew out and slapped his forearm. "Did you just say Acronus?"

"Yes, the Cup of Acronus. Why?" he asked.

The tension in the room was palpable, and both stared at me, waiting.

Heat burned in my chest. "Since I got back from Australia, I've been doing research, trying to find out what the rest of the relics are and then pinpointing their location. I came across the name Acronus, but I hadn't yet figured out what it was or if it had a link to my parents' murders. I guess you've done that bit for me."

"Oh my, this is a lot to take in." Jordi exhaled heavily.

"I can't believe you were doing all this for my birthday."

Jordi paced the small confines of Tyler's office. "That's all well and good, but you know as well as I do the High Council forbade anyone to help Evelyn solve the mystery of her parents' death, and it's pretty clear they were murdered because of the Sphere. They hid the relics so no one would find them, and in the end, it got them killed. You helping her find them goes against their instructions, and you could get her killed."

My breathing sped, and my eyes watered. Had Tyler crossed the line?

He swivelled in his chair and looked at Jordi. "No, you're wrong. I may have started looking into the relics of the Sphere to help Evelyn find them, but it was Blair who helped me put it together with the verse she was pointing to, and that is a murder I am permitted to solve."

"My research tells me that the cup resides in a place called the Gateway. I believe it's connected to the Sphere and your parents' deaths, but I don't know how. That's for you to find out. I gave you a head start, that's all."

I threw my arms around his neck and kissed him with as much love as I could share knowing my best friend was watching. "Thank you. This is the best birthday ever."

I planted a lip-smacking kiss on his lips, and he reciprocated deepening the kiss until I was lost in his euphoric world of bliss. He pulled me onto his lap and his arms warmed around me and I closed my eyes holding onto his love, our hearts beating as one against each other's chest. A smile plastered on my face, I sighed in the comfort of his embrace.

Peeling my eyes open, my gaze landed on a pale-faced Jordi standing a few feet away on the other side of the room, an inward gaze that crushed my heart. I gulped back a spoonful of guilt and pushed away from Tyler retaking my position in the chair opposite him.

Sensing the awkwardness, he cleared his throat and returned to his research. "I was talking to my mother last week, and she was telling me about her tarot cards and how she had them read, and that's where I got the idea from. I've been curious ever since we got back from Australia. I guess the cup is like the holy grail for witches or something like that."

"This is great. Thank you, Tyler," I said, my insides all gooey and warm as I looked at him.

Jordi huffed, tutted, and rolled her eyes. "Even if this cup is related to the Sphere, we still need to find its location before we can do anything."

"And I know just the witch to ask—the woman who has been there for me since forever," I said, looking Jordi in the eye.

A smile spread across her face, and we said in unison, "Aunt Edie."

"That's my cue to leave," Jordi said, moving around the back of Tyler's chair and stopping by the door.

I spun and swallowed the lump in my throat. "What are you talking about? I can't do this without you. You're coming too."

"What?" Her expression fell, as she looked at me and then at Tyler.

He held his hands up and shook his head. "Hey, don't look at me, I just do as I'm told."

She reached for my hands and squeezed them. "Evelyn, I'm okay, you don't need to babysit me. If Wade has found love with someone else, I'm happy for him, I truly am. I'm not going to do anything drastic like shift into my raven and poop on her head, now that would be childish."

I laughed, but a corner of my mind wondered if she was being serious. "It sure would."

"Are you sure you're going to be all right?" I asked, giving her one last hug.

"Yes, I'll be fine. If I'm not, you will be the first person I call. Deal?"

"Deal," I said smiling.

"Catch you later, Tyler," Jordi said, play-punching him in the upper arm then shaking her hand and applying pressure to it. "Aw, what do you have in there, a brick?"

He winked her way and sent her a loving smile. "One hundred per cent pure muscle, my friend." He paused and flexed his muscle for show, and the room filled with laughter. "You never know when I'm going to be called to save one of my girls from the evil forces at play."

She rolled her eyes and waved. "Bye."

Tyler stood and gathered his notes into his folder. "You ready to go see Aunt Edie? We can pick up your car on the way if you like."

I nodded. "Sounds like a plan.

***

I parked behind Tyler outside The Melting Pot Café, Aunt Edie's personally designed witch-themed café. What better place for a witch to work than a café disguised as a witch's den? Residents of Saltwater Cove know who the witches are, but it keeps the visitors to town guessing. Even though the sun's rays warmed my skin through the car window, a blustery blanket of wind shot through me as I stepped out of the car. Pausing on the way in, I noticed the occupied police vehicle parked on the corner opposite The Melting Pot. Martins sat in the driver's seat. It was odd, but not unusual considering Aunt Edie's reputation as a master baker could not be disputed.

I wonder what they want?

Pushing through the door, I was surprised to see it so quiet, but then again it was a Tuesday, and by all the tables laden with empty plates, it had been a busy lunch rush.

A woman with her back towards the door stood at the counter fiddling in her bag, and then she picked up two plastic bags full of takeaway containers and turned.

Tiffany?

She glared at me, her head tilted, and her lips pouted like she was going to tell the teacher on me.

She stormed towards me, the bags swaying as she moved. Stopping in front of me, she hiked the bags up onto the nearest table and leaned on the tops. "Some private eye your boyfriend turned out to be."

"Excuse me?"

"He left me sitting at that police station. I had to endure hours of questioning and trying to convince those knuckleheads I had nothing to do with Misty's death. They wanted my alibi, but I couldn't tell them without exposing you know who."

"Tiffany, Tyler told you he would do what he could. He never said that he would take your case, only that he would look into it and that's exactly what we're doing. You'll be pleased to know that we have a few leads we are checking out, and he hopes to be able to report back to you within the next few days."

She huffed, picked up her bags and walked around me to the door. "Don't go out of your way, I convinced them to let me go home as long as I agreed to put a block on my magic, stay under house arrest at home and be monitored twenty-four hours a day until either my name is cleared, or another suspect comes to life."

"That's good I guess." What else could I say?

She held up the bags. "Hence the takeaway meals and my personal escort sitting out front. I'm out of here."

I watched her exit and breathed the tension from my shoulders as she left. That woman was like a whirlwind wherever she went.

Harriett bounded from the kitchen with the dishes bucket ready to collect a new batch of dirty dishes from the tables. Her eyes beamed when she saw me. "Evelyn, what are you doing here? According to Eli, you swapped shifts with him. You shouldn't be in for at least another hour."

The door banged shut behind me, and I jumped.

"Sorry, wind took it out of my hands," Tyler said, moving up to stand beside me. He looked at me and whispered, "Was that Tiffany who rushed past me?"

I nodded and mouthed, "I'll explain later."

I turned towards Harriett. "Have you seen Aunt Edie?"

She shrugged. "Last time I saw her she was heading inside to the house with Detective Huxton."

"Great. Thanks." I leaned into Tyler and whispered, "Let's do this before I have to start work."

He nodded and followed.

As I got closer to the connecting door between The Melting Pot Café and the kitchen of our home, my gut tightened. An unusual commotion was coming from the other side. Aunt Edie's panicked voice stuck out like a sore thumb.

The hairs on the back of my neck stiffened, and my entire body cramped up.

What the hell is going on?

I pushed the door open, Tyler at my back, to see Aunt Edie's face as red as a ripe tomato, her breath racing. She glared at Detective Huxton, her arm outstretched and pointing towards the door.

"You get out of my house this instant Micha Huxton. The wedding is off. I'll not marry a liar. Get out. Get out. Get out. Don't make me say it again."

"Edith, listen to me," Detective Huxton said from the corner of the kitchen.

"No, no, no." Aunt Edie's hands covered her ears, and she squeezed her eyes shut, shaking her head from side to side. "You're lying. Get out. The wedding is off. Get out of my house before I do something I'll regret." She dropped her hands and sent him a cold resentful stare. Her fingers began to curl, and her body began to shake which was not a good sign.

My chest clamped tight as though each word or action from Aunt Edie was turning the clamp a notch tighter. My eyebrows pulled together sending a shooting pain from my head down to my heart.

I stepped forward and held my hands out between the two adults. "Whoa, whoa, whoa, everybody calm down a moment. I don't know what is going on here, but surely it can be resolved without saying or doing something one of you will regret."

Aunt Edie stormed towards me, her face and neck red. She pointed at Detective Huxton. "Tell that man he can take his marriage proposal and give it to some other woman who is happy to marry a liar and a scoundrel."

"Hey, that's not fair, Edith, and you damn well know it," Detective Huxton said, stepping forward but keeping the table between them.

Tyler's back stiffened and he moved to the other side of Aunt Edie.

"Get out," she screamed. Her arm flew out to the side as a blue stream of crystal energy let loose from her fingers and sailed across the room colliding with the plates hanging on the wall. The plates smashed to the floor in a loud, frightening crash. Her other hand shook as she pointed it towards Micah. It was the first time I'd seen fear register in his eyes. He held his hands up and slowly moved backwards. Her fingertips glowed crystal blue, and my entire body tensed as I bolted in front of her hand blocking her view of Detective Huxton.

"Get out of the way, Evelyn," she demanded.

I shook my head. "Aunt Edie, I have no idea what is going on, but he's not worth losing your powers over. Detective Huxton loves you; I can't imagine what he has done to deserve this. It's obviously upset you a great deal, but this is no way for it to end."

"He…he…lied," she stuttered. "I'll not marry a man I cannot trust."

"You can trust me, Edith. I am not lying, and I can prove it."

"Prove it? Ha. You can't prove it," she snapped.

Detective Huxton's spine stiffened, and he folded his arms across his chest. "I'm not leaving here until you see the evidence, Edith, and then maybe you'll know that I'm not lying. I would never hurt you intentionally. I love you with all my heart, but I can't ignore the evidence."

"What is the evidence?" Tyler asked.

A heavy cloud of silence hung in the air around Tyler's question.

"Go on, tell them what you told me," Edith demanded, standing behind Evelyn.

"Aunt Edie, look at me...look at me." It was a few moments before Edith withdrew her focus from Micah and refocused on my voice. "Explain this all to me, I am totally confused. Why have you turned on Detective Huxton?"

"Because his evidence is wrong...wrong I tell you."

I looked at Detective Huxton, and one word passed my lips. "Explain."

Detective Huxton held his hands out in a placating manner. "There's no easy way to say this, so I'm just going to be totally honest with you as I was with Edith. We found several sets of fingerprints on the font, but one in particular caught our attention."

"Lies, I tell you," Aunt Edie snapped.

I put my arm around her shoulders and held her tight. "Shh, Aunt Edie, it's okay. Go on."

"We're pretty sure black magic is involved in Blair's death, but there was one set of fingerprints in particular that caught my attention—those of Rosalyn Peyton."

Aunt Edie tensed in my arms, and I held her tight. "Who is Rosalyn Peyton?"

She sucked in a breath and then whispered, "No one of importance."

"That's where you're wrong, Edith. You know and I know it. She's someone of great importance." He stood his ground, placing his hands on the table and leaning in. His cheeks glowed a crimson red. "I'm right, aren't I?"

Pain shot down my jawline. "Does someone want to tell me who Rosalyn Peyton is?"

In a deadpan voice, Aunt Edie said, "My older sister. My older *dead* sister."

CHAPTER FOURTEEN

The air rushed from my lungs, and my eyes stung. I blinked, and my body swayed. My knees wobbled, and I rubbed my forehead.

I have another aunt?

"I have another aunt...I have another aunt." Each time I said the words, my chest constricted. I turned square-on, holding Aunt Edie by the shoulders. "Aunt Edie, how could you keep this from me? I have another aunt. Why don't I know about her? Why didn't anyone tell me?"

"Had, Evelyn, I..." Tears streamed down Aunt Edie's cheeks, and I pulled her into my chest and held her tight until her breathing calmed and the crying subsided.

Detective Huxton cleared his throat and spoke in a soft tone. "Rosalyn Peyton was the eldest of the three Peyton women, six years older than Edith."

Aunt Edie pulled back and brushed my hair behind my ears. "You have her eyes just as Brianna did." Her eyes watered over, but she kept the tears from making an appearance.

"I'm sorry you had to find out this way," she said. "You were never meant to know about her at all."

"How could you say such a thing?" Her words stabbed me in the heart as sure as she'd driven the knife in with her own hands. "I have a right to know I had another aunt."

Detective Huxton had edged his way around behind Aunt Edie and pulled a chair out for her. He stood, bracing for another outburst, but she simply sank into it pulling me down onto the chair beside her.

Tyler and Detective Huxton occupied the two chairs on the opposite side of the table.

I wasn't sure if the flutter in my belly was excitement or nausea. "Aunt Edie, what happened to her?"

"Oh, love." She wiped her wet eyes with the back of her hand. "Ros." She paused, unable to say her sister's full name. She swallowed hard and sucked in a deep breath. "Rosalyn was my older sister; she was twenty-one when she died."

Tears pricked my eyes, and my hand cover my mouth.

"Detective Huxton says they found her fingerprints in the church on the baptism font. That's only five years old. The math does not add up. I'll not marry someone who lies."

"Edith, you should know I would never lie to you, but the evidence is the evidence. I am as baffled as you are. I have no idea how they got there, but it is my job to find out."

Aunt Edie pushed her chair back and stood. "This is just too much. I can't dredge it all up again."

My limbs were heavy, but I reached up and held her hands. "For me, Aunt Edie. Please. Tell me about my Aunt Rosalyn."

"You know, Edith, she has a right to know about her ancestry," Miss Saffron's purring voice rang out from the corner. Aunt Edie and I glanced at the furball in question, and she arched her back and slinked her way towards the table. She jumped up on Tyler's lap and nuzzled her whiskers under his chin for a scratch.

"Hey there, Miss Saffron, you want in on the action too, huh?" Tyler asked giving her a tickle under her chin.

"You have no idea." She purred and sprang onto the table and sat smack bang in the centre. Purring and sitting tall, her gaze focused on Aunt Edie. "Edith, somehow Rosalyn's fingerprints have turned up in Saltwater Cove, we don't know why or how, but wouldn't it be better if everyone knew the whole story, so they were properly informed?"

A fresh tear ran down Aunt Edie's cheek, and she sniffed it back. "I'm sorry, but some memories are too painful to rehash."

"Does her death have anything to do with my parents' murder?" I asked, knots forming in my stomach.

Aunt Edie and Miss Saffron both shook their heads, and a sigh escaped my lips.

Miss Saffron spoke and put it as plainly as she could. "You know how persistent your niece is, Edith, just like you. If you don't tell her the truth, she'll find out somehow and then who knows if they will tell her the truth or some distorted version of it."

Aunt Edie threw her arms up in resignation. "All right, but we take it slow, and we do this my way." Everyone sat with their ears at the ready waiting for Aunt Edie to speak.

She fiddled with the edge of her fingernail, and a warm smile lit up her eyes. "Rosalyn was the life of the party, a witch like me and Brianna, but she had more power than both of us put together. She had the most amazing, addictive laugh. You couldn't help yourself. When she was near, life was better."

Detective Huxton joined in, a smile turning his lips up. "She was twenty-one. Edith was fifteen, and Brianna was thirteen."

"How come Mom didn't mention her?" I asked.

"After the accident, the whole world fell apart for all of us. It was too hard to look at her face without bursting into tears, so all her pictures were removed. They're in the attic somewhere, I've avoided going up there for so long—and then life happened, and I had no need to go up there."

I squeezed her hand. "Go on."

"It was her twenty-second birthday, and that year Mom and Dad decided we would pick our own birthday outings. Rosalyn wanted to go sailing. Of all things…sailing. She'd shown an interest in the activity and had been doing some training, but when she suggested we go out on our own, it freaked me out. She'd only ever been out with an instructor, but she was all gung-ho and everything and promised she could handle it."

"We warned Rosalyn about the approaching storm, but she refused to believe how bad it was and insisted they still go as it was her birthday, and it was her right to choose," Miss Saffron said wiping her eye with her paw.

Aunt Edie swallowed; her skin was all red and blotchy. "She promised to stay close to the shoreline, and then the storm hit. It turned out to be a big one. Rosalyn insisted she had it under control, and we were to follow her instructions to the letter. We did, but it was no match for the storm front."

"Why didn't you use your powers to get yourselves safely back to shore?" Tyler asked, his hand stroking Miss Saffron under her chin.

"You'd think that would have been the obvious solution." Aunt Edie's eyes grew dark. "We tried, but unbeknownst to Brianna and me, Rosalyn had put a blocking spell on both of us. Our powers were useless. If only she hadn't done that, she'd still be alive today."

"Why would she do that?" I asked.

Aunt Edie smiled. "Rosalyn was all about establishing that females were just as capable as men. I guess she wanted all three of us to prove her point."

The heaviness in my chest weighed down my heart. Between the ringing in my ears and the light-headedness, I wasn't sure if I was going to vomit or pass out. "I can't believe this. I can't believe no one ever told me about her."

Aunt Edie wiped the tears from her eyes. "It was by my mother's decree that all pictures and memorabilia relating to Rosalyn be either given away or burned. She was never to be talked about or discussed again. It was far too painful for my mother."

My jaw dropped and my hands flattened against the table. "Burned? Why would you burn all the memories?"

"She didn't want to be reminded of all she'd lost," Aunt Edie said, glancing at me through glazed eyes. A smile broke, and she looked at me with a warm loving smile, and she patted my hands. "And then you were born. Mother was so excited, and for a while she was happy. She replaced Rosalyn's memory with new ones of you laughing and playing and being the mischievous child, you were."

I slid my hands along the table bringing them to rest on my lap. "I don't remember her."

Aunt Edie shook her head. "No, you wouldn't. Then you started showing signs of witchcraft and that was it for Mom and Dad—they couldn't lose another child or grandchild. They gave both of us an ultimatum; choose witchcraft or them, but we couldn't have both. I think our choice was obvious, it's who we are. I know I couldn't turn my back on the very essence of who I am, and neither could Brianna.

"They renounced all connections with the supernatural and moved away, and we lost contact. It was only a few months later that Brianna decided to move away from Saltwater Cove and let you live your life as a normal child. She wanted you to decide if you wanted to be a witch or not."

Detective Huxton piped up. "It was one of the worst times Edith has endured. I was there for her then, and I'll be here for her now." Aunt Edie caught his eye. A moment passed between them, and she nodded.

I sighed, pinching the bridge of my nose. "Hold up a second. I'm confused. When I asked Mom about my grandparents, she told me Dad's parents were in heaven and that her parents had also gone away, far, far away. I took that to mean they were also in heaven, and now I'm finding out they're alive."

Aunt Edie brushed the hair off my face and rested her warm hand against my cheek. "I'm so sorry, sweetheart. I remember having a conversation with Brianna the week before she was killed. She told me she'd touched base with Mom and Dad and that they were going to come and visit, to meet you. After the accident, I found their number when I was going through Brianna's things. I rang and told them what happened. They refused to come to the funeral to mourn another child and wanted no more to do with her, me, or you."

Nothing to do with me? But they don't even know me.

I felt the blood drain from my face and bile coated the back of my throat. "I see."

Aunt Edie clasped my hands in hers and held them tight, a single tear escaped her eye. "I'm so sorry, sweetheart," she said again. "We all thought it was best you didn't know about any of this. They are the ones who walked out on us. They don't deserve to know you, to know what an amazing, talented wonderful witch you turned out to be. I could not be prouder of you. I love you to the moon and back a gazillion times over."

"Thank you." I wrapped my arms around her shoulders and hugged her until I went numb on the inside and out. I buried my face in her neck while uncontrollable tears flowed, soaking her neck and blouse.

"It's going to be okay; let it all out," she whispered, stroking my hair as a mother would when comforting a distressed child.

The tears finally stopped, but the ache in my chest and heart had left a big hole. I pulled away from Aunt Edie and wiped my wet eyes on my shirt sleeve. "Let me get this straight. What you're telling me is that I have grandparents alive out there somewhere who know I exist, but don't want anything to do with me because I'm a witch?"

I looked into the hollow eyes of Aunt Edie and Detective Huxton. Their silence was confirmation. I was right. I straightened my spine and licked my lips. "The way I see it is if they can't be bothered to get to know the amazing witch I am, I couldn't give two hoots about them. As far as I'm concerned, they're not a part of my life, and that's the way it's going to stay." I reached out for Aunt Edie's hand and Tyler's and gifted them both a smile to light up their hearts. "I have all the love I need right here."

Aunt Edie pressed her lips together and a new stream of tears ran down her cheeks. This time they were happy tears. I could tell.

Tyler picked up my hand and kissed the back of it so gentleman-like that it made me giggle. "Damn straight," he said. "You'll never be without love in Saltwater Cove, Evie girl. And let's not forget Harriet and Jordi, you know both of them love you like a sister."

"Thank you all." Heat radiated through my chest. "There is one thing I am not sure of."

"What's that, love?" Aunt Edie asked.

I turned to Detective Huxton, and his brows shot up. "You said you found Rosalyn's fingerprints on the baptism font and that's why Aunt Edie was so angry with you."

Aunt Edie shot up from her chair and planted her hands on the table. She leaned into Detective

Huxton, her body towering over his. "That is why you are wrong." She stormed over to the kitchen sink and gripped the edge, her head dropping forward.

Detective Huxton stood and moved up behind her. "Edith, you of all people know how good I am at my job. I checked and double-checked. Do you think I would have said anything if I weren't a hundred per cent sure?"

She flexed her fingers against the edge of the sink, and her shoulders rose up and down faster than normal. "You and your team have made a mistake. Rosalyn is dead, so they can't be hers."

"Edith," he said in his detective authoritative tone. "The font is only five years old, there is only one way her fingerprints could have gotten there, and that is by Rosalyn putting them there."

"This is all getting too much." Aunt Edie spun, and her wide eyes drilled Detective Huxton. She opened her mouth to speak, and she paled, her head shaking from side to side in small movements. Within a split second, her eyes rolled back, and her head lolled, and her knees collapsed from under her.

Chapter Fifteen

"Aunt Edie," I yelled as she fell into Detective Huxton's arms. He scooped her up and headed into the lounge room. I swung Miss Saffron into my arms and raced in after them.

He placed her delicately on the three-seater lounge, kneeling beside her. Tyler stopped behind me placing his arm around my shoulder and pulling me close to his side. The thrashing of my heartbeat against my temple was loud enough to send a shooting pain across my forehead. "Aunt Edie?" I whispered.

"Give her some space," Detective Huxton said, brushing the hair from her forehead. He repeated the soothing action along with a shushing sound that calmed my racing heart. I hoped Aunt Edie could hear him.

Her erratic breathing scared the hell out of me, but then she reached out and Detective Huxton held her hand close to his chest. "It's okay, Edith, you're all right. Everything is going to be all right."

"Micah," she said through her husky tone, tears seeping out the corners of her closed eyes.

He squeezed her hand and brushed the back of his hand down her cheek. "Yes, love. I'm here."

"I'm sorry." She dropped her head to the side, and her eyelashes fluttered open to focus on her love. "Please forgive me, Micah."

"There's nothing to forgive, Edith. You had a shock, that's all."

"Aunt Edie, it's Evelyn. You'll be fine." I leaned my head onto Tyler's shoulder, and Miss Saffron sprang onto the armrest of the lounge. She purred and spoke so clearly in my mind Aunt Edie must have heard it. "Evelyn, either Rosalyn has risen from the dead or someone is out to make it look like she's alive. You have to find out what is going on."

I will, don't worry. If she's alive, then I'll find her, and if it's someone playing with Aunt Edie's mind, I swear I will make them suffer. I don't care if I have to use my magic to do it.

"Who would play such a horrible prank on me? What did I ever do to them?" Aunt Edie mumbled, her voice sluggish.

"I'll find out." Detective Huxton leaned in and kissed her forehead. "I promise, Edith. I promise I'll find out what is going on."

She lay a moment and refocused her breathing. Her eyelids flicked open, and she pushed herself into a sitting position.

"Easy there," Micah said, joining her on the lounge. "How do you feel?"

"I'm okay. My head's throbbing but nothing a few painkillers won't fix."

Tyler took a step away towards the kitchen. "I'll get them for you."

I smiled and mouthed, "Thank you."

Aunt Edie glanced at me, Micah, and then Miss Saffron and smiled. "I expect I look worse than I feel." She grabbed Micah's hands and squirmed in her seat. "Micah, can you ever forgive me for my outburst? I know you were only doing your job, and I should have realized that. With all my heart, I still want to marry you if you'll have me."

"If I'll, have you?" he repeated, his brows creased into a monobrow. "Like I would ever let you get away from me again. I let that happen once, and there's no way it's going to happen again. I'll be marrying you if I have to carry you down the aisle over my shoulder. One way or another you will be Mrs Micah Huxton."

Aunt Edie burst into happy tears, and she hugged the life out of him. He may be police—but as long as he made her happy, that was all that mattered to me.

"Here you go," Tyler said, handing her two tablets and a glass of water.

"Thank you, Tyler." She knocked them back and then handed her glass to Tyler who placed it on the table. "I'm sure they will kick in soon. I cannot believe someone in Saltwater Cove would stoop so low to play such a cruel joke. It has to be someone who was here when Rosalyn was alive, so that should narrow it down a bit."

"Edith, darling," Detective Huxton said, brushing her cheeks with his hands.

Darling? The endearment is a little too sweet for my liking. I'm sure there will be plenty more once they're married.

I moved around to sit on the single lounge chair opposite Aunt Edie.

"How are you feeling?" Detective Huxton asked, frowning.

She patted his knee and smiled. "I'm okay, love, it was a shock; that's all."

I looked over at the detective and said, "I was hoping we might be able to talk about the Misty slash Blair case."

"Oh," he said and sat back on the sofa being sure to keep his hand and Aunt Edie's locked together. "I'm listening. A change of subject might be good."

Tyler sat on the armrest of my chair, his closeness warm and comforting.

I cleared my throat and looked Detective Huxton in the eye. "As I came in, I bumped into Tiffany on her way out of The Melting Pot. She said you questioned her, and she's allowed out, but her powers have been blocked, and she is under twenty-four-hour house arrest. Is that right?"

"I'm afraid it is." He turned and looked Tyler up and down. "She said she's enlisted your services to help prove her innocence."

Tyler nodded. "Yes sir, she has, and I believe she is innocent."

Detective Huxton scratched at his jawline and cocked his head to the side. "Since when have you and Tiffany been pals?"

"We're not pals," Tyler said, shifting uncomfortably on the armrest. "She hired me to do a job. If I find evidence she's guilty of the crime, you can rest assured I will report it to you at once."

"I see." He paused, frowned then returned his focus to me. "To answer your question, yes. We questioned her, and it was like listening to a broken record. She has no alibi but confirms that she was in the salon and picked up the trophy to hand it to Misty when she asked for it."

Tyler ran his hand down to his knee and leaned forward. "Tiffany said she had no alibi for the time of Misty's murder?"

"That's correct." Detective Huxton nodded. "She said she was at home, alone, and we all know that is no kind of alibi. We held her for as long as we could but had to let her go when another print was found."

"You found another print on the trophy?" I asked, my words flowing from my lips more rushed than I expected.

Could it be the print from the person who ran from the church?

"Unfortunately, it was too smudged to make a clear identification, but it is definitely not Misty's or Tiffany's."

Tyler stood and clasped his hands together. "That's great. It proves another person was present and could have committed the crime."

"Not so fast, son. It might be another print, but Tiffany is still our number one suspect at present."

"What about the person we saw running from the church?" Tyler asked his arms outstretched. "Surely, Wade told you about them."

Detective Huxton nodded. "He did, but as yet there have been no more sightings, and the lead's running cold."

"Tyler, it's not like you to get so uptight about something like this. What's going on?" Aunt Edie asked, concern etched on her brow.

That's just like my aunt, she gets the scare of her life, yet she still puts others before herself. I live with the coolest aunt in the world, and she's all mine.

"For once, I believe Tiffany is innocent, and she's getting a bad rap for it just because she's done some stupid things in the past. This time is different."

"That may be so," Aunt Edie said, looking up at Tyler. "But her actions in the past haven't left her in good favour with the townsfolk, it's hard to believe Tiffany would do anything good for another person."

The scarred and tormented image of Johanna flashed across my mind, and a new bout of nausea swished around in my stomach. Tiffany gave her life for her sister, and no one but Tyler and I knew about it.

I wriggled to the edge of my seat and pressed my hand to my hardened stomach. "I don't mean to change the subject, but the reason we actually stopped by was that Tyler came across something interesting in his research today, and we wanted to run it by you and get your opinion."

"Does it have anything to do with Misty's murder?" Detective Huxton asked.

I shook my head. "No, not at all."

He raised his eyebrows. "Blair's murder?"

I paused and looked at Tyler. He shrugged and gave a small nod. "Possibly, we're not sure."

"All right, let's hear it then." He looked up at Tyler and waved him down. "Take a seat for goodness' sake, man, you're making the place look untidy."

Tyler smiled and sat on the only spare lounge chair. "While we were in the church today, Evelyn noticed something about the positioning of Blair's body."

"Is that so?" Detective Huxton reached for his notepad and pen. "Go on."

Tyler looked at me and nodded. I bit the inside of my lip and returned the nod. I sucked in a deep breath through my nose and let it out along with the nerves clogging up my system. I related the whole scenario from the moment we found the bible beneath Blair's body until the point Tyler decoded her dying message.

Tyler took up the tale, outlining what he'd learned about the cup. "As Evelyn said, I also believe it's connected to the Sphere and possibly her parents' deaths, but I don't know how. That's why we came to you, hoping you might know."

Detective Huxton finished his frantic note scribbling. "What happened to our two-way street, Evelyn? You were supposed to come to me when you made a discovery. That was the deal."

"The deal was, I come to you when I had something to tell you. I didn't; Tyler did, and once we put it together, we came straight here, I think that's close enough," I snapped. "That's as far as we got. We're hoping you can help us work it out."

"We haven't exactly been doing nothing over at the station," Detective Huxton said.

"It isn't something I am aware of, but that doesn't mean I can't help you," Aunt Edie said, her voice calm and comforting.

"Thank you."

"You're welcome, sweetheart." She glanced at the clock on the wall, and her body jarred in her seat. "Oh my goodness, is that the time? We're supposed to be on our way to Vivienne's for her new jam tastings."

Detective Huxton frowned and placed his hand on Aunt Edie's knee. "Are you sure you're up for it, love? I'd hate you to push yourself too much too quickly. The jams can wait."

Oh no, they can't, Miss Saffron interrupted my thoughts, prancing up onto the top of the table.

I couldn't agree more. You know you're Vivienne's number-one jam taster.

I sure am.

"Enough chitchat," Aunt Edie said, gathering Miss Saffron up in her arms and rubbing her nose against her tummy fur. She turned to Micah and plonked her into his arms. "If you take Miss Saffron here out to the car, I'll grab my jacket and keys and be out in a jiffy."

His lips spluttered, and he grabbed the fur from his mouth. "Easy there, I've had my daily intake of calories." He was on his way out of the kitchen in seconds, pausing by the door. "Evelyn, one more question. Do you think Misty and Blair's murders are related?"

His question rolled around in my mind and churned around in my gut. "If I'm honest, I have to say yes. I feel they are related somehow."

"Thank you for your honesty." Miss Saffron's tail whacked him in the face, and he coughed fur balls as he closed the door behind him.

"Poor Detective Huxton." Tyler muffled his laugh as his gaze followed him out. "I hope he can handle life being married to a witch."

I pinched my lips together and poked him in the belly once, twice, three times before he pulled back and rubbed his tummy. "How do you think you're going to do being married to a witch? What makes you think your life will be any easier?"

"Hey, I already know what I'm getting into, I have since high school, and I say bring it on." He stood with a cheeky smirk on his face and his hand out, fingers beckoning me closer. I stepped in, and he picked me up and twirled me in the air, my giggles and his laughter joining as one.

"What has gotten into you two?" Aunt Edie asked as she shuffled past and headed towards the door.

Tyler put me down, and I gasped for some much-needed air, still smiling at his antics. "Nothing, just having some fun. See you later."

"Bye," she called over her shoulder as she opened the door. She winked, "Don't wait up."

Ew, what an image to put into my mind. It was bad enough I was going to have to live with the detective once they were married. I didn't want to know when they were getting down and dirty. I squeezed my eyes shut and shook the image from my mind when a sharp knock at the door snapped me out of it.

"I'll get it," Tyler said, his chuckle still hanging around in the air. He opened the door, and a bitter coldness worked its way into the room disintegrating the jovial atmosphere instantly.

"Ashlyn, what are you doing here?" Tyler asked.

The fear embedded in her eyes couldn't be ignored. She wiped her hands down her jeans and looked straight through me as if I were a ghost. "Evelyn, I need your help. I believe I'm marked for death."

CHAPTER SIXTEEN

"Marked for death? What are you talking about?" I asked, my temperature rising.

Her shaking body stood on the doorstep while she glanced over her shoulder several times. "Please, Evelyn, can I come in?"

"Of course." Tyler and I stepped to the side, and she bolted across the room planting herself in the doorway leading to the main house.

She rocked from side to side, moving in sharp, jerky movements and biting her fingernails. The woman was as nervous as a newborn colt. She rubbed the back of her neck and eyed the exit door as though looking for others following her.

"Ashlyn." I held my breath and took a small step towards her holding my arms out in front of me.

"Firstly, I need you to take a few deep breaths and calm down."

She paced the small confines of the kitchen, her gaze darting around. The room was on high alert.

"Ashlyn, can you do that for me?" I asked again.

But instead, her agitation grew, and she started rubbing the skin on her forearms, her fingers twitching and jumping on and off her skin, unable to keep them still.

"Ashlyn!" I snapped, and she froze. She spun her head to glare at me. It was the first time she noticed Tyler, and her eyes widened as she stumbled back against the doorframe.

My breath caught, and I wanted to reach forward and catch her, but she righted herself. "It's all right, you know Tyler; he won't hurt you."

Ashlyn's posture perked. She looked at Tyler and then back at me. "I know he won't hurt me, but others might. Evelyn, I need your help," she blurted, clutching her coat to her chest. "I need a protection spell for me and my family."

"A protection spell? Why do you need one, and why for your family?" Now she had my full attention.

She threw her hands up in the air and rolled her eyes. "Duh, where have you been for the last two days? Blair is dead, and I'm sure I'll be next. I need a spell or concoction to help protect me from them— my family as well. They need protection."

"From whom?" I asked, edging myself forward.

"From whoever killed Blair, that's who." Her voice rose to a screech, and I cringed.

"Is that the same person who killed Misty?" Tyler asked, speaking for the first time since she arrived.

"All right, no need to shout. I get it." Ashlyn paced, one hand holding her stomach and one hand on her hip. "I have no idea who killed either of them, and I'm not lying. I want to say Tiffany, but I can't be a hundred percent sure it was her."

Tyler tutted and crossed his arms. "You are full of it, Ashlyn. We happen to know that Tiffany has a solid alibi for Misty's death."

"Which is more than I can say for you when it comes to alibis." I walked over to the table and pulled out a chair. "How about you sit and tell us about how you skipped out on lunch with Blair on Sunday right around the time of Misty's murder? Sounds pretty suspicious to me."

Ashlyn toyed with the ring on her finger and shook her head, her eyes wide enough that the whites were showing. "No, no, I did not kill Misty. I swear."

"What were you doing for thirty minutes then? That's plenty of time to nip back, kill Misty and be back in time for more food."

She moved to stand behind the chair and leaned against the back. "You've got it all wrong. Yes, I slipped out and made a phone call, but I did not kill Misty. How many times do I have to say it?" She pushed off the chair and paced behind it. I looked at Tyler, and he shrugged.

Ashlyn stopped and clapped her hands together then rested them against her sternum. "I can clear this all up. I stepped out to make my phone call and about ten minutes into it, Marlana from The Four Brothers walked past on her way to work. I waved, and she waved and then we chatted for a few minutes. There is no way I could have made it from The Esplanade Café to Salty Snips, kill Misty, make my phone call, talk to Marlena, and get back to lunch with Blair in thirty minutes. There—it proves I could not have killed Misty."

Tyler sat back in his chair. "Only if she can corroborate your story."

Ashlyn nodded with pleading eyes. "And she better because it's the truth. Now, will you help me? Please help me protect my family?"

My brain was working overtime, but there was some logic to Ashlyn's story if it checked out with Marlana. I wiped the beads of sweat from my forehead and contemplated Ashlyn's request. It was Tyler's voice that made me pause just as I was about to agree to her request.

"Ashlyn, have you told us the whole truth?" Tyler asked. "Every detail you know about Misty and Blair, either of their murders or why someone would want to murder them? Because if Evelyn helps you and gives you this protection spell and we find out that you lied to us or haven't told us everything, what do you think her answer will be next time you ask for help?"

Ashlyn's back straightened, and she looked at me, the desperation disappeared from her eyes, and she lowered her gaze dipping her chin. A blush worked its way across her cheeks, and I clenched my jaw. Tyler's words had obviously triggered Ashlyn's guilty conscious.

"Um…" She bit her bottom lip and slid into the chair, her gaze cast downward. "There was this one other thing. The morning she was killed, Misty had two other visitors. Slade, Mercer's nephew from The Four Brothers, brought her a lunch delivery. That's not unusual as she often ordered her lunch in. There was also a woman, but I couldn't work out the voice. They were out the back behind closed doors having a rather animated conversation. I have no idea who it was, but I know I'd never heard her voice before. That's all. I swear that's all there is."

How could she have kept something so important from the police?

I sat in my chair seething at the audacity of the woman in front of me. I wanted to shake some sense into her, but there was always the catch that maybe I wouldn't stop shaking. I glanced at Tyler, and he shook his head as though he were thinking the exact same thing.

I pushed up from my chair and glared at the woman. "Okay, I'll do a protection spell for your house, and that should cover your family as well, but if I find out you have lied to me—"

"You won't," Ashlyn said, beaming from ear to ear.

Standing tall, I crossed my arms and kept my gaze glued to her. "I'd better not." Moving into Aunt Edie's pantry I paused and let the combination of aromas treat my senses to a blissful awakening. My nose itched as the spices struck all at once. Aunt Edie's pantry was heaven for any witch or cook. Imagine having the Hogwarts potions classroom at your fingertips. Well, that was Aunt Edie's pantry, Normal food on the left-hand side and on the right, every potion ingredient a witch could possibly need, clearly labelled and in its allocated spot.

I gathered the ingredients Ashlyn would need, some sage, four copper pennies, a candle and some of Aunt Edie's special incense and placed them in a hessian bag. Closing the door behind me, I was quick to make sure Ashlyn knew exactly what to do. "For this spell to work, you must do exactly as I say, is that clear?"

Ashlyn nodded. "Absolutely. I'll do it all exactly as you tell me."

I handed her the hessian bag and jotted down the instructions on a piece of paper, including the last one which was to burn the piece of paper once the spell had been completed. "Have a read and let me know if you are unclear on any part of the instructions?"

Ashlyn frowned as she read. "I have to stay inside and not leave my house?"

"Yes, this is a protection spell that will keep not only you safe but your house and those in it. No harm will come to you if you follow the instructions as I have written them."

"Thank you," she said and moved towards the door. Pausing, she turned and grabbed my hand. "I knew I could count on you. Bye."

"Bye, Ashlyn and good luck," I said, closing the door behind her. I looked into Tyler's eyes and huffed, shaking my head. "Why does life have to be so complicated all the time?"

"Ah, the life of a witch, never dull or boring," he said, his soft lips connecting with my cheek. "Something I was well aware of before we started dating. At least I know you'll always have me on my toes ready and waiting for the next adventure."

I'm glad he's excited about it. I wish I could go back to bed and restart the day.

"Oh no," I said, bypassing Tyler and grabbing an apron from the hook embroidered with The Melting Pot Café logo. "I should have been at work over half an hour ago, Eli and Harriet are going to be furious with me."

"No problem. I'll pop home for a while." Tyler pulled his car keys from his back pocket and jangled them on his right ring finger. "It'll give me a few hours to follow up on some things. It's your birthday eve. What do you say I pick you up for dinner when your shift is finished? We can head to The Four Brothers. That way we can speak to Marlana and confirm Ashlyn's story and also Slade's and have a bite to eat. Killing three birds with one stone as they say."

"Why is it you always know the right things to say?" I asked, threading my arms around his waist, and resting my head against his tight chest. Breathing in his musky scent, it was as though I were floating in his arms. His arms pressed against my back, and my chest warmed. A feeling of security washed over me. "I love you," I whispered.

He placed a delicate kiss on the top of my head and held it there for a moment. "I love you too, Evie girl."

***

I flicked the last light off at The Melting Pot, locked the door behind me and breathed out a huge sigh. "Thank goodness that shift is over. The end could not have come soon enough." I love working in The Melting Pot when it's busy but shifts like that one where the customers are few and far between make the evening drag.

After I updated Eli and Harriet on the fingerprint findings of my long-lost presumed dead aunt, Rosalyn, and the Ashlyn saga, Eli forgave me for being late and left. With limited customers there was no use having two people twiddling their thumbs, so Harriet was happy when I sent her home early. It did give me time to decide what to do for my birthday. A flutter moved through my belly. It might be my birthday tomorrow, but what better way to shock everyone than throw my own surprise party? That was the last thing everyone would be expecting.

A manic gust of wind swirled around my legs and up my shirt tingling my spine as it went. Pulling my jacket tight around my chest, I hightailed it down the front path towards Tyler's car and jumped in.

A blast of heat hit my icy skin, and I squinted against the force of the airflow. I held my hand up in front of my face. "Gee, I know the air can be a little chilly at night around this time of year, but do you need it on full blast?"

"Sorry, I just wanted it to be warm when you got in," he said, flicking a few switches on the dashboard. The airflow dropped to a steady manageable stream. "Better?"

I nodded and gifted him a smile. "Much better, thank you." He pulled away and headed towards The Four Brothers. "Any luck finding the location of the cup?"

He shook his head. "Nope, it's proving harder than I expected. How was your shift?"

"Boring as ever. We had a few customers. I decided to let Harriet go early. It was nothing I couldn't handle by myself. Although,"—I paused and pulled my knee up on my seat so I could face him— "I've finally decided what I want to do for my birthday tomorrow."

He kept his eyes on the road, but his brows raised adding a few more creases to his forehead. "That's great, am I allowed to know?"

"As long as you can keep a secret."

Tyler nodded and turned down the road where The Four Brothers was located.

I was excited to tell him. "I'm going to have a special surprise party for those close to me, except I'm the one giving the party. What do you think?"

"I think it sounds great, and it will satisfy those grumbly bums who insist you have one. This way it's on your terms."

"Exactly," I said, energised by the adrenaline flowing through my body. "I get to organise it all, so it will be exactly what I want. Your job will be to ensure everyone is there but knows not to be at The Melting Pot until six-thirty tomorrow night."

"Done." He smiled and squeezed my hand. "Let me know if you need me to do anything else."

"Will do."

Tyler finally found a parking spot at The Four Brothers—it was unusually busy for a Tuesday night, and then it dawned on me. Tuesday was trivia night, a popular evening among the locals. "Looks like trivia is another hit tonight. Mercer must be doing something right since he started dishing out the workload to others."

"I guess so." Tyler grabbed my hand, and we were about to head through the main doors when Hannah emerged, swishing her ginger locks over her shoulder. My hand brushed her icy skin, and a shiver danced up my arm and across my shoulder blades.

"Oh, my goodness. I'm so sorry, Evelyn. I didn't mean to run straight into you like that. I'm just pleased to have finished my shift." Hannah frowned, and her emerald-green eyes glowed sorrowfully. That was if a vampire could look sorrowful. Hannah oozed beauty no matter what she was wearing—a pair of trendy faded jeans, a nondescript t-shirt, Doc Martens with pick shoelaces and of course, no jacket because vampires don't get cold.

"Pfft," I said swishing my hand in the air. "Don't mention it; these things happen."

Hannah flicked the hair from her forehead and sighed. "You're too kind."

"But now that I have you here, I was wondering how things were going with you and Slade."

Her eyes fluttered, and her expression turned into a scowl. "Don't talk to me about that loser."

Loser? Oh, this should be good.

"I don't even want to talk about that man." She beckoned us over to the side of the walkway as though she didn't want anyone else to hear our conversation which suited me just fine.

"I don't understand," Tyler said, his head tilted and his eyebrows squishing together. "I thought he was the one."

"Gosh no." Hannah pulled back, her expression one of disgust. "He is the most arrogant, self-absorbed man I have ever met in my life."

"No way." The words escaped before I could hold them back. "I had no idea."

She folded her arms across her chest. "Believe it, but not at first. He'll woo you, dine you until he has you wrapped around his little pinkie and then WHAM." She clapped her hands together, and Tyler and I jumped backwards. "He'll go in for the kill. I was lucky I saw through him before he could dig his claws into me."

I smiled at the irony of her statement. "I thought it was vampires who had the claws?"

"Oh, we do, and the sharp teeth." She pinched her lips together, and her eyes thinned. "I tell you, I have never wanted to take a bite out of someone more than I wanted to rip into Slade's neck. But I couldn't do it, the thought of tasting human blood had me dry-retching."

"I guess you're lucky your mother is human, saves you having to snack on Slade or any other town visitor. How do you work with the guy, assuming he's still working here?"

She nodded and rolled her eyes. "He is—we stay away from each other. He knows what's good for him. I may not be able to snack on him, but that doesn't mean I can't rip him limb from limb if he makes me angry. Most people at work know there will be hell to pay if they push too far, that's why we get on so well. Except for Slade, that is."

"Sounds like you have it all sorted," Tyler said. "Remind me not to get on your bad side."

A cutesy giggle pierced the air, and she play-punched Tyler in the shoulder. "You are so funny,

Tyler. Anyway, I'm done for the night, was there anything else you needed?"

I pressed my lips together and held back my internal laugh. It was the first time I'd seen Tyler flinch. Who knew a female vampire was intimidating and strong enough to make him nervous?

"Nope," Tyler said before I had a chance to reply.

"See you later," Hannah said over her shoulder as she moved off.

"Night," I said, following Tyler inside.

The energy of the place buzzed, and the excitement of the patrons flowed within the room. Jazzamay rocked out her tunes while Talen backed her up on the guitar. Their soulful music worked its way through your body like a musical addiction. You couldn't help but move and wiggle along to the tunes.

"Wow, trivia night has drawn the crowds this evening," Tyler said, leading me to the back of the bar area where it was quieter. "I can't remember when I've seen this many people here on a Tuesday evening."

I glanced around at the familiar and unfamiliar faces and smiled at the good time beaming on their faces. "I'm glad. Mercer's been working hard to bring it back after Florence Chesterfield almost destroyed it."

Tyler's head flinched back slightly. "Why would you bring that woman up? First, she's obsessed with me then she tries to kill me, remember?"

"How could I forget?" Thinking of Tyler passed out lying in a pool of blood on the floor of the cellar here at The Four Brothers brought a flood of bile up to the back of my throat. A shiver ran across the back of my neck.

"There she is." I followed Tyler's arm as he pointed to the woman on the far side of the restaurant.

Marlana rushed around from table to table like a woman on a mission. She appeared to be the only one working the tables. Poor woman. "Come on." I made a beeline for her, pulling Tyler along behind me.

Stopping by her side, I dropped his hand and tapped her on the shoulder. "Marlana, how are you doing?"

She looked at me as though I were her worst enemy then frowned. "Evelyn? What is it? Is there something wrong with your meal?"

"No, we haven't eaten yet."

She picked up an armful of dirty dishes, careful to balance them on her forearm. "As you can see, I'm a little busy. Since Keelin left to go work at The Melting Pot, we've been run off our feet. Excuse me," she said shuffling past us into the kitchen.

I followed her and waited until she re-emerged, Tyler sticking close to my side. "Sweetheart, why don't you go and find Mercer or Slade and see if you can chat with him about his delivery to Misty the morning she was killed?"

He nodded. "Okay but keep your phone on you and call me when you're finished."

"Bye." I reached up and planted a kiss on his lips, and he headed off toward Mercer's office. My gaze was glued to his pants hugging his tight derriere a glove. I licked my lips and smiled.

Yummy.

The door to the kitchen flew open, and Marlana walked straight into me. Thankfully her arms were empty. "Marlana."

"Evelyn, what are you still doing here?" she said, her hands on her hips and her foot tapping away double time. A pinched expression creased her forehead. "If I'd had a tray full of food, it would be all over you by now."

"I'm sorry." I clasped my hands in a prayer position in front of my chest. "Can I have a few moments of your time, even less? I just have to ask you one question about Ashlyn. I promise to be quick, and then you don't have to see me for the rest of the night. Oh, unless we're in your serving area for dinner."

Marlana dropped her arms, and her eyes dulled. "Okay but be quick about it. What is it you want to know?"

"Thank you," I said, the tension releasing from my chest. "Ashlyn swears that she was nowhere near the salon when Misty was killed. She said that she was out back of The Esplanade Café on a phone call, and you walked by and chatted for a while. Is that right?"

"When did you say this was?" Marlana asked, rubbing her bottom lip with her finger.

"Um, about, lunchtime I think."

Marlana's eyes widened. She snapped her fingers and nodded. "Now that I think about it. Yes. I ran into her on my way to work. I remember…she was on the phone, pacing, and we walked straight into each other. She got off the phone, and we chatted a moment, and then I went on my way."

My heart sank. "Are you sure?"

"Of course, I'm sure," she said, her back stiffening. She let out a noisy impatient breath. "Is there anything else because I really have to get back to work?"

I shook my head, deflated. "No, that's it. Thank you. I appreciate your time."

She gave me an abrupt nod, turned, and flounced away.

I guess that answers the question about Ashlyn's alibi.

I pulled my phone out to call Tyler, and my hand vibrated at the same time. His gorgeous picture came up on the screen, and I smiled deep down in my belly.

"Hey, good-looking, how did you go? I came up with a dead end I'm afraid."

"I've found something interesting. Are you anywhere near Mercer's office?"

I spun around and headed down the corridor to the other side of the bar. "Be there in two minutes." The soulful sounds of Jazzamay had finished, and my head was being pounded with the drumming beat of tribal music with a modern upbeat twist.

I rounded the corner of the bar and walked past a semi-packed gathering of men and women around the bar, some waiting to be served, some chatting and a lot of jovial laughter from all. I eyed Tyler waiting a few meters past Mercer's office, pretending to look at the *What's Happening* Noticeboard. His eyes caught my attention and his back stiffened.

"Hey, there," he said, handing me a glass of red wine and then cupping my hand and dragging me towards Mercer's office. He paused and leaned against the wall and placed me on the other side.

What is with all the pulling and pushing?

"What are you doing?" I asked, shaking my head.

He threaded his arms around my waist and angled our bodies together our glasses touching. "Tyler, what are you doing?"

He placed a finger over my lips. "Shhh, just follow my lead."

"Ooo-kay." My breathing hitched as he ran the back of his finger down my cheek. He leaned in and kissed behind my ear sending a multitude of tingles and shivers across my back and down my torso. My shoulder pulled up to my neck, and I couldn't help but giggle. "Tyler, you know I'm ticklish behind my ears."

His sultry eyes looked down at me, and he winked at me.

I whispered, "You don't need to flirt with me. I'm a sure thing when it comes to you."

He took a sip of his drink and smiled. "I know Evie girl. I hate to break it to you, but we're here because I want you to see if you can get a glimpse of the black jumper hanging over Mercer's chair in his office and tell me if you think it's the same as the one the person wore running out of the church this morning."

An undercover mission? I love it.

Adrenaline infused my body at the thought of getting caught. I stretched my hand with the wine glass up over Tyler's shoulder and eased my body closer to his. I pushed up on tippy-toes and placed my lips on his cheek, while my gaze darted over the top of the semi-glazed glass into the office.

In seconds I'd located the black jumper and knew instantly it was the one. The red stripe across the shoulder and down the arms gave it away. "Yes, that's it. I remember that red stripe as clear as day."

"That's what I thought too. I wanted to have you confirm before I try to find Mercer."

I eased away from Tyler and took a sip of my wine, the strawberry and grape sweetness clung to the back of my throat. I coughed and cleared the bitter taste away. "Now I remember why I like white wine instead of red."

"Sorry, I just grabbed two as I walked past the bar. You don't have to drink it if you don't want to, just hold it if you like. Here's as good a place as any to wait for Mercer."

"Did someone say my name?"

Tyler spun, and I stepped to the side of him to see Mercer standing behind him holding a plate of freshly cooked garlic prawns delicately sitting on a pile of jasmine rice. The mix of aromas was scintillating. I licked my lips and looked at the steam coming from the plate. My stomach grumbled and groaned, demanding to be fed. Drooling was not the best look, so I diverted my gaze to Mercer.

"Mercer, yes. We were hoping to have a quick chat if you're available," Tyler said maintaining his authoritative tone.

He shrugged and opened his office door and walked in. "Sure, as long as you don't mind me having a bite for dinner as we chat. Tonight's really picked up. I can't believe how successful these trivia nights are, especially when the first prize is a hundred-dollar bar tab."

Tyler and I followed, Tyler taking a seat on the purple velour lounge chair. I took the green one.

"I'll come straight to the point," Tyler said, one hand resting on his thigh and the other on his knee. "Is that your jumper behind you on the back of your chair?"

With the door closed the smell of the garlic prawns filled the entire room. My tastebuds were having a conniption, demanding a taste of the succulent dish.

Focus, Evelyn. Focus.

Mercer leaned forward and looked over his shoulder. "Nope, it's Slade's jacket."

"Do you know where he is? We'd like to talk to him," Tyler asked.

Mercer paused the next mouthful and replaced his fork on the plate. He glanced up, his head tilted, and eyes narrowed. "He's out doing home deliveries. May I ask what this is about?"

Tyler rubbed his hand down his pant leg. "Both Evelyn and I are pretty sure we saw him running in that jacket,"—he paused and pointed to the one on the back of the chair— "running from Blair's body in the church this morning. That red stripe down the sleeves is a dead giveaway. We'd like to question him about it if that's all right with you."

Mercer threw the fork down on his plate with a sharp clang and leaned back in his chair rubbing his forehead. "That's it. I'm done. Question him as much as you like. I've had enough of his attitude and lack of respect. That boy was supposed to clean up his act while he was here, but he's done nothing but argue, belittle, and disrespect me and the other staff."

Mercer's face grew redder. "This was his last chance, come here, work for me, and clean up his act or face jail time. I had hoped his time here would change him…guess I was wrong. You're welcome to wait for him or when he returns, I'll keep him here and give you and Detective Huxton a call."

Tyler stood and held his hand out. "We'll wait. Thank you." Mercer shook his hand. "Evelyn and I are staying for dinner. If we haven't managed to catch you or him during the night, we'll touch base before we leave."

A deflated Mercer nodded and sank back down in his chair. Tyler closed the door behind him on the way out.

"That was interesting," I said, my hands rubbing together. "Did you know any of that, about this being his last chance? I wonder what he did to get jail time?"

Tyler followed close behind as we entered the crowded bar area. "If he got jail time for it, it can't be that good, but it probably means we have our killer unless he can provide an alibi. Time will tell."

"Evelyn," Mercer's voice called from behind, and we both turned in unison to see Mercer approaching. "I forgot to tell you there's a lady waiting for you up in the back corner of the bar by the old fire."

"Oh." I squinted and glanced through the crowd to the back of the bar and vaguely saw the outline of someone wearing a hooded cloak and sipping a drink. "Who is it?"

Mercer shrugged. "Stuffed if I know. She said to let you know when you got here and that she only wanted to speak to you, and you alone."

"Thanks." Heading into the bar area I pulled up in a spot with a clear view of the table then turned to Tyler and placed my hands on his chest. His racing heart beat against my hand, and a warmth melted my hand to his chest. I looked into his dreamy eyes and smiled. "You wait here. It has a perfect view of the table."

"What?"

"Tyler, she said alone. The last thing we want to do is scare her off if she has information about Misty or Blair's murders, and if she sees you, she might clam up or worse, run."

"Okay, I get it." He huffed and leaned his elbow against the bar.

"I'll be back as soon as I can. It's probably just someone who has some gossip to share." I turned and headed towards the table, my insides a ball of fury.

CHAPTER SEVENTEEN

M y palms turned sweaty, and my heart kicked into triple time as I edged myself closer to the table. The woman's head was lowered, all mysterious and brooding-like. She sipped from the tall glass in front of her. How does she fit into the puzzle? I stepped in front of the table, and her head popped up. My gaze connected with hers, and my lungs seized. I gasped and swayed, struggling to suck in enough air to breathe. It was as though I were looking at an older version of Aunt Edie. Same bone structure, same brown hair, same gorgeous complexion.

Is this my Aunt Rosalyn?

My hands clenched into fists, and the hollowness in her honey-brown eyes clawed its way into my heart. She smiled, and it broke me, tears streamed down my cheeks, and it took every ounce of my energy to keep my body upright. Instinctively, I took a step back, and her hand reached out.

Evelyn, please don't go. It's me, Rosalyn, Edith's older sister. I know this is a shock, but please stay and hear me out.

Her voice pierced my thoughts like a knife slicing through satin. Smooth and straight to the point.

I know you can hear me, all those with Peyton blood running through their veins have the gift. I'm assuming you carry it too. Please don't go. I need you to hear me out—it's a matter of life and death.

My chest ached from the constant heaviness restricting my breathing.

Rosalyn, is it really you? My Aunt Rosalyn?

Her jaw dropped, and her eyes widened before a warm smile spread across her face.

Aunt Rosalyn? I never thought I would ever hear those words grace my ears. I like it.

I'm not used to having telepathic conversations out in public. Here in Saltwater Cove, we try as much as we can to live normal lives.

"Oh, sorry," she said pulling back in her chair. "I'll have whatever type of conversation you wish as long as you'll stay and hear me out."

"Why…where have you been? You're supposed to be dead. Aunt Edie went crazy when your fingerprints were found on the baptismal font in the church. I don't blame her."

She dropped her shaking head and rubbed her forehead with her fingers. "I'm sorry, that was a mistake on my part. My prints were never meant to be there. It all happened so fast."

I edged myself onto the stool and clasped my hands together on the table. Primarily so they wouldn't shake. Here I was sitting across from my supposedly dead aunt. *I'm not crazy, am I?*

"No, Evelyn you're not crazy." She shuffled in her seat, her skin flushed. "I don't have long, and you're my only link to Edith. I need you to explain what happened."

"Why don't you tell her yourself?"

She shook her head. "It's too dangerous. I need to explain so she'll forgive me."

The jitters in my belly started, and I pressed my hand against it. "Why do you need her forgiveness?"

"It's best I start from the top, but it will have to be the abridged version as I don't have much time."

I nodded waiting patiently.

She began, "When I was in my late teens, I fell in love with the man of my dreams, he was everything I ever wanted in a man, and he liked me in return. He was charming and caring, and I fell hard. We kept our relationship secret from Edith and my parents, I knew they wouldn't approve. I should have listened to my gut. Turns out, when he showed his true colours, he was the complete opposite. I was in way too deep by then with no way out. He was ruthless and one of the cruellest men I'd ever met. He's so good at his job that he works for Salis van der Kault."

"No," I gasped, and my hand flew to cover my mouth.

"But I didn't know it, I swear, and by the time I figured it out, it was too late. You have no idea how hard I fought to escape his hold over me, but he's too powerful. I took all I could take, and I wanted to leave. I told him so. It ended in a massive argument, and he gave me an ultimatum; my life or those of my family. I either stayed with him, by his side forever, or he would kill every one of my family members in a slow and painful death in front of me. And he would do it, I have no doubt."

Bile hit the back of my throat, and I clenched my muscles and coughed it back. "That's horrible. How could he ask that of you?"

She rolled her drinking straw between her fingertips, her eyes downcast. "It took me less than a second to give him my answer. I'd do anything to protect my family, now and forever. Consequently, I've been with him ever since."

"But now you can escape, right?"

"No, no," she said, her hands darting and grabbing mine. "No, I can never leave if I want to keep you all protected. That was the deal, and I'm not about to play Russian roulette with your lives." Her skin paled, and her chin trembled. "I'm here to warn you and to tell you the truth."

"Warn me?" I said, my head dizzy and running over with all this new information. "What is going on?"

"I will do whatever it takes to save my family even if it means a life with a man I despise and detest. I'm here to tell you Salis is after the Sphere."

I rolled my eyes. "Tell me something I don't know."

She continued. "The man I'm tied to—"

My agitation grew at Rosalyn's inability to name this her captor. "Who is this man? You keep talking about him, but who is he? What's his name?"

She shook her hand at me. "Who he is, is not important. What's important is that he is in charge of obtaining the relics and destroying anything and anyone in his path. That's why I had to take this chance. Evelyn, you must stop looking for the relics. Your parents split them up and hid them around the universe to protect you so that you could live a safe and normal life."

"Safe? Normal…Ha. My life has been anything but safe and normal. They may have split them up and hidden them, but it still got them killed in the end."

"You're alive and that's all that matters. Alive to live out your life with Edith," she said, her words practically pleading with me to be satisfied with life as it is.

I blinked, and the vision of my parent's car disappearing over the edge of the cliff startled me. The image reignited the slow burn for vengeance deep in my belly. "What do you know of my parent's death?" I pushed the words out past the thickness clogging the back of my throat. "Did you have anything to do with it?"

"Of course not, you must believe me," Rosalyn begged. The pain in her voice knotted my chest.

"I do."

"It took me a long time to find out the truth. It was Salis who gave the command for their deaths, but the deed was carried out by his henchman, and by the man I once loved. I had no idea there could be such evil out there in the world. I was disgusted and mortified by his actions. After they were killed, I couldn't even look at him. I refused to follow his commands any longer. I locked myself away in my chamber, I refused to eat or drink anything."

"What happened?" I sat on the edge of my stool holding on to every word she said.

"For a while, he left me alone, but he knew my one weakness. My family—and there were still you and Edith to consider. He said that if things didn't go back to the way they were, he would tell Salis I'd gone back on my word, and you both would be killed."

My skin heated and itched at the thought. Pressing my lips together I pushed my fist against my lips, holding back the nausea coating my esophagus.

"I wanted Edith to know the truth. I saw my moment at the church. It was being back on my home turf that had strengthened my powers, so I took a chance with the baptism font and then I slipped out the secret passageway under the communion table." She paused. "Will you pass everything onto Edith,

Evelyn? I need Edith to know that I did it for her, to keep you all alive. I love them all so much."

I nodded and gripped her hand. "Yes, of course."

Rosalyn's smile wavered. "Can you also apologize for what it did to Mom and Dad? My death and then Brianna's drove them away, and that's on me—a burden I have to endure every day for the rest of my life."

"Aunt Rosalyn, I made a promise to bring my parents' killer to justice, and I intend to keep it." Her mouth opened, and her head moved in short sharp movements from side to side. I held up my hand before she had a chance to respond. "You can argue all you like, but I will keep my promise. I will find the relics and the Sphere and destroy them all before Salis can get his filthy hands on them." I bit my bottom lip and breathed in a lungful of air. "'To change one's destiny, one must first discover the hidden truth.' That was written on a magic medallion my mom tried to hide at the North Pole. If I can find that, I can find anything. It's my destiny."

Rosalyn sat in silence; her gaze never wavered from mine. Her eyes dulled, and her shoulders slumped. She gave one long exhale and nodded.

"I believe it's your destiny too. You are going to be a great and powerful witch one day, Evelyn Brianna Grayson."

A burst of adrenaline shot through my insides, and I sat tall, soaking up this special moment with my lost aunt. She raised my hands to her lips and kissed my fingers.

"I have to go, but before I do, I want to give you something to remember me," she said, replacing my hands on the table. "It's something every witch should own, especially if she's turning twenty-five and going to receive her full witch qualifications."

My forehead pulled tight. "You've lost me." Rosalyn brushed her finger underneath my chin, and I smiled at her loving gesture.

"I'm going to miss your smile. It's so much like Brianna's." She reached over and brushed her warm fingers down my cheek. My skin tingled under her light touch. "I want to give you something, both for your birthday and your graduation. When you have a moment, go to the bank, and ask for safe deposit box twenty-one. The password is Fallen Angel. I want you to have what's inside. Use it; perfect your craft and know that I will always love you."

She stood and retied her hooded cloak around her neck.

My heart jumped into the back of my throat. "Please don't go."

"Oh, love, I have to." She squeezed my hands once more, and my chest burned under the heaviness laden upon it.

My pulse sped, and I jumped up and wrapped my arms around her neck and held on. Silent tears flowed down my cheeks as she encased me in her arms. "Thank you for everything you have done. I won't ever forget it. After I've dealt with the Sphere, I'll do my best to find you and bring you home." My body jerked backward, and she held me at arm's length.

"No, no you must promise me that you will not look for me or come after me. Promise me, Evelyn?" Her voice choked with emotion. My shoulders stung as her hands squeezed tighter. "Promise me."

"Okay, I promise I won't come after you." The words tasted metallic as they passed my lips.

Rosalyn visibly relaxed and sighed, her hand flattening against her chest. "You had me going there for a moment." She stepped back and kissed her fingers then held her palm flat and blew me a kiss. "Goodbye, Evelyn."

"Goodbye, Aunt Rosalyn." And then she was gone, disappeared into the crowd gathered at the bar. I stood, my feet unwilling to move from their spot, my eyes still watching the door, praying she'd come back.

While she never did, a familiar figure entered and headed towards the back of the bar area near the wine cellar.

Bingo. Nice of you to grace us with your presence, Slade.

Keeping my eye on him, I moved toward his location and ran straight into Tyler as he appeared from the other end of the bar. "You saw him too?"

I nodded. "Yes, the timing couldn't have been better." The energy of the bar patrons shot up ten notches as we passed, fuelled by copious amounts of alcohol they'd consumed.

"Who was it? Are you okay?" he asked, concern etched in his tone.

"Yes, I will be. It was my Aunt Rosalyn."

Tyler stopped still, and his hand caught my shoulder, spinning me to face him. "Your aunt? The dead one whose fingerprints Detective Huxton found on the baptism font?"

I nodded and bit the inside of my cheek.

"That can't have been easy. Are you sure you're, okay? Do you want to talk about it?"

I nodded. "There's no time to talk about it now. I'll explain later. Let's get this Slade questioning out of the way."

"Gosh, I don't know how I'd feel if I found out my long-lost aunt wasn't actually dead."

Probably like me. As though one of your limbs has been severed.

"Tyler…Evelyn, this way." Mercer stood with one foot inside his office and the other in the walkway waving us toward him. "I have Slade in here."

"That's more like it," Tyler said, rubbing his hands together. "I'm here if you need to talk. Let's get this over and done with as soon as possible. If I don't feed my grumbling stomach monster, I won't be held accountable for the consequences."

I cringed and glanced up at him. "You did not just say that?"

Tyler winked and placed his hand on my lower back as we arrived. Mercer held the door open, and

Tyler and I entered coming face to face with a grumpy and annoyed Slade. He stood with his arms folded across his chest and his lips pinched together. A murderous glare in his eyes.

"What the hell is going on?" Slade snapped. "I don't have time for chitchat."

Mercer's hand shot out, and he pointed directly at Slade an inch or two from his nose. "Watch your mouth, young man. You're in enough trouble as it is."

"What?" he spat. "What did I do?" His lips turned down, and his eyes grew darker if that were possible.

"I'll cut to the chase," Tyler said, stepping forward. "Were you at the church this morning where Blair's body was found?"

"What?" He looked Tyler dead in the eye. "What are you talking about? I was nowhere near the church this morning." He said it with such conviction that I even believed him.

Tyler's brows pulled together. "You weren't running out of the church?"

He shook his head. "Hell, no. The last time I was in a church was for my mother's second wedding to that douchebag she calls a husband. I prefer the term dead-beat loser."

Mercer's cheeks glowed a cherry red as he stepped in next to Slade. "Watch it. That's my sister you're talking about there."

Slade's jaw tensed, and his lips turned up into a snarl. "So…what do you care? You live here in your own little perfect world. You have no idea what it's like."

"That's enough," Mercer snapped. The veins in his temple pulsed and twitched.

My gut tensed, and I stepped forward. "Okay, let's keep this a civil conversation. It's quite simple. Slade, if you weren't at the church this morning, where were you?"

Slade stood still, his tense, fevered stare glued to his uncle. "Not that it's anyone's business because it was my morning off, but I was over in Hallows Creek. I got back about an hour before my shift started. I had an early breakfast at Isla's place before she went to work and then fixed up the back fence for her. It was damaged in the last storm, and I'm handy with the tools. You can ask her if you don't believe me."

My forehead pulled tight. "You and Isla are seeing each other?"

He nodded and stuck his jaw out. "We are, do you have a problem with that?"

"No. I just wasn't aware that you were dating after your breakup with Hannah."

Slade rolled his eyes and huffed. "I wouldn't call what Hannah and I did 'dating.' It was more like she was the princess, and I followed. Not my kind of relationship."

"I see," Tyler said, rubbing his chin. "Will Isla confirm this?"

"Of course. I don't know what you think I did, but you are dead wrong," Slade said, picking up his jacket from the back of Mercer's chair. "Now, if there is nothing else."

"One more thing," Tyler said. "Where were you Sunday lunchtime? Do you have an alibi for Misty's time of death?"

Slade pinched his lips together and shook his head. "You people never give up, do you?"

"Just answer the question." Mercer barked.

"I was with Isla most of the morning then I called into Noble Crest to have lunch with her." He gave Tyler a brazen expression throwing his jacket over his shoulder. "I'd like to get back to my deliveries as I'm sure they've piled up by now."

"Of course," Tyler said. "Thank you for your time."

Mercer nodded and stepped aside, and all three of us watched Slade as he left the office. A samurai sword could have sliced the tension in the room.

Mercer shrugged. "I'm sorry he couldn't be any more help to you. Looks like the need to have a serious chat with my sister is long overdue."

Tyler's warm hand grabbed mine, and he led the way out of the office. "Thanks, Mercer. I still need to confirm the details with Isla, but it sounds as though he was far away from the church at the time in question."

Back to the drawing board. If it wasn't Slade running out of the church, who then?

CHAPTER EIGHTEEN

Exhaustion played havoc with my body. My muscles ached like I'd run a triathlon. Twice. *Like that is ever going to happen in my lifetime.*

Tyler had dropped me home after dinner, and the shower beckoned, what could I do but obey its calling? The massaging pellets of water droplets pulverized my back, and the tension stored in my muscles floated away. Freshly showered and in my pyjamas, I sat at the kitchen table, a steaming hot chocolate in hand and my furry familiar spread across my knees.

"I guess it's you and me tonight, Miss Saffron." I took a sip and watched as my voice barely registered, although I glimpsed her ears flicker ever so slightly. "I know you can hear me, cheeky girl," I said, scratching behind her ear. She looked up and licked her paw then settled back down.

"I don't blame you. If I was comfortable, I wouldn't want to move, but..." I paused and lifted her onto the centre of the table, and a dissatisfied grumbly purr echoed. "We need to talk."

Miss Saffron arched her back and rolled her neck stretching her joints one at a time. "You could have quite happily chatted while I was on your lap," she said, unfolding into a sitting position.

I tapped my finger on her nose, and she blinked. "I know, but this way I get to look into your gorgeous golden eyes while we chat."

She tutted and licked her paw. "Flattery will get you everywhere."

"How was your visit to Vivienne's? Did you pick out her next winning jam?" I asked sarcastically as if I didn't know.

"Of course," she said slyly. "Since when don't I pick a winning jam?"

"True." I sipped my hot chocolate. "Some birthday eve?"

"Have you decided what you are going to do for your birthday yet?" she asked, tilting her head.

"Yes, I believe I have," I said, my chest lightened happy with my decision. "I'm going to throw my own surprise party for the special people in my life."

"I hope I'm included in there somewhere," she said, brushing her paw over my hand.

Ruffling the fur on her head, I said with a chuckle, "Of course you are. You've been a part of this family much longer than I have.

"I've asked Tyler to make sure Harriet and Jordi come to The Melting Pot at six-thirty tomorrow night. I'll get Aunt Edie to make sure Eli and Detective Huxton are there, and you and I will round it up nicely."

"Sounds like you have it all planned."

My scalp prickled, and a shiver ran through my torso. "I may have it all planned, but how am I supposed to enjoy it or my graduation when there are two unsolved murders and an aunt who has mysteriously returned from the grave."

Miss Saffron's ears spiked before turning and flattening. Her head stretched up, showing me those inquisitive golden eyes. "What are you talking about? Who has returned from the grave?"

Resting my chin on my hand, I sighed. "Aunt Rosalyn, that's who. I met her this evening at The Four Brothers. It's a long story, but she's alive."

Miss Saffron's eyes widened and her back stiffened, the hair running down her spine stood to attention. "No way. Rosalyn Peyton is alive? Are you sure?"

I nodded, wiping the chocolate from around the rim of my cup and licking it off my finger. The sweet taste rolled around my tastebuds. "Yep, I saw her with my own eyes and talked to her. It was strange but comforting at the same time."

"Tell me more," Miss Saffron said, her body dropping low. She held my gaze in hers.

"The crux of it is she fell in love with the bad boy and when she wanted out, he refused and gave her an ultimatum—go away with him or watch her family die a horrible death." I pressed my hands flat on the sides of my cup. "She chose that latter and faked her own death to save her family, an honourable choice if you ask me. I'd do the same, but thankfully, I've fallen for Mr Right."

"Rosalyn is alive. Are you going to tell Edith?" she asked, crawling closer to my arms. She dropped her chin on my forearm and looked up at me with her cutesy golden eyes.

I shrugged. A hot flush zoomed up my neck and cheeks followed by a rush of icy coolness. "I don't know. I know she wanted me to. She wanted her to know the truth."

I swallowed the final droplets of my hot chocolate and pushed up from the table. Mulling over the situation in my head, I rinsed my cup and placed it in the dishwasher. Spinning, I clasped my hands together and smiled at Miss Saffron. "I know what I'll do. Surely Aunt Edie and Detective Huxton won't be at dinner much longer, I'll simply watch a movie and wait for her to get back, and then we can talk about what our next steps should be."

"Do you think that's wise?" Miss Saffron asked, licking her paw. "After all, it is your birthday tomorrow and you do need your beauty sleep."

I scooped her into my arms and blew a raspberry on her belly. "I'll get my beauty sleep. Don't you worry about that. Just for that comment, you can keep me company while I watch a movie."

Walking into the lounge room, I ruffled her fur under her belly. The range of purring, hissing, and meowing made me giggle. "What'll it be, some Hugh Grant in *Love Actually,* or do we want some Thor action in the form of Chris Hemsworth?"

I flinched as Miss Saffron let out a growl and squirmed her way out of my arms and onto the carpet. She turned her nose up and glared at me.

If they are my two choices, count me out.

Miss Saffron's sassy tone rang loud and clear in my mind.

"Have it your way, but I'm in the mood for a little muscle. Bring on Thor."

She rolled her eyes and slinked back through the doorway and out of sight. Fine by me.

Curled up on the couch with the blanket snuggled under my chin I was set for the night, just me and Thor. "Thor may not be a Greek god like a certain promise-ring-giving, witch-loving hunk, but he's running a close second."

Between the action scenes and the dazzling effects, my brain begged for a time out, and it wasn't long before my head lulled to the side with my eyelids heavy.

The click of the front door closing woke me with a start, and I flicked my legs over the edge of the lounge and called out, "Aunt Edie, is that you?"

"Yes, sweetheart, it's me." She popped her head through the doorframe and smiled. "What are you doing up so late?"

I wiped the sleep from my eyes and stifled a yawn. "I was watching a movie. I was waiting for you to get home. I guess I must have dozed off."

She sat on the end of the couch and patted my leg. "I'm sorry, love. If I'd known you wanted to talk, I would have come home earlier. Is everything all right? Is this about your birthday tomorrow?"

"Kind of," I said with a half-hearted smile. My insides squirmed at the thought of mentioning Aunt Rosalyn. "Do you trust me, Aunt Edie?"

She huffed and pulled back, crossing her arms. "What kind of question is that? Of course, I trust you."

"And you know that I would never lie to you or say or do anything to hurt you?"

"Evelyn, what is going on?" she asked, her forehead creasing and her brows drawing together. "You can tell me; I won't be upset or angry."

Oh, somehow, I think you will.

"Why don't I make us a fresh pot of tea before you get started?" she said, the idea sure to bolster her confidence. But the longer I waited the more the storm in my belly grew and thrashed around rolling and building into an internal tornado.

My hand reached out and grabbed hers and held it in mine. "No, please. I'd like to chat now. The sooner I get it off my chest the better."

"Okay, love." She patted my hand.

I pressed my lips together and added one more stipulation. "Promise me, you'll listen and wait until the end before reacting?"

Her posture perked up, and her nose wrinkled just a fraction, and then she nodded. "Okay, I promise."

I took a deep breath and filled my lungs before diving headfirst. "I can confirm Detective Huxton was correct in his assessment of the fingerprints found on the baptism font. They were indeed Rosalyn Peyton's, and I know this because I spoke to her this evening at The Four Brothers."

I held my breath, waiting for an outburst, but nothing. Aunt Edie went completely still except for her hands which clenched into fists as she pressed them into her lap.

By the time I finished, Aunt Edie had gone pale, and her breathing had quickened, her shoulders rising and falling at a hurried pace. My heart constricted, and all I wanted to do was take her pain away, but it was more important she realise the truth and the risk to Aunt Rosalyn's life.

"I don't understand," she whispered, absently wiping her lips.

"There's no easy way to say this."

"Just say it, Evelyn," she said, her muscles jumping under her skin.

I nodded. By the time I finished explaining in detail, I felt nauseous, and Aunt Edie looked like she was going to throw up all over the carpet. She bolted from the couch and shot across the room letting out a strangled cry of frustration. She grabbed her stomach and rocked back and forth. Tears rolled down my cheeks, and I ran over and threw my arms around her and held her until her weeping stopped and her breathing resembled normal.

I stood holding her in my strong embrace for a good ten minutes until I felt her hand pat my arm. "Thank you. Thank you for telling me the truth. That can't have been easy."

You have no idea.

"Now that you have, we can put a plan in action to bring her home."

Her words sent a bolt of fear thrashing through my body. I released my arms and spun her around. "No, no we can't. It's too dangerous. He will kill her. She was adamant that I couldn't go after her."

Aunt Edie shook her head, and her eyes darkened. "That's crazy. She's alive and should be here with her family, not with some crazed lunatic."

Fire roared within my body, and my words shot out louder and stronger than I expected. "No. Over my dead body will you go after her. You may not believe me, but I'm the one who saw and felt the fear in her eyes. He will kill her, and that means he would kill you in the blink of an eye. I'll not lose another member of my family. I just won't. I've not asked much of you, but you have to promise me you will leave it alone. Knowing that she is alive has to be enough. It just has to be."

My lungs burned, and my head throbbed. It pained me to breathe through the massive knot in my chest. Aunt Edie stood staring at me as though she were looking at someone she'd never met.

"Okay," she finally said, her hand cupping my cheek, and a tear rolled from the corner of her eye. "I understand, but I won't give up on her. She's my sister and I love her."

"As do I. I'm not giving up on her either, but what do you say we make sure Misty's murderer is brought to justice first? Then I can return to finding the relics and destroying the Sphere, which should lead us to Salis, and we can both work out a way to take him down?"

Aunt Edie laughed even though tears still streamed down her cheeks. "Tell me, how did you get so smart?"

"I had a good teacher." I winked at her, and she pulled me into a hug. I melted in her arms. "Aunt Rosalyn mentioned a safe deposit box over at the back. Did you know she had one?"

She shook her head and a gazillion thoughts of what might be in it went through my mind. "She gave me the password and said she wanted me to have what was inside as a birthday and graduation present."

"Then we must make sure you get it." She pulled back and wiped her eyes, sniffing back the tears. "It's late and someone needs to get their beauty sleep before tomorrow."

Again, with the beauty sleep comment.

I slapped my forehead. "That reminds me, I was wondering if you could arrange for Eli and Detective Huxton to come to The Melting Pot tomorrow night but not before six-thirty?"

"Do I detect a birthday party in the planning?" she said, a soft smile lighting up her face.

I shrugged. "Sort of, for my closest family and friends. I'm going to decorate it my way, and the surprise will be on them."

"Sounds perfect." She placed a kiss on my forehead. "I'll tell you what—since I'm opening tomorrow, I'll take care of the food for tomorrow night while I'm on shift, so all you have to do is the decorations, how does that sound?"

Warmth radiated through my chest. "You really are the best aunt in the world. Thank you." I pushed up on my tippy-toes and planted a kiss on her damp cheek.

"Right." She clapped her hands and performed a shooing action towards the staircase. "Off to bed with you. Don't forget you have the High Council visit at ten in the morning."

How could I forget that? My whole future depends on that one appointment.

***

"Evelyn?" Aunt Edie's voice vaguely called me, but it was my birthday, and the crystal-clear water of the ocean was so inviting it had me mesmerised. I took my sundress off and dove straight in. The icy freshness of the water caught my breath, and I coughed and sputtered.

"Evelyn, wake up," she yelled, and I shot up in my bed disorientated.

I gulped a lungful of air and blinked until my focus returned and registered that I was in the familiar surroundings of my bedroom. No beach and no water.

Aunt Edie stood at the door, arms folded and her foot tapping away. "What are you still doing asleep?"

"What? What's wrong with a sleep-in on my birthday?" I asked, stretching the kinks and aches out of my body. I flopped back on my bed and closed my eyes.

Today is the day. Bring it on.

"It wouldn't be an issue if you didn't have the High Council rocking up on your doorstep in thirty minutes."

My eyes snapped open, and I bolted upright in my bed. "What? Thirty minutes?"

"Didn't you set your alarm to be up in time to get ready?" she asked, panicked. "I hadn't heard from you, and I was worried. I popped in from The Melting Pot to check on you. Lucky I did."

I ran a hand through my hair and swiped my phone from my bedside table. Three messages from Harriet, Jordi, a blocked number, and a missed call from Tyler. I bit my bottom lip as I checked the alarm. "Oh my goodness. It's on silent, and I set it for eight p.m. instead of eight a.m."

Aunt Edie tutted and shook her head. "You quickly get ready, and I'll have a coffee waiting for you downstairs."

I nodded and pulled a collection of clothing items from various drawers and bolted for the shower. The steaming water barely touched my skin but tickled and stimulated my body all the same. In and out in less than ten minutes, I dried and dressed and was on the way downstairs to be greeted by the scintillating scents of spice cinnamon and pumpkin.

"Oh wow, what is that smell?" Pausing, I finger-brushed my hair up into a messy bun and pulled the wispy bits above my ears down. "My taste buds are drooling over here."

Aunt Edie turned and held a cup towards me, the steam rising in a swirly dance that smelled divine. "Here, have a taste. I'm trying out a few ideas for the Halloween menu next month. This is a spiced pumpkin latte. Let me know what you think?"

I took a sip and let the sweet liquid ooze down my throat leaving a fiery trail in its wake. I closed my eyes and drifted off in a moment of euphoric bliss which wasn't to last very long.

A resounding thump on the door sent my heartbeat pounding against my temple. My eyelids opened, and I looked at Aunt Edie. "That's them, isn't it?"

Polly Holmes

She nodded and relieved my shaky hand of the coffee and headed for the adjoining door that led through to The Melting Pot Café. "Best of luck, sweetheart. I know you'll do great." And she was gone.

"Thanks," I said as the door closed. Clearing my throat, I rolled my shoulders back and sucked in a deep breath through my nose and shook off the nerves. Brushing my hands down my pants, I straightened my top and paused by the closed door.

"Let's get this over and done with." I plastered on a smile and opened the door.

My smile dropped, and I stared at the woman in front of me, my mind spinning. "It's you."

CHAPTER NINETEEN

"**G**ood morning, Evelyn. I believe you are expecting me?" The woman's perky voice took me by surprise.

It was the woman from my dream. The one standing next to my mother.

I stood staring at her blonde pixie haircut and her big blue eyes. She looked just as she did in my dream, right down to the burgundy cape.

"Are you going to keep me waiting out here, or am I permitted to come in?" she asked, an air of impatience in her tone.

"Yes, of course." I jumped out of the way and extended my arm, guiding her inside. "Please forgive me."

She tilted her head, gave a blunt nod, and then entered the kitchen as though she were floating, her beautiful cape swaying as she went.

Closing the door, I wasn't sure if I was supposed to curtsey or bow, or what the protocol was when addressing an Officer of the High Council, so I bit my tongue and waited.

She walked around the room, taking in the homey features of the kitchen, her expression unreadable. "It's interesting how your guests enter through the kitchen door."

What's wrong with it? This is the best room in the house.

"When I was eleven, I came to live with Aunt Edie after my parents were killed, and she was in the middle of renovating. She was putting in the connecting door that leads to The Melting Pot Café and decided at the same time to make the kitchen the focal point of the house since this is where we usually spend most of our days experimenting and cooking for the café next door. It works for us."

"I see," she said as a smile brightened her demeanor. "Well, I must say I do love what Edith has done with the place. We haven't met." She thrust her hand out. "Zahlia Velio, Radiant Officer of the High Council."

Radiant Officer? That sounds important.

I clasped her hand and shook it. The power emanating from her touch refreshed my inner energy. "Pleased to meet you. Actually...I have seen you before."

She laughed pretentiously. "I highly doubt that since I have never before today set foot in Saltwater Cove."

"It was in a dream, and you were with my mother, before she died, that is."

She looked at me and flinched as though someone had walked across her grave.

Maybe it was my mother's ghost taking a walk?

"Shall we get started?" she asked, pointing to the kitchen table and chairs.

I nodded and took a seat opposite her at the table, my churning stomach a pile of nerves.

She cleared her throat and began firing one question after another, each addressing some aspect of my magic, my life, or my relationships. She gave several hypothetical scenarios I might find myself in and wanted to know how I would get out of them. Of course, none came close to the dramas I'd already faced. I answered them with ease.

"It appears you have a response for everything," Zahlia said, sitting back in her chair. "I only have one more question for you."

I shuffled in my seat and stuck my chin out.

Bring it on.

"How will you defeat Salis Van Der Kolt?"

The heat in the room had suddenly quadrupled, and I pulled at the collar of my shirt. "Um…I…um."

She pushed up from her chair. "Let's take a walk, Evelyn." And she was off toward the door, her arm lifting the edge of her cape into a full swing and wrapping it around her shoulders.

I sat dumbfounded by her question.

How am I going to defeat Salis Van Der Kolt? That is a very good question. I have no idea...yet.

"Are you coming?" Zahlia's voice called me back to reality and my gaze caught her waiting by the door.

"Sorry, yes, of course. A walk sounds great." I bolted from my chair, opened the door, and followed her out. "What did you mean back there?"

She walked at a brisk pace toward the empty playground as though she hadn't heard me. I doubled my step to catch her and said once more, "What did you mean back in the kitchen?"

"All in good time, Evelyn." Zahlia looked back at the house, slowed her pace, and turned to me. "Thank you for going along with me."

The skin on my forehead pulled tight. "What are you talking about?"

"The dream you had wasn't a dream, it was a memory. A memory of when I was at your place with your mother." She grabbed my hand and pulled me down on the closest park bench at the back of the playground, out of view of nosy onlookers.

I rubbed my fingers against my temples and then pressed them above my eyebrows against the stabbing pain behind my eyes. "What is going on?" I muttered under my breath. "You said you hadn't stepped foot in Saltwater Cove."

"It's true, I haven't. Your parents' left Saltwater Cove to give you a normal life, to give you the choice to be a witch or not. They moved in two doors down from me. I was one of the few witches in town, so as you can imagine, we became good friends. I was devastated when I heard about the accident. I had suspected foul play was at hand, but I had no idea how to prove it. Should you choose witchcraft, your parents knew you would be a powerful witch one day, as did I. The way I could honour them was to be in the best possible position to help you when the time came." She paused and opened her arms. "And here I am. As a Radiant Officer of the High Council, I was able to request this mission to assess you and deem you worthy of your full qualification. That was never in question. On more than one occasion in recent years, you have demonstrated your worth as a witch and your dedication to your craft and your family."

"Are you saying what I think you're saying?" I asked, my heart in the back of my throat.

She smiled and nodded, and tears blurred my vision. My chest was on fire, but in a good way. "You mean I pass? I can graduate to a full witch?"

She nodded, the sparkle in her eye broke me, and I fist-pumped the air. "Yes!"

Zahlia giggled and opened her hand. "Congratulations."

"Thank you," I said, shaking it vigorously.

"Easy there. I'd like to keep my arm, thanks."

"Oops, sorry." I cringed, letting go of her hand and running mine up and down my thighs.

"Now we have that out of the way, I have something more important to talk to you about." Her tone turned cold, and a shiver squelched my happy vibe.

"Does this relate to Salis Van Der Kolt?"

She nodded and continued. "After your parents were killed, I made it my mission to find out what happened to them and the best way for me to do that was to become an officer of the High Council. That's where the power is, and that's where I needed to be. It took me a long time, but I finally worked my way up in the ranks to a senior position. I now know Salis Van Der Kolt was behind their deaths."

That matches Aunt Rosalyn's version.

A chilled numbness coated me, and despondent, I let Zahlia do all the talking.

"There is animosity and unrest among some senior members of the High Council. While they don't believe Salis has the power to affect them, they are aware his following is increasing and that could pose a problem should he or one of his henchmen get their hands on the relics or the Sphere. We know you are close and have already found some relics, but we also know Salis and his henchmen have made an appearance here in Saltwater Cove."

They sure have. Poor Blair.

"I agree." Nausea rolled around in my belly. I baulked at the images of the blue stream wrapped around Blair's neck, her body gasping for air, yearning to live. "I know for a fact, one of his henchmen killed a woman here in town the other day. Apparently, it was Salis's right-hand man."

Zahlia's palm covered her mouth, and she paused for a moment. "Are you positive?"

I nodded. "Yes."

I doubt Aunt Rosalyn would lie to me.

"Do you know his name?" I asked. "The one who does Salis's dirty work?" I waited on the edge of my seat, desperate to know who had control of Aunt Rosalyn, the man who would kill her family at the snap of his fingers.

"Yes, Amorant Morren. He's not to be trifled with," she said. My stomach hardened at the conviction in her tone.

"The council is aware of his growing presence and is concerned he may get too big for his boots and would like him dealt with before he gets out of hand. Not only was it unanimous you be granted full witch status, but the senior members also recognised the power that runs through your veins being of Peyton descent. They believe you are the one to stop him in his tracks."

"Really?" I asked. My chest puffed out, and I sat tall in my seat. "They said that?"

She nodded, flipping her hair from her face. "They did. Nothing gets by the High Council. When they granted you and you only permission to look into your parents' deaths, they knew your determination would be one of your biggest strengths. And you have never given up."

"And I never will."

"That's why the president of the High Council made a new ruling supported by the senior executive. He declared you may now utilise others to help you in your quest while you continue investigating at Master Witch level One status."

I stared at Zahlia as though she had just spoken her words in gibberish. "Excuse me?"

Master Witch Level One? No way.

She held up her finger and shook it in my direction. "There are a few stipulations. You may tell Edith of your new status, but she is the only person you may tell. You will need her help to navigate the master witch world. You will get your wand, which has been upgraded to level one. The senior members feel with these new powers and resources at your fingertips, it will hold you in good stead if and when you do come up against Salis or Amorant."

My forehead tightened. "My wand?"

She nodded and grinned. "Yes, your wand. Every master witch has a wand."

"Aunt Edie doesn't have one," I blurted.

She let out a muffled giggle before pressing her lips together. "Edith has a wand. She chooses not to use it, and that's understandable at her master witch level. Her powers are stronger without it, as I'm sure yours will be one day. A wand is there to support the witch, and some choose to use it constantly. Others, like Edith, choose to only use it when necessary."

My mind was blown by this new information, and I just sat there letting it all soak into that spongey mind of mine. She placed her hands open on her lap. I followed her gaze as it dropped to her hands. Her fingers twitched and sparkles rose from them and swirled in figure eights above and then disappeared. A box with a gorgeous wand materialised in her hands. My head swam with the notion that one day I'd be able to do spells just like Aunt Edie and Zahlia.

She held the box out toward me. "Here, use it wisely."

She shot from the chair and brushed her hands together as though dusting off breadcrumbs. "That concludes our business. I trust you will adhere to all the terms we have discussed here today?"

"Of course." A fresh bout of adrenaline soared through me, energising my body like it was my first day at school.

She stepped out and clasped her hands together at her waist. "Wonderful, then I shall report back to the High Council that all messages have been received loud and clear. If you'll excuse me, I must—"

"Wait," I said, catching her before she left. "I need your help. Have you ever heard of the Cup of Acronus?" I watched a multitude of expressions cross her face, the last one leaving an odd tense knot in my chest. "You have, haven't you?"

She drew back and slipped her hands into her pockets. "I have heard of the existence of the Cup of Acronus." She paused and visibly started gnawing at her bottom lip.

A-ha, you do know something.

I stood and closed the gap between us. "Tyler, my boyfriend believes the cup is connected to the recent town murder and also the Sphere but trying to pinpoint its location has left us at a dead end. All we've been able to ascertain is that it is located at the Gateway."

Zahlia's eyebrows shot up, and her eyes widened. Her brow wrinkled, and she deliberately diverted her gaze from mine.

Bingo.

"Come on, Zahlia," I pleaded. "If you know something, tell me."

She turned and spun on her heel. "I'm only supposed to approve your graduation and pass on the messages from the High Council, that's all."

"Did they say you couldn't help me?" I asked, moving around to stand in front of her.

She shook her head as though my question had just sunk in. "No."

"Did they say I could...how did you put it... 'utilise others in my quest?'" I asked, upping the stakes.

Zahlia shook her head again. This time she had a cheeky glint in her eye, and the corner of her lip was edging into a smile. "Yesould."

"Then we aren't breaking any laws, are we?"

Her eyes brightened, and her spine straightened. A soft smile lit up her face like a crystal. "You do have a way with words, Evelyn. I'll give you that much."

"Thank you," I said, giving her a mock bow. "Now, will you help me?"

She nodded. "The Cup of Acronus is indeed one of the relics, and as far as I know, it is located at the Gateway."

Tyler was right. I wanted to fist-pump the air and do a happy dance. "Where is the Gateway?"

Her expression dropped. "I'm afraid I can't help you there. Only the Watchman can help you find the Gateway."

Great, another dead end.

CHAPTER TWENTY

I tucked my new wand under my arm and headed back to The Melting Pot, my mind running through the morning events once more. The day was half gone, but it wasn't every day you graduated and jumped straight to master witch level one status. I wanted to celebrate, but time wasted celebrating was time I could spend working out who the Watchman was and where I could find him.

I popped back home and dropped my wand on the kitchen table before heading through the connecting door to The Melting Pot. I froze, the air draining from my lungs. My gaze caught the gigantic *Happy Birthday Evelyn* sign hanging above the main seating area above the candelabras. Heat covered my neck and cheeks, growing to a boiling point.

Somebody is going to pay for this, mark my words. I bet it was Eli.

I held my breath and made a beeline for the kitchen.

"There she is. There's the birthday girl." A female voice called from the back of the café.

I stopped and let out a big sigh. I caught Aubrey Garcina standing by her table and Olive seated next to her, both clapping their hands, their faces boasting huge smiles. My chest relaxed, and I grinned at the woman. Aubrey Garcina and her sister, Olive, were both retired witches from The Elder Flame Coven. They arrived in Saltwater Cove to help find the murderer of one of their own and had stayed close by ever since.

A cheerful chorus of 'Happy Birthday' led by Aubrey rang out across the café, with most patrons joining in. I stood and soaked it up. It was the least I could do knowing how much those two women had helped my witch skills develop over the past two years.

Cheers from the patrons erupted, and I bounded over and engulfed Aubrey in a huge hug. "Thank you. That was a lovely surprise."

"Ha, I knew it would be," she said, hugging me back with a gigantic squeeze that I was sure cracked a rib or two.

She pulled back and, after a breather, Olive's arms pulling me into an embrace replaced hers.

"Happy birthday, Evelyn," she said, rocking us from side to side.

"Thank you," I squeezed out while her shoulder was digging into my neck. I stepped back and my gaze moved from Olive to Aubrey and back again. "Thank you, guys, so much. I'm still in shock. I was so not expecting that."

Their smiles beamed from ear to ear, and my heart filled with warmth. It may be my birthday, but if I can make two dear friends smile that big, then I'm all for it. "I'm going to head out back and see Aunt Edie now, but that is one rendition of 'Happy Birthday' I won't forget."

"Enjoy your day, love," Aubrey said.

Olive added with a squeeze of my hand. "Yes, have a wonderful day."

I nodded and moved off towards the kitchen accepting birthday wishes from guests and random people. Entering the kitchen, I spotted the nearest chair and collapsed into it, my head spinning. Wiping my forehead, I huffed out a breath and turned to see Aunt Edi and Eli staring at me.

Eli looked at me with a sheepish smile, then reached over and handed me a wrapped present. "Happy Birthday, Evelyn. I'll forgo singing you the song at this point."

"Good idea," I said, between gritted teeth.

"And congratulations on receiving your full witch qualifications." He paused and tilted his head. "You did get your full witch qualification, didn't you?"

I stared at him and pursed my lips together. I watched his Adam's apple move up and down his neck before I smiled and nodded. "Of course."

I sure did, and more.

Aunt Edie cleared her throat, and Eli stepped back. "Sorry, I guess you guys have witchy stuff to talk about. Why don't I look after the floor, and you two can do whatever you need to?"

I gifted him a smile. "Thank you, you read my mind."

Aunt Edie pulled up a stool and sat waiting. She licked her lips and then pressed her hands together in her lap. The silent tension hung thick in the air.

"Oh for goodness' sake, are you going to make me beg?" she asked, throwing her hands in the air in a huff. "What happened?"

I smiled and said, "You are not going to believe it." I fidgeted with the tablecloth hanging over the edge of the bench while I explained in minute detail everything Zahlia had said, finishing with the information about the Watchman and the Cup of Acronus located at the Gateway. My throat dried from the excessive swallowing, and I grabbed a glass of water from the pitcher on the counter.

Aunt Edie sat and stared at me. A wash of heat filled my cheeks. "What's wrong?"

"I'm not happy about you going after Salis and getting deeper involved with finding the Sphere. It scares the pants of me."

I opened my mouth to offer my rebuttal, but she stopped me with a single hand up. She tilted her head to the side and a warm glow filled her eyes. "Before you argue with me, I said I hated you getting deeper involved, not that I wouldn't support you. I know your determination to get to the bottom of your parents' death, find the Sphere and destroy it, but it doesn't mean I won't worry and get anxious you're putting your life at risk."

My chest ached. "Thank you. I'd be lying if I didn't say I wasn't a bit apprehensive myself, but I have to do this, for them, for you and for me and the future of our world." My back straightened and I winked. "I've got a lot of support behind me and let's not forget I am a fully qualified master witch level one now." I stopped and gave her one huge hug, squeezing as much love into her as possible.

"I'm so proud of you, Evelyn. Jumping straight to master witch level one is a true testament to your growing abilities as a witch and your knack for solving a murder or two." Aunt Edie paused, then frowned, tapping her finger against her chin. "Are you sure she said Watchman?"

"Of course, I'm sure. Why?"

"If she indeed said Watchman, I know exactly who she is talking about."

I coughed and caught my breath on a mouthful of water. My hand covered my mouth, preventing a disaster in the making. "Sorry, that was the last thing

I expected you to say. I don't understand. You know who the Watchman is?"

"Yes." Aunt Edie's expression screamed caution. "Zahlia confirmed the Cup was one of the relics?"

"Yes, she did, which means I am one step closer. I just have to find the Watchman and get him to tell me where the Gateway is."

Aunt Edie huffed. "Easier said than done."

I ran my hand through my hair and gripped the back of my neck. "What are you talking about? And please give it to me straight without the riddles."

She pressed her lips together and nodded. "The Watchman lives in the old cabin by Swallows Bridge near Dead Man's Hollow. You, Tyler, Jordi, and Harriet used to play on the banks of the river, so you must have seen it."

I racked my brain trying to place the cabin, but it was like trying to find a jellybean in a tub of fairy floss.

She continued. "For as long as I can remember, his job has always been to guard the Gateway. He keeps to himself and is self-sufficient, living off the land as he likes to put it. As far as I know, he goes by the name Old Man Alexio more than the Watchman these days. On the occasions he ventured into town, he would always stop by the café for some of my rhubarb and chocolate pie. I can't remember the last time I saw him. I wouldn't even know if he's still alive."

The Watchman has been living on my doorstep all this time, and I never knew it.

"I always say, there's no time like the present to reacquaint yourself with the past," I said, bolting from my chair. "It's time I paid a visit to Old Man Alexio. Maybe he's the missing piece to the puzzle."

"Since when have you said that?" Aunt Edie asked, frowning while moving over to the centre counter to start sorting empty dishes.

"Since now," I said with a giggle. "Time isn't going to stand still just because it's my birthday and neither will Salis. Do I need to remind you he is also after the Sphere, and I'd like to be the one who finds it first? Maybe it has something to do with it controlling the universe and falling into the wrong hands, etc."

"No need to get cheeky," she said, swatting me on the backside as I walked past. "But I do understand why you have to see him. I'm happy to tell you I've completed all the cooking for your surprise party this evening, so that's one less thing you have to worry about."

"What about Eli and Detective Huxton?"

"They are all set to be here at six-thirty. I told Eli we were opening for a special night dinner slot, and I'd rostered him on. He wasn't happy about it, let me tell you."

She let out a cute little giggle, and I couldn't help but smile at her shrewdness. "And Detective Huxton?"

"Micah was a little harder to convince. I told him to pick me up here at six-thirty for a date night at the movies. He was adamant I should be spending it with you, so I had to think on the spot, and as far as he knows, Harriet and Jordi are taking you out for dinner."

"You are positively sinful, Aunt Edie, and I love it."

"Why thank you." She dipped her head forward and put on a fake curtsey, then burst out laughing. The sound of her happy was the best birthday present I could ask for.

"I'll wrap up a piece of pie for you to take with you. Rhubarb and chocolate pie just happens to be on the menu this week. I'm sure as soon as Old Man Alexio smells it, you'll have him eating out of the palm of your hand."

"Thank you." I felt more alive than I had in a long time, rejuvenated by this new lead and one step closer to finding the Sphere. Aunt Edie handed over a brown paper bag, and the zingy earthy aroma accosted my nostrils. "See you tonight."

***

"No, no, no, don't you dare come on," I said, glaring at the empty petrol gauge. Ding. The orange warning light lit up the corner of the dashboard. "I could have sworn I had more petrol in my car. I should be able to make it to the nearest petrol station on the way home."

As I walked up the crumbled pathway to the front door of the cabin, my stomach knotted. The place was overgrown with trees and hedges, and the cabin itself looked like something you'd find in the back of a forest.

I sucked in a deep breath and knocked.

"Go away," a grumpy voice called.

You're not getting rid of me that easily.

I knocked again.

"Didn't you hear me the first time? I said go away." His voice grew darker by the second.

"Yes, I heard you," I said through the wooden door. "But I'm not going anywhere until you and I have a chat about the Gateway."

I strained to hear the muttering being spoken inside, and then the door flew open, and I was standing opposite a frowning man who could have passed for Santa Claus complete with old age and a long white beard.

"Hello, I'm Evelyn Grayson," I said, putting on my best greeting smile and ignoring his grumpy demeanor. "I'm not going to waste your time. I'll come straight to the point. I'm here to discuss the whereabouts of the Cup of Acronus. I'm told you might be able to help me locate the Gateway."

"Is that so?" He folded his arms and stood his ground.

This might be harder than I thought. Time to up the stakes.

I held out my hand holding the brown paper bag. "I have pie, rhubarb and chocolate pie from Edith Payton at The Melting Pot Café."

His arms slowly lowered, and his eyes widened. "Pie from Edith?"

I nodded.

A smile broke out across his face, and he waved me inside. "Why didn't you start with that in the first place? Come in, come in."

A sigh of relief escaped my lips. I stepped inside and the succulent scents of a roast lamb kick-started my grumbling stomach. It was only then that I noticed he was about to sit down to lunch. "I'm sorry, I didn't mean to interrupt your lunch. Would you like me to wait in the lounge until you are finished?"

"Oh, pishy-poshy," he said, swatting the air with his hand. "You'll join me for lunch. It's been so long since I've had a visitor that it will be nice to have someone to talk to."

Lunch? It does have a mouth-watering smell to it. The day had gone by so fast, I didn't even know it was that time of the day. It would be rude of me to turn down a perfectly good invitation. I gifted him a smile and nodded. "I'd love to join you for lunch. After all, a girl's gotta eat."

He laughed and punched his fist in the air towards me. "That's what I'm talking about." He whizzed around the table and pulled out a chair.

"Madam," he said with a gentlemanly bow.

"Why thank you, kind sir," I said, playing along with the pompous action. "It sure smells wonderful."

"Thank you. I grow it all here. I'm as self-sufficient as they come these days. I rarely go into town." He looked at the brown paper bag in the centre of the table. "If anything can lure me back, it's a piece of Edith's chocolate and rhubarb pie."

"Do you mind if we talk while we eat?" I asked as he served up the meat and vegetables.

"Of course not. I'm interested to know what brought you here."

I hesitated a moment and then rolled my shoulders back and jumped in feet first. "I'm here because I'm trying to find the Cup of Acronus, and I was told by a very reliable source that it's located at the Gateway." He put a plate of food in front of me, and I paused, the delectable smells wafting around my nose.

Ignoring the grumble in my stomach, I lifted my gaze from my plate and forced myself to continue. "I was told the Watchman would know where the Gateway was. Aunt Edie said you were the Watchman, so…" I shrugged, "here I am, hoping you can tell me how to get to the Gateway."

There I said it, now time to eat.

I licked my lips and dug into the food in front of me while I waited for his reply. He kept eating as though contemplating what I had just said. I didn't mind. My mouth was in heaven.

"It's true, I am the Watchman, and would have been able to tell you once, but alas, I no longer possess the ability to see the Gateway. My power was destroyed by evil."

"No way," I whispered.

He continued, "I will forever be the Watchman until my replacement arrives, but as to the whereabouts of the Cup of Acronus, I am at a loss. I'd like to be able to help you, but the sad truth of it is, I cannot."

My heart sank. "Are you sure?"

He nodded and popped another bite of baked potato into his mouth. "I may once have had the knowledge, but it was taken from me by a spell."

A spell?

"What spell are you talking about?" I asked, wiping the gravy from my plate with a piece of white bread.

"It was a few centuries back—"

"A few centuries?" My forehead pulled tight above my brow, and I held my hand up. "Wait, how old are you?"

"Tsk, tsk, tsk. Don't you know it's never polite to ask someone how old they are?"

I stared at him, unsure if he was joking or not. I thought it best to keep quiet and let him explain.

He shuffled in his seat and put his fist to his mouth. He coughed and cleared his throat. "As I was saying, it was a few centuries ago when evil paid me an unexpected visit one night. The consequences left me with my memories of the Gateway erased, along with other memories that were taken from me."

"How terrible for you," I said, my chest aching for the burden he must endure day in and day out. "I'm so sorry, and here I am, drudging up the past."

"You had no idea."

"I know, but I still feel like a total douchebag." I placed my knife and fork together in the centre of my plate and patted my full belly. "That was one of the best roasts I've ever had, and I've had a few."

"You're welcome, Evelyn. Glad you enjoyed it."

I reached across the table and squeezed his hand. "I know this is not much comfort, but somehow I will find the Gateway and the Cup of Acronus, and when I do, I'm going to make sure you're there to see it. It will be as much your find as it will be mine."

Tears glazed his eyes, and he squeezed my hand in return. "Thank you. That means a lot to me."

Time was ticking away, and it was now mid-afternoon. The day had practically gone. I still had no clue where the Gateway was. Old Man Alexio wasn't in a position to help, but I wouldn't ever forget his generosity. "You have been the most amazing host, but if I'm going to get through my to-do list, I need to get going."

"I'm not giving up. I'll try to remember."

"That's the spirit," I said, rising from my chair and heading for the door. I paused and turned, preparing to hug the man, but he beat me to it. His arms were around my shoulders, and he held on, letting his warmth bleed into my soul.

"Come back and visit anytime," he called from the doorway as I drew closer to my car. "And bring that aunt of yours, too."

I drove off toward the service station with a huge smile on my face and a full heart.

***

I replaced the nozzle of the petrol pump and closed the cap on my petrol tank, thankful I made it to the service station in time. Tyler would not have been happy if he'd gotten a damsel-in-distress call. Grabbing my bag from the front seat I moved double time inside to pay. After all, I still had a café to decorate for the arrival of my guests at six-thirty.

Walking with my head stuck in my bag searching for my debit card, my body collided with another, and I jolted backward. I looked up to see a teary Isla staring at me, complete with smudged mascara and wide watery eyes. She quickly sniffed and wiped her tears away, but it was too late, my heart had already gone out to the woman. "Isla, what is it? What's wrong?"

She pretended to smile as though nothing was wrong. It was an epic failure. "I'm fine, really. Just some dirt blew into my eye, that's all."

"Yeah, and I was born in the last shower of glitter." She gave me a half-hearted smile while her shoulders heaved up and down as though she'd burst into tears at any second. I guided her back into the store and down an aisle out of the view of customers and the counter where the cashier stood counting chewing gum packets on a shelf behind the counter.

I fished a clean tissue packet out of my bag and handed her one. "I know a woman scorned when I see one."

"Thank you," Isla said, grabbing the tissue and swiping her eyes dry. "Is it that obvious?"

I stuck my bottom lip out and nodded. "Can I do anything? I hate seeing you so upset."

She huffed, and her puffy eyes teared up again. "It's my fault. I've never had much luck with men. We can't all get it right like you. You picked a winner with Tyler."

"Thank you. Are you telling me you are upset over a guy?" I asked, giving her a new tissue. She nodded, blew her nose, and I cringed. The sound was like running fingernails down a chalkboard. "But aren't you and Slade seeing each other? At least that's what Hannah said when we bumped into her last night."

Her lips quivered, tears ran down her blotchy red cheeks, and she nodded. "Yes, we're supposed to be seeing each other, although I don't know if you'd call what we're doing 'seeing'." She wiped her teary eyes. "Correct me if I'm wrong, but one would assume 'seeing each other' means spending time with one another, would it not?"

"I believe so."

"Well, looks like I'm doing it all wrong then."

This is worse than I thought. That man has a lot to answer for.

Her chin trembled, and she hugged her waist with her arms. "Oh, Evelyn, you don't need me dumping my boyfriend troubles on you."

Oh, yes, I do, especially if it's about Slade.

I wiped the wet strands of hair from her face. Isla's bleak mood fatigued my inner strength, but I ignored my falling energy levels and pushed forward. "What I know is that a man should cherish a woman and never make her cry, and if they do, it's on them not the woman." I paused, giving her a moment to calm down. "So, you and Slade are an item, you just haven't been spending all that much time together?"

She nodded and wiped the tissue under her nose.

How interesting.

"Exactly. I heard rumours of his odd behaviour, but when he was with me, he was different, so loving and gentle and then it all changed just like that." She paused and clicked her fingers. "He started asking me to run his errands just because I worked in Hallows Creek, and he kept cancelling our lunch dates telling me something important had come up or Mercer has asked him to work."

Heat burned my cheeks, and a surge of newfound energy flowed through my body. "Didn't he fix your fence for you yesterday morning?"

Or did you lie about that, Slade?

She shrugged. "Yes, he fixed it, but I couldn't be sure of the exact time because I was at work. Wait a minute, my neighbour called me to complain about the noise, and I think that was about sevenish in the morning. I rang him to tell him to leave it until a bit later, but it went straight to message bank."

Adrenaline kicked in, and all the pieces were falling into place. "So you have no idea what time he left your place yesterday morning?" She shook her head. "For all you know he could have left there and been back in Saltwater Cove any time before nine a.m.?"

She shrugged. "I suppose so."

That's one of Slade's alibis shot to smithereens.

My back stiffened, and I turned to face her head-on. "Isla, this is very important. What time did Slade call in to your work and have lunch with you on Sunday?"

Her expression blanked. "He didn't. He was going to and then cancelled and said he had to stay in Saltwater Cove. Slade wouldn't tell me why. He said it was no big deal and that I should keep it to myself."

Oh my, oh my, oh my, this is pure gold. First, he lies about the time he fixed her fence and then he cancels lunch on her and lies about that too.

He lied because it was Slade who ran out of the church, and it was Slade who killed Misty. I'd bet my life on it.

The question is why?

CHAPTER TWENTY-ONE

"**P**ick up, pick up," I muttered to myself, my heart racing a gazillion miles an hour. "What good is a two-way street if you don't pick up your phone." The wheels screeched along the bitumen as I took the corner like an experienced race car driver.

"Huxton here." His voice boomed down the line.

"Detective Huxton, it's Evelyn. It's Slade, he killed Misty," I blurted.

"Woah, slow down, Evelyn," he said, his tone calmer than mine. "Where are you?"

My hands gripped the steering wheel, turning my knuckles white. "In my car on the way back from Hallows Creek. I've got you on speaker. I stopped in to get petrol and ran into Isla, and one thing led to another. She confirmed Slade lied about the time he said he built the fence, and he also lied about his whereabouts when Misty was killed."

"How interesting. This is definitely a step in the right direction, but I don't want you to get your hopes up. He could just as easily have a legitimate reason, but it's worth having a chat with him, anyway."

"It's him. I know it is," I said, the conviction in my voice surprising even me. "It's too coincidental to be anything else. Why lie unless you are doing something illegal?"

"Where's Isla now?" he asked.

"I told her to go straight home and stay there and expect a call from the police as you were going to want to know more about Slade's whereabouts."

"Good girl. You said you were on the way back from Hallows Creek?"

I could hear papers and mutterings down the line like there was a commotion at the police station, and it made it hard to hear his words. "Sorry," I said. "What was that? I didn't get all of it."

"I said." He cleared his throat. "Are you still on the way back from Hallows Creek?"

"Yes, this day has gone faster than I expected, and I'm heading back to The Melting Pot now." My insides were as jumpy as a swamp of grasshoppers. "Maybe I should head straight to The Four Brothers instead to see—"

"No, Evelyn," he snapped. "You should stay out of it from now on and let the police take it from here.

You've done enough. If Slade is the murderer, the last Edith or I want is to have you anywhere near him."

Oh great, play the aunt card with me. How am I supposed to refuse that?

"But…"

"I've already dispatched a car to The Four Brothers and one to his home. I'll contact Mercer and explain the situation. Getting to the bottom of this is my focus. I must apologise to Edith in case I don't make our dinner date this evening, but I'll do my best even if I'm late. Thank you, Evelyn."

"You're welcome. Good luck." A droning tone blared in the car as he hung up. My fingertips itched as I pressed end call. Pulling into our driveway, I grabbed my phone and bag and hightailed it into the house. I couldn't wait to tell Aunt Edie I solved the puzzle.

Dropping my bag on the kitchen bench I called, "I'm home."

An eerie silence met my call, and a shiver danced up my spine. I glanced across the kitchen to the basket in the corner. Empty. I couldn't even share my find with my trusty familiar. "Where are they?" My eyes caught the piece of paper sitting alone in the middle of the table.

Dear Evelyn, I've popped out to do some last-minute errands before this evening. Miss Saffron is with me. Everything is all ready for tonight, and you'll find it in the fridge at the back of the kitchen. It's all locked up and ready for you to work your magic on the place. Good luck with your decorating and Micah and I will see you at six-thirty. Love you. Aunt Edie.

"Of course, she's doing last-minute errands."

I called Tyler next as I headed through the connecting door to The Melting Pot, and my hand fisted by my side when it went straight to the message bank. "Tyler, it's me, and boy, do I have some news to tell you. I'm not sure where you are but I did it, I solved Misty's murder. Call me back as soon as you get this message. It's almost five now, and I'm at The Melting Pot about to get this place ready. Love you."

I whipped around and placed decorations in various spots, and in no time, I was standing in the Mad Hatter's Tea Party. A bead of sweat trickled down my temple as I attached the *Happy Birthday* banner across the wall above the counter. I stepped down from the ladder and wiped my brow with the back of my hand surveying my handy work.

"This is perfect, and who would have thought a Mad Hatter's tea party would have turned out so well? I must remember to thank Aunt Edie for keeping the customer birthday cupboard well stocked."

A tap on the glass window startled me. My heart catapulted into the back of my throat, and a coldness shot through me. I turned to see Wade waving through one of the front windows. Unlocking the front door, I smiled. "What are you doing here? Why aren't you out helping Detective Huxton bring Slade into custody?"

"Last time I talked to him he said he said he had it all under control, and he'd call me if he needed me. I haven't heard from him. Evelyn, I know this is bad timing, but I really need to talk to you," he said, his pained expression calling to the concerned citizen in me. His five-o'clock shadow was thicker than normal.

Go, Detective Huxton. That was a quick arrest.

"Of course, come in." I stepped aside and closed the door behind him. "What can I do for you?"

His gaze scanned the café, and he spun around and glared at me. "You're having a birthday party, aren't you? And I've barged in on it." His lips pressed together, and he ran his hand through his dishevelled hair. "Trust me to screw it up for you."

"Wade, I can see there is something on your mind, and you're already here, so you may as well let me help you."

He smiled, but it was a minimal effort, it barely reached his eyes. "It's about Jordi."

My heart fell, and my stomach bottomed out. My hands gripped my tight chest. "Oh my gosh, what happened? Is she all right?"

His hands shot out, and his eyes widened. "No, she's fine. I just wanted to talk to you about her."

Tears welled behind my eyes, and I gripped the nearest chair to keep my jelly knees from collapsing. "Far out, Wade. Way to scare the hell out of someone."

"I'm sorry, that was never my intention," he said, his brows drawing together in a haunted expression.

"I'm at a loss, and I know you and she are best friends. I was hoping you could help me out."

My back straightened. "Help you out? How do you mean?"

He huffed and paced the floor as though he had the weight of the world on him.

"Wade, what you say here is between us," I said, hoping to ease his apprehension about sharing. "I promise, what's said inside The Melting Pot stays inside The Melting Pot."

A half smile turned his lip up, and he nodded giving over to my charms. "Okay, Evelyn, you win. As you know, I'm engaged."

The word sent a hot shudder up my neck to my cheeks. "I do. Congratulations."

"The thing is." He paused and bit his lip.

His gaze caught mine, and the sincerity echoed in his eyes caught my breath. "What are you trying to tell me, Wade?"

"Not being able to see Jordi and let her know how I feel about her is killing me."

I shook my head. "No, you shouldn't have any feelings for her when you are engaged to another woman."

"That's just it, I'm not," he blurted.

My brow tightened and my head pounded. "Not what?"

"Engaged."

I rubbed my aching forehead and squeezed my eyes together. "I'm confused. First, you say you're engaged and then you say you're not. Make up your mind which one it is because I'll not let you break my best friend's heart all over again. I'd rather turn you into a four-legged rat than let that happen. And I would do it too."

"Ease up," he said, holding up his hands as a barrier between us. "Yes, I'm engaged, but it's not what you think. I shouldn't be telling you this, but you promised it would stay between us."

I nodded and folded my arms across my chest, waiting.

"I'm going crazy not being able to let Jordi know how I feel. My engagement is a cover. The woman is a witness to a crime, and the engagement is only until she testifies next week. My job is to keep her hidden and out of the public eye until the trial."

I stared at him, and my lips parted, my head swimming in light-headedness with this new spill of information.

It's all fake? The relationship, the engagement—but not his feelings for Jordi.

Mixed emotions screwed with my heart. I wanted to use every ounce of my being and turn him into a rat anyway for putting my best friend through hell, but I knew it was his job. If nothing else, he was committed to his job.

He stood there, his hands shoved in his pockets staring at me. "Say something."

I placed my hand on my chest and couldn't contain the smile that broke out across my face. "I'm relieved…happy… excited for the time ahead. But most of all thrilled you feel about Jordi the same way she feels about you, which tells me there's hope for the future."

And it's only for another week until she testifies. I can keep Jordi's spirits up until then.

Wade blushed, and his gaze wandered up towards the heavens. If I didn't know better, I would have said he was communicating with someone. He was a necromancer who could talk to ghosts, so he may be saying thank you to someone *out there.*

He cleared his throat. "I know you won't say anything, and if Detective Huxton finds out I told you about my assignment, I'm screwed. But I had to tell someone, and it was a chance I was willing to take."

I made a locking action across my lips and then threw the imaginary key over my shoulder. He laughed. The joyous sound warmed my heart. "I'm having a little surprise birthday party for a few of my closest friends. Why don't you stay? You can finish helping me set up. All I need to do is get the food table ready and bring out the cake from the fridge in the back of the kitchen."

"I'd love to." He bounded towards the kitchen entrance. "Why don't you set up the snacks table, and I'll get the cake?"

"Sounds like a plan." He disappeared out back, and I busied myself opening packets of lollies and tipping them into jars. The light shone off the sapphire ring on my finger and I held it up to admire. I was suddenly hyper-aware that my pulse was racing knowing my love for Tyler is as strong today, as the day I said those three magic words to him.

Moments later, the whole building went black. "Oh no. Are you okay out there, Wade?"

"No problem," he called.

"Looks like a fuse has blown." I dropped packets of chocolate bullets on the table, pulled out my mobile and booted up the flashlight app.

Wade called from the kitchen. "I'll pop out the back door and take care of it. In the meantime, can you create some mood lighting?"

Mood lighting? Mmm.

I tapped my finger on my pursed lips, and my mind lit up with the possibilities. There's no time like the present to test out my new master witch skills. I stood and held my hand out toward the candelabras and spoke in a clear voice.

"In the darkness I now shall be but make this room a place to see. With this spell ignite the spark, bring forth the light from the dark."

My fingers tingled like they were thawing out from frostbite. Amber streams of glittered sparkles flew from my fingertips around the room and circled the candelabras. It only lasted a few seconds. The residual tingles vanished from my fingers, and I waited a moment with my hands clasped together and looked at the candelabras. A soft warm glow rose from the bottom of the candle and ignited the flame.

I fist-pumped the air. "Yes! I did it." Overjoyed with my newfound abilities, I lit a few more candles and watched them come alive right in front of me. I clapped my achievements and hugged my hands to my chest. "Now, that's what I'm talking about. Mood lighting…tick."

I turned and jumped at the sight of Jordi standing just inside the door, my hand flattened against my racing heart. "What the hell, Jordi? You scared me. You're not supposed to be here for another forty minutes."

I stood frozen to the spot, staring at me, her arms behind her back. Was she hiding a present or something in her hands? Our gazes locked, and it was then I zoomed in on her rapid breathing and trembling lips. A gush of shivers ran through my body, and my chest locked up. "Jordi, is everything okay?"

The wrinkles in her forehead doubled, and she did a minute head shake.

What is that supposed to mean?

Even under the warm glow of candlelight, I could see her skin had turned ashen white. "Say something, you're scaring me."

She opened her mouth to speak, but it was a male voice. "Good. About time you got a taste of your own medicine."

Slade?

My breathing sped up, and I swallowed hard to show minimal recognition of the voice. My hands grew clammy, and shivers shot across my neck, bolting the hairs upright. A flicker of candlelight glinted along the edge of a long blade as it crept around the front of Jordi's neck. My heart seized. The unshaven, scruffy face of Slade inched out from behind her, and his nostrils flared.

My hand shot out in front of me. "Slade, what are you doing?"

"Call it payback," he said. Jordi's back straightened as he forced the knife into her chin.

"Stop," I yelled, swallowing the fear radiating from Jordi's eyes. "What is going on, Slade? I don't understand. If you have a beef with me, then take it up with me. You don't need to include Jordi."

"That's where you're wrong," he yelled, his eyes bulging. "It's only fair I destroy one of your relationships just like you did mine."

"What are you talking about?"

"Isla," he screamed, shoving Jordi forward and away from the door, her body jarring as she stumbled. He yanked her up close to his body and held the knife against her abdomen. One thrust to the hilt and my minimal healing powers wouldn't be able to save her.

"You and your big mouth. What was it she said you told her…that's right. 'A man should cherish a woman and never make her cry, and if they do, it's on them, not the woman'?"

He threw my words back in my face. "Yes, I said those words to her, but you're going to have to explain it to me, Slade."

"The woman is supposed to stand by her man no matter what. I thought Isla would be different, but no, she was the same as Hannah and all the others." Jordi gasped as he pushed the knife against her stomach. "Then you get in her ear, and she rings me and dumps me. Me! How dare she think she can dump me."

"You know, I was all set on coming in here and making you pay for destroying my life and then this shifter arrived at the same time which worked out perfectly because now I can watch you suffer as I dissect her one limb at a time."

Wade, I hope you can see all this.

"Wait, wait a minute." Jordi spoke for the first time. "If I'm going to be the one to die, the least you could do is explain why. I can't imagine it's the first time you've been dumped."

"Jordi, what the hell are you doing?" I asked, my voice strained.

Baiting him right now may not be the best option.

She looked at me with pleading eyes. "I just think that if I'm going to die, I have a right to know why, and that *all* of us should hear it. I mean there's no reason to *wade* through all the useless information."

Wade through…she knows Wade's here. I have no idea how, but I'll go with it.

"I suppose you have a point." I tensed my muscles and glared at him.

Silence hung in the air, and my insides were about to erupt. "The ball's in your court, Slade."

He shrugged. "Why not. After I finish with you two, no one will be able to recognise your bodies, anyway."

"Then what are you waiting for?" Jordi asked.

He moved the knife up to Jordi's cheek and ran the tip of the blade down towards her neck. She gasped and screamed out in pain as the tip pierced her skin and a trickle of blood emerged. "Patience…patience."

My stomach squirmed, and bile shot up the back of my throat. "Okay, okay enough. Isla dumped you. We get it, but what's the rest of the story?"

"She didn't just dump me; she blabbed to you and blew my alibi. If only she'd kept her mouth shut. Isla will pay with her life for what she did, but she's disappeared somewhere to wallow in her tears. For now, she can wait. I know how smart you are, Evelyn. I'm pretty sure you would have put the pieces together and worked out it was me running from the church and me who killed Misty. My suspicions were confirmed when our trusty detective put the call out for my arrest. Police scanners are a wonderful invention, aren't they?"

"You killed Misty?" Jordi said in a whisper. "Why?"

"It really was a misfortunate incident," he said, waving the knife in front of her face. "I pride myself on being a shrewd businessman, and I wanted in on the black market trade here in town. There's a lot of money to be had dealing in illegal contraband. I knew it was being distributed through Salty Snips and I was under the impression Misty was the head honcho."

Salty Snips is a front for dealing illegal drugs?

"Turns out I was wrong, and she had no idea about the trade. She kind of went crazy and said she would move heaven and hell to find out who it was. Then she threatened to turn me in to the police. Well, I couldn't have that, could I? She had to go. I suppose you could say it was a crime of convenience."

"And the church?" I asked.

"Seems someone got to Blair before I could, there was no use in my hanging around. I'm just glad I can run faster than Tyler." He paused and then looked at both of us in turn, wielding the huge blade around. "Right, who wants to go first? I'm sure I can make it look like a robbery gone wrong."

The blood rushed to my head, and my mind blanked. I stepped forward just as Slade tuned to face Jordi and pulled back the knife, ready to thrust it into her chest. She closed her eyes tight and braced for impact just as a shatter of glass echoed from the other side of the café.

My gaze transfixed on my best friend, I yelled, "No."

Slade screamed out in pain, and his hand shot to his neck. He froze mid-movement. Like he'd been hit with a freeze spell. Within seconds, the knife dropped from his hand and clattered to the floor. His body followed, crumbling in a heap at Jordi's feet.

"What happened?" My hand flattened against my forehead, my gaze staring at the heap on the floor. I rushed to Jordi and threw my arms around her, squeezing tight. My racing heart matched hers. Cold chills went through me as I held her shaking body.

"Evelyn, thank goodness you're okay." She leaned her head against my shoulder a moment and then asked, "Do you think you can untie my hands?"

I nodded biting my lip, "Of course." I pulled her away from Slade's body and kept my gaze half on Jordi's hands and half on Slade's still body. "What do you think happened?"

The door flew open, and Wade emerged carrying what looked like a weird style of gun.

"Wade?" Jordi said, through teary eyes. "What is that?"

"This..." He held up the gun and smiled, blowing across the top of the barrel as they did in the movies. "Is my trusty tranquilliser gun."

Jordi's eyebrows raised. "You shot him with that?"

"I had to. I didn't have my gun with me as I hadn't intended to stay long—so I had to improvise. This was left in my car from my last assignment." He paused and looked at Slade. "I guess he won't be joining the birthday celebrations."

I looked at Jordi, then Wade and then Slade. If the situation hadn't been so serious, I may have seen the funny side of his comment. "Thank you," I said, gifting Wade a smile from the bottom of my heart. I turned to Jordi, "You knew he was here, didn't you?"

A grin broke out across her face. "I saw him sneak past one of the windows outside, so I figured I'd stall, and between the three of us, a solution would present itself. I was right."

"Does someone want to explain why there is a man slumped on the floor in the middle of my café?" Aunt Edie's voice boomed from the door where she stood, one arm holding a groomed Miss Saffron, the other on her hip, her toes tapping.

"I can explain," I said.

"Well, someone had better, and fast."

***

I sat next to Aunt Edie in one of the conference rooms at the bank with my head in my hands and waited for the bank manager to return with Aunt Rosalyn's safe deposit box. The constant thumping of my headache was like some little man inside my head beating my brain with a hammer.

"That will teach you," Aunt Edie whispered. "If you're going to consume that much alcohol, then there are consequences to pay."

I sat up and squinted from the bright light. "I know, but you have to admit, it was one hell of a party."

A mischievous smile spread across her lips, and she nodded. "That it was, my dear. You young people sure know how to party."

"It's not every day you graduate to master witch level one status, catch the murderer *and* turn twenty-five," I said, my words a little on the gloating side.

She nodded. "Yes, all right. I'll give you that one."

My mind wandered back to the previous night, and while technically not a party, I couldn't have asked for a better ending to my birthday. Celebrating with those who mean the world to me.

The door clicked open, and the bank manager returned, a metal box securely tucked under her elbow. "Here we are, box number twenty-one." She set it in the middle of the table and placed the paperwork in front of me. "All right, if you could just sign at the bottom indicating you are taking the contents from the box with you, we'll be all done."

My hand twitched as I signed and shuffled, restless in my seat. I glanced at Aunt Edie, and she sat twisting her engagement ring back and forth.

"Here we are. These copies are yours." She smiled and handed them over. Last, she placed the key in my open hand. "I'll leave you to it. I'll be in my office. Feel free to utilise this room as long as you need it."

I stood and shook her hand, my stomach a nervous swarm of butterflies. "Thank you."

Both of us sat in silence looking at the box. It looked like it could fit about three bottles of wine in it. It was deep, and I wracked my brain trying to work out what could be inside.

"This is crazy," Aunt Edie said, tutting. "There is no way to predict what's inside, and the last time I looked, neither of us possessed X-ray vision. Best just to open it."

I nodded and breathed in a deep gulf of air. Unlocking it, I lifted the lid, and my lips parted. My gaze landed on the most beautifully decorated book I'd ever seen.

Tears formed in Aunt Edie's eyes as she ran her fingers over the fabric-covered book. "It's been a while since I've seen this."

"What is it?"

She smiled, and tears ran down her cheeks. "It's Rosalyn's grimoire. It's like a textbook for a witch. It's used for spells and personal notes. We both had one. After she died, I destroyed mine. For a while, I didn't want to think about magic. Then as time went on, I decided not to get a new one. I just keep all my spells in my recipe book in the pantry."

I withdrew the book from the box and a shot of electricity rushed up my arms as though I'd been given a new lease on life. "This is beautiful. I'll treasure it forever."

"It's yours now, she wanted you to have it. It's time you had your own grimoire, this way, you have a part of our heritage that you can add your own spells to."

I placed my hand over hers and squeezed. "I love you."

She wiped the tears from her face. "I love you too."

"I couldn't think of a better way to start the next chapter of my life," I said, my smile beaming at the coolest aunt in the world.

Thank you for reading
Black Magic Murder
If you enjoyed this story, I would really appreciate it
if you would consider leaving a review of this book,
no matter how short, at the retailer site where you
bought your copy or on sites like Goodreads.

YOU are the key to this book's success and the
success of **The Melting Pot Café Cozy Mystery
Series.** I read every review and they really do make
a huge difference.

THE MELTING POT SERIES

BUY LINKS FOR PUMPKIN PIES & POTIONS #1

Amazon US   Amazon AU
Amazon UK   Amazon CA

BUY LINKS FOR HAPPY DEADLY NEW YEAR #2

Amazon US   Amazon AU
Amazon UK   Amazon CA

BUY LINKS FOR MUFFINS & MAGIC #3

Amazon US   Amazon AU
Amazon UK   Amazon CA

BUY LINKS FOR MISTLETOE, MURDER & MAYHEM #4

Amazon US   Amazon AU
Amazon UK   Amazon CA

BUY LINKS FOR A DEADLY DISAPPEARANCE DOWN UNDER#5

Amazon US   Amazon AU
Amazon UK   Amazon CA

CONNECT WITH POLLY

You can sign up for my newsletter here:
https://www.pollyholmesmysteries.com/

Keep up to date on Polly's book releases, signings, and events on her website:
https://www.pollyholmesmysteries.com

Follow her on her Facebook page:
https://www.facebook.com/plharrisauthor/

Check out all the latest news in her Facebook group:
https://www.facebook.com/groups/217817788798223

Follow her on her Instagram page:
https://www.instagram.com/plharris_pollyholmes_author/

Follow her on Bookbub:
https://www.bookbub.com/authors/polly-holmes

ABOUT THE AUTHOR

Polly Holmes is the cheeky, sassy alter ego of Amazon best-selling author, *P.L. Harris*. When she's not writing her next romantic suspense novel as *P.L. Harris*, she is planning the next murder in one of Polly's cozy mysteries. She pens food-themed and paranormal cozy mysteries and publishes her books solely with Gumnut Press.

As *Polly Holmes*, *Cupcakes and Corpses* was a finalist in the Oklahoma Romance Writers of America's <u>2019 IDA International Digital Awards,</u> short suspense category. *Cupcakes and Curses* claimed second place and *Cupcakes and Cyanide* gained third place making it a clean sweep in the category.

She won silver in the <u>2020 ROAR! National Business Awards</u> in the *Writer/Blogger/Author* category and for the second year in a row, she was a finalist in the <u>2021 ROAR! National Business Awards</u> winning bronze in the *Writer/Blogger/Author* category with Gumnut Press taking out the gold in the *Hustle and Heart* category.

2022 saw Polly Holmes' books *Muffins & Magic* and *Mistletoe, Murder & Mayhem* long-listed in the Davitt Awards, a prestigious award run by the Sisters of Crime, Australia. *Muffins & Magic* also placed in the finals of the cozy mystery category in the Nashville Silver Falchion Awards.

When she's not writing you can find her sipping coffee in her favourite cafe, watching reruns of Murder, She Wrote or Psych, or taking long walks along the beach soaking up the fresh salty air.

BOOK 1 OUT NOW

Witches, cats, pumpkin pies, and murder!

I'm Evelyn Grayson and if you'd told me by the time I was 23, I'd have lost both my parents in a mysterious accident, moved in with the coolest Aunt ever, lived in a magical town, and I was a witch, I would have said you were crazy. Funny thing is, you'd be right.

Camille Stenson, the grumpiest woman in Saltwater Cove is set on making this year's Halloween celebrations difficult for everyone, but when she turns up dead and my best friend is on the suspect list, I have no choice but to find out whodunit and clear her name.

Amongst the pumpkin carving, abandoned houses, and apple bobbing, it soon becomes apparent dark magic is at play and I must use all my newfound witches' abilities to find the killer before another spell is cast.

Step into Evelyn Grayson's magical world in the first book of the Melting Pot Café series, a fun and flirty romantic paranormal cozy mystery where the spells are flowing, and the adventure is just beginning

***

Read on for an excerpt of book 1.

.

CHAPTER ONE

"Oh, my goodness, breakfast smells divine," I said, bounding down the stairs two at a time toward the lip-smacking scent streaming from the kitchen. Rubbing my grumbling stomach, I peeked over Aunt Edie's shoulder at the green gooey concoction boiling on the stove. I've been living with my aunt for the past eleven years since my parents died, and not once have I questioned her cooking abilities. Until now. I folded my arms and leaned against the kitchen bench. "I know it smells amazing but are you sure it's edible because it sure as heck doesn't look like it."

Aunt Edie frowned and her eyebrows pulled together. Her classic pondering expression. She snapped her fingers and looked straight at me with her golden honey-brown eyes glowing like she'd just solved the world's climate crisis.

"Popcorn. I forgot the popcorn. Evelyn, honey be a dear and grab me the popcorn from the second shelf in the pantry. The caramel packet, not the plain."

Caramel popcorn for breakfast? That's a new one.

I shrugged. "Sure." Walking into Aunt Edie's pantry was like walking into the potions classroom at Hogwarts. Every witch's dream pantry. Normal food on the left-hand side and on the right, every potion ingredient a witch could possibly need, clearly labelled in its allocated spot. Aunt Edie would always say: a place for everything and everything in its place.

"I can't believe Halloween is only three days away," I called, swiping the caramel popcorn bag off the shelf. Heading back out, the hunger monster growing in my stomach grumbled, clearly protesting the fact I still hadn't satisfied its demand for food.

Aunt Edie's cheeks glowed at the mention of the annual holiday. "I know. It's my most favourite day of the year, aside from Christmas, that is."

"Of course." I handed her the bag of popcorn and made a beeline for the coffee machine. My blood begged to be infused with caffeine. Within minutes, I held a steaming cup of heaven in my hands. As I sipped, the hot liquid danced down my throat in euphoric bliss.

"I love how Saltwater Cove goes all out for Halloween. Best place to live if you ask me."

She paused stirring and glanced my way.

"I'm so glad you're back this year. *The Melting Pot* hasn't been the same without you. *I* haven't been the same without you."

The pang of sadness in her voice gripped my heart tight.

The Melting Pot is Aunt Edie's witch themed café. Her pride and joy. We'd spend hours cooking up delicious new recipes to sell to her customers. Her cooking is to die for, I guess that's where I get my passion from. My dream was always to stay in Saltwater Cove and run the business together, but she insisted I travel and experience the world. Done and dusted.

I glanced around the kitchen, my gaze landing on the empty cat bed in the corner. "Where is my mischievous familiar this morning? Doesn't she usually keep you company when you're cooking?"

Miss Saffron had been my saving grace after my parents died. She'd found me when my soul had been ripped out, when I had nothing more to live for. Thanks to her friendship, I rekindled my will to live, and love.

It isn't uncommon for a witch to have a familiar. It's kind of the norm in the witch world, but none as special as Miss Saffron. My diva familiar, of the spoilt kind. Her exotic appearance with high cheekbones and shimmering black silver-tipped coat still dazzles me. They say the Chausie breed is a distant cousin of the miniature cougar. She certainly has some fight nestled in her bones. But Miss Saffron's best features are her glamourous eyes. More oval than almond-shaped with a golden glow to rival a morning sunrise.

"Oh, I'm sure she's around somewhere. She's probably found some unexplored territory to investigate. I'm sure she'll turn up when it's time to eat or you get into mischief."

Although not completely wrong, I ignored the mischief comment. "Speaking of eating, what is that?" I asked, leaning in closer, my mouth drooling at the sweet caramel aroma. A cheeky grin spread across Aunt Edie's face.

Oh no, do I want to know?

"Well, Halloween's not for everyone and some of the kids were complaining last year certain townspeople were grumpy when they went trick or treating so it got me thinking. I thought I'd spice things up a bit this year with a happy spell."

My eyebrows went up. "A happy spell?"

She nodded and scooped a little spoonful into a pumpkin shaped candy mould. "When I'm done, we'll have cheerful candy to hand out for all the grouchy Halloween spoilers out there. Within ten seconds of popping one of these little darlings in their mouth, their frown will turn upside down and they'll be spreading the happy vibes to all. I'm going to make sure this year is as wonderful as it can be."

"Aunt Edie, you can't." My stomach dropped and I gripped the edge of the kitchen bench with one hand. The disastrous implications of her words sent shivers running down my spine. "You know it's against the law to use magic to change the essence of a person. You could be sanctioned or worse, have your powers stripped."

"Relax, sweetie," she said, pausing, her smile serene and calm. "This falls under the Halloween Amendment of 1632."

"What are you talking about…The Halloween Amendment of 1632? I've never heard of it."

A subtle puff of air escaped her lips. "Halloween wasn't exactly your favourite holiday growing up, especially after your parents died, and then you missed the last two or so travelling."

"But I was back by last Christmas."

She smiled. "Yes indeed. And it was the best Christmas ever. But Halloween was always a reminder you were different."

"Yeah, a witch."

"Yes."

She placed her hand on mine. A sigh left my lips at the warmth of her reassuring touch.

"A day when young girls dressed up as witches. Where their fantasy was your daily reality."

Aunt Edie's words were like a slap in the face with a wet dishcloth. "Was I really that self-absorbed?

I'm so sorry to have dumped it all on you. I guess I was pretty hard to live with at times."

"Hard? Never," she said, her jaw gaping in mock horror. "Challenging, now that's a definite possibility."

She burst into laughter and my heart overflowed with warmth as the sweet sound filled the room.

I threw my arms around her and squeezed. "I love you, Aunt Edie."

"I love you too, sweetheart."

I pulled back and drilled my eyes into hers, wanting answers. "Now, what is this Halloween Amendment of 1632?"

Her eyes sparkled like gemstones and she resumed filling candy moulds with green slimy goo. "The amendment is only active for five days leading up to Halloween and finishes at the stroke of midnight October thirty-first. It allows any graduate or fully qualified witch to enhance the holiday using magic as long as it is temporary, no harm or foul comes to the object of the spell or intentionally alters the future."

"Are you serious? That means me. I'm a graduate witch," I said. My inner child was doing jumping jacks.

Aunt Edie tutted. "True. A graduate witch who is still learning the ropes and until you receive your full qualification at twenty-five, even then, you must always strive to be the best witch you can be. We can't afford another mishap like graduation."

If it wasn't for my three besties, Harriet, Jordi, Tyler and, Aunt Edie's guidance and training, I may never have made it to graduation. My mind skipped back to the disastrous end to the graduation party. It wasn't exactly my fault the party ended in rack and ruin. Who knew having a shapeshifter for a best friend could cause so much havoc?

I caught the upturned lip of Aunt Edie and chuckled. "Oh, come on, even you thought it was funny when Jordi shifted into a raven and chased that cow, Prudence McAvoy around the ballroom. She's had it in for Jordi ever since I moved to Saltwater Cove. I guess she pushed one too many times, I mean, no one taunts Jordi and gets away with it." I giggled, the blood-red face of Prudence covered in banoffee pie was the best graduation present, ever. "Besides, my involvement came down to wrong place, wrong time. Prudence eventually owned up, it was all on her. But I get the message. Be a good witch."

"That's my girl." Aunt Edie huffed, dropping the spoon back in the empty pan. She wiped her sweaty brow with the back of her hand and smeared the remains of the gooey green substance on her hands down her apron. "There all done. Time to let them set."

"How do you know the spell works? I mean, will they work on everyone?" I asked.

Aunt Edie crossed her arms and pinched her lips together, her cheeks glowing a cute rosy pink. "Of course, they'll work on everyone, even those beings of the paranormal kind. Since when *hasn't* one of my spells worked, young lady?"

True. You don't earn the title of master witch by doing terrible spells that fail.

She rubbed her chin and continued. "But I wouldn't say no to testing them before Halloween rolls around."

"Have you got a guinea pig in mind?" I paused at her sly grin. "All I can say is, it better not be me."

***

Daily life was made a whole lot easier since The Melting Pot joined Aunt Edie's house. Walking next door to work suited me just fine. Kind of like an extension of her kitchen. She loved to share her passion for cooking delicious food with the rest of the world. A passion we both shared.

I twisted my wavy, blue-streaked chestnut hair into a messy bun on top of my head and shoved it under my witch's hat. Glancing at my reflection, I saw it screamed modern classy-chic witch in an understated way. My dainty black satin skirt fell just above my knees showing off my trendy black and orange horizontal strip stockings. A slick black short sleeve button-up blouse fit perfectly covered in an orange vest, the words The Melting Pot embroidered above the right breast pocket in white. To add the finishing touch, I slipped my size seven feet into a pair of black lace up Doc Martin ankle boots and tied the black and silver glitter laces in elegant bows. I surveyed my reflection one last time in the mirror and grinned. I mean, who else gets to dress up every day as a witch to go to work. "Me, that's who."

An electric buzz filled my blood as I pushed open the door and stepped into The Melting Pot, closing it swiftly behind me. A clever tactic on Aunt Edie's part to design her café like a witch's cave. Everywhere I looked shouted witch heaven. Cauldrons of various sizes and candelabras standing high on their perches framed the seating area. Pumpkins scattered among the witches' brooms and replica spell books. Potions and brews strategically placed high on display shelves gave off the perfect image of a witch's cave. Best not tell anyone they're real. Aunt Edie insisted on an element of authenticity. Every child's Halloween dream all year round. I squeezed my hands together in front of my heart. "Gosh, I love my job."

A purr echoed from the floor to my right and glancing down, I saw my four-legged feline slinking elegantly in a figure eight between my legs. "You love it here too, don't you, Miss Saffron?" She stretched and catapulted up onto the counter, her agility and poise qualities to admire. Her big yellow eyes stared at me, and she purred. "I swear you know exactly what I'm saying."

Aunt Edie's merry voice trailed into the main serving area from the kitchen. "I've got a wooden spoon here dripping with the last of my famous chocolate-strawberry sauce. Unless someone comes to claim it in the next ten seconds, I'll have to wash it down the sink."

"Shotgun," I whispered in Miss Saffron's direction then took off dodging tables and chairs in record time to make it to the kitchen. "Don't you dare. You know it's my favourite."

Miss Saffron sat tall on the counter, her beady eyes keeping a firm gaze on the chocolate covered spoon in my hand. My insides salivated as I licked it clean. "Oh my God. A-MA-ZING." The best part of my childhood was beating mum to the spoon and bowl when Aunt Edie was cooking up a storm. My gut clenched. I missed my mum and dad so much some days the hurt was unbearable.

The cowbell above the main entry door jingled and I jumped, startled by the unexpected intrusion. I glanced at the antique wall clock. Eight fifteen. We weren't even open yet.

"Anybody here?" Barked a familiar grouchy pompous voice.

Great. Why does today have to start with a visit from the Queen of Complaints?

"Evelyn Grayson. Stop scowling right this instant," said Aunt Edie. "You look like you're sucking a lemon. It may be fifteen minutes before we open, but you know my policy, every customer deserves a warm witch welcome."

My chest hollowed out as Aunt Edie's words curbed my inner snob. "Of course, you're right. I'm sorry," I said, dropping the spoon in the sink and wiping the chocolate sauce from my face.

"But…" Aunt Edie paused and handed me a plate. The cheeky twinkle in her eyes confused me. "It wouldn't hurt Saltwater Cove's town grouch to be happy once in a while."

I looked down at the plate and a gasped in jubilation.

Green happy candy.

"Why Aunt Edie, you are positively sinful. I love it. But I'm not even sure a happy spell will work on Camille."

"Worth a try. After all what better guinea pig could we ask for?"

I nodded and grabbed the plate. Plastering on a smile I headed out ready to see if one happy candy can soften the most bad-tempered creature I've ever had the pleasure of meeting.

"It's about time. What does a woman have to do to get service around here?" Camille Stenson snapped. "What sort of business are you running, making customers wait so long?"

I bit my tongue and held back the cynical comment chomping at the bit to get out. "I'm terribly sorry to have kept you waiting, Miss Stenson. What can I do for you?"

Her jaw dropped and a fiery shade of red washed over her pale complexion. I pursed my lips tight together to stop the laugh growing in my belly from escaping.

"It's Wednesday or have you forgotten?" She asked, her eyebrows raised, showing the stark whites of her eyes.

A shudder bolted through my body.

Scary. Yes, I know, Mr Bain's dinner, of course.

Why he can't come in and get it himself is beyond me. She's supposed to be the loan's officer at the bank, not his wife. The sarcastic tone fuelled my inner desire to squash her like a petulant fly.

Perfect guinea pig.

I eased the plate of yummy caramel scented candy in front of Camille's nose. "My sincere apologies. Please accept one of Aunt Edie's treats as a peace offering. She made them especially for the Halloween season."

"Pfft, Halloween is a waste of time if you ask me." Camille leaned in to examine the plate and frowned. Her brows crinkled together in an unattractive monobrow. "Mmm, you're not trying to poison me, are you?"

Poison? No. Cheer you up so you can stop making everyone else miserable? Yes.

"How could you say such a thing?" I said, feigning hurt. "You know Aunt Edie's food is the best for miles around. That's why people keep coming back."

"Fine." She rolled her hazel eyes to the roof, huffed, and popped a candy in her mouth.

I stood frozen, waiting, my pulse pulverising my temples as if I was standing on the edge of a cliff ready to jump. One…two…three…four. Camille stared at me, her hazel eyes clouding over. Five…six…seven. Nothing, absolutely nothing. Eight…nine. My eye caught Aunt Edie peeking in from the kitchen and she shrugged. I guess it doesn't work on people whose core being is made up of such deep-set crankiness. Ten.

"Evelyn, my dear precious Evelyn." Camille's tone shot three octaves higher. A smile flashed across her face as electric as a neon sign in the dead of night. "You look positively radiant as always. I never seem to tell you enough how beautiful you are. Just like your mother. God rest her soul."

My mother? How did she know my mother?

I swear I'd been transported into an alternate universe. "Um, thank you. That is kind of you to say. But how…"

"Pfft, nonsense," she interrupted with a sashaying movement of her hand. "It so great to have you back in Saltwater Cove. I bet your aunt is pleased you're home?"

Did she mention my mother? Maybe I imagined it. I made a mental note to follow up Camille's comment about my mother with Aunt Edie.

"I…." Stunned by Camille's reaction to the spell, my words caught in the back of my throat.

"That I am," Aunt Edie said, threading an arm around my waist. With her head turned from Camille's view, she gave me a cheeky wink.

She handed a paper bag to Camille and smiled. "Here you go, Mr Bain's dinner. His usual, just how he likes it."

"Perfect. He doesn't know how good he has it eating your wonderful meals four nights a week. He's off to some big Banking Symposium at Dawnbury Heights this afternoon but insisted I still pick up his dinner so he can take it with him. He can't stand hotel food, mind you, who can? Makes him all bloated." Camille said, placing the food inside a bigger tapestry carpet bag.

It kind of reminded me of Mary Poppins' bottomless bag. She turned toward the exit and waved.

"Ta-ta now. You ladies have a wonderful day, and may it be filled with all the magical wonders of the world."

The cow bell rattled as she left. My jaw dropped, and I stared at the closed door in silence. I looked at Aunt Edie and within seconds we were both into hysterical fits of laughter.

"Well I'd say...that spell...is a winner, wouldn't you?" I said, barely able to speak between giggles.

She nodded and cleared her throat wiping a tear from her eye. "I hope she stays that way for the next hour and a half. But who knows, it all depends on the individual person."

I laughed so much a stitch stabbed my side. "Aw," I said, pressing against the pain. "Okay, I give up, why do we want it to last an hour and a half?"

"Because Vivienne has an appointment with Camille in about thirty minutes regarding her loan application. If all goes well, she'll be able to expand her business just like she's always planned."

Vivienne Delany and Aunt Edie have been best friends since primary school. Aunt Edie ran The Melting Pot and Vivienne was the proud owner of *Perfect Pumpkin Home-Made Treats* where she made every kind of dish out of pumpkins one could dare to conjure up. And even though they both ran food business; they'd die before letting harm come to the other. That's what best friends do for each other.

"Let hope your spell does the trick." The cow bell jiggled over the door, signalling the beginning of the morning rush. "I guess we'll have to wait and see."

Buy links for Pumpkin Pies & Potions #1

Amazon US
Amazon AU
Amazon UK
Amazon CA

BOOK 2 OUT NOW

Never in my lifetime did I think I'd spend New Year's Eve knee-deep in mischief, magic, and murder!

When my high-school nemesis, Prudence McAvoy, chooses The Melting Pot Café to host her New Year's party, I know I'm courting trouble by accepting her booking. The trouble begins with Prudence turning up dead, face down in a pond, and the finger for her murder is pointed directly at my shape-shifting best friend, Jordi.

Determined to clear Jordi's name and bring the real killer to justice, I pool resources with Harriet, Tyler, and my cheeky familiar, Miss Saffron, to find out what happened to Prudence. As the clock counts down to midnight, time is running out in more ways than one.

Can we find the killer before another body drops? Or will Jordi's new year begin in the pokey?

If you like witty witches, talking cats, and magical murder mysteries, then you'll love Polly Holmes' light-hearted Melting Pot Café series.

Buy links for Happy DEADLY New Year

Amazon US
Amazon.AU
Amazon UK
Amazon CA

BOOK 3 OUT NOW

What's a witch to do when faced with protecting the ones she loves against an unimaginable evil?

Ever had one of those days when everything is going too well? When you have that sense that the other boot is about to drop? Welcome to my day.

It's the Annual Saltwater Cove Show, and this year there are more rides, show bags, food stalls, and competitions than ever before. Witches from worlds near and far have descended to try their hand at winning the prestigious Witch Wonder Trophy for best witch baker

When Seraphina Morgan from the Coven of the Night Moon turns up dead, all avenues lead to last year's reigning champion, Aunt Edie, as the guilty party. Dark magic is lurking, and I'm determined to get to the bottom of it and clear Aunt Edie's name before the unthinkable happens, and she's found guilty. Enlisting the help of my two best friends and drop-dead Greek-god gorgeous boyfriend, we set about finding the real killer before Aunt Edie's goose is cooked. Or pie is baked as the case may be.

If you like witty witches, talking cats, and magical murder mysteries, then step into the fun and flirty romantic paranormal cozy mystery world of the Melting Pot Café series where the spells are flowing, and the adventure is sure to leave you craving more.

Buy links for Muffins & Magic

Amazon US
Amazon AU
Amazon UK
Amazon CA

Book 4 Out Now

Christmas is Saltwater Cove's favourite holiday of the year, but that didn't stop murder and mayhem from making an unscheduled visit.

The festive spirit is out and about, the eggnog is flowing, mistletoe is hung, and the town is pumped for the most exciting event on the Christmas calendar, the Annual Concert. This year aunt Edie decided it would be a brilliant idea to volunteer me and my best friend, Harriet, to run both Santa's photo booth *and* the refreshment stall.

As the celebrations kick-off, things turn complicated fast when my childhood friend, Trixie Snowball, winner of the Elf of the Year contest, reveals she's lost Santa's list and is desperate to find it. I agreed to use my magic to help, but things take a turn for the worse when the runner-up of the contest turns up dead behind the refreshment stall, and Trixie is the number one suspect.

Christmas day is fast approaching, and now I'm in a race against time to find a murderer, clear Trixie's name, bring the real killer to justice and find the list before disappointment rains down on children all over the world. How, oh, how did I get myself into such a predicament?

Buy links for Mistletoe, Murder & Mayhem

Amazon US
Amazon AU
Amazon UK
Amazon CA

BOOK 5 OUT NOW

Solving the disappearance of my best friends' parents was NOT one of my New Year's Resolutions…

A trip to sunny Australia in the scorching summer wasn't in my holiday plans, but when Jordi rings in a state of utter panic revealing her parents failed to turn up at the annual Shapeshifters Conference held in country Western Australia, what's a girl to do?

Despite having solved a murder or two in my time, I am completely out of my comfort zone in the harsh Aussie outback where not only the sun, insects, and snakes bite, but the locals do too.

The search is interrupted when the body of Harridan Reef local and chairman of the Shapeshifters Executive Council, Shayla Ramos, turns up dead in a sheep paddock at the local country show. I'm convinced her murder is linked to Jordi's missing parents. But what if I'm wrong?

Forbidden to use magical powers in a town where the supernatural is concealed from view, it becomes apparent the locals have their own secrets. Secrets someone is willing to kill to keep hidden.

Together with Aunt Edie, Detective Huxton Harriet, Jordi, Tyler and my trusty furry familiar, Miss Saffron, we must all work together to uncover the truth. With a blazing bush fire threatening to destroy all in its path we must race the clock to unlock the secrets before Jordi's parents pay the ultimate price.

Buy links for A Deadly Disappearance Down Under

Amazon US
Amazon AU
Amazon UK
Amazon CA